G000252574

THE VENETIAN

ALSO BY SHANI STRUTHERS

EVE: A CHRISTMAS GHOST STORY
(PSYCHIC SURVEYS PREQUEL)

PSYCHIC SURVEYS BOOK ONE:
THE HAUNTING OF HIGHDOWN HALL

PSYCHIC SURVEYS BOOK TWO:
RISE TO ME

PSYCHIC SURVEYS BOOK THREE:
44 GILMORE STREET

PSYCHIC SURVEYS BOOK FOUR:
OLD CROSS COTTAGE

JESSAMINE

This Haunted World:
Book One

THE VENETIAN

SHANI STRUTHERS

This Haunted World: Book One, The Venetian
Copyright © Shani Struthers 2016

The right of Shani Struthers to be identified as the Author of the work has been asserted by her in accordance with the Copyright, Designs and Patents Act 1988. All rights reserved in all media. No part of this publication may be reproduced, stored in a retrieval system, or transmitted in any form or by any means, electronic, mechanical, recording, photocopying, the Internet or otherwise, without the prior written consent of the copyright holder, nor be otherwise circulated in any form of binding or cover other than that in which it is published and without a similar condition being imposed on the subsequent purchaser.

Authors Reach
www.authorsreach.co.uk

ISBN: 978 0 9935183 7 9

All characters and events featured in this publication are purely fictitious and any resemblance to any person, place, organisation/company, living or dead, is entirely coincidental.

For Jack Struthers, destined to be one
of life's great explorers.

Acknowledgements

The first in a brand new series, getting it right has proved an arduous task but so many have helped me along the way. First up, my incredible band of beta readers, they see so much that I don't and make me change so much too – but all for the better! Huge thanks to Louisa Taylor (who read it through twice!), Rob Struthers (who I made read it through twice!), Lesley Hughes, Alicen Haire, Sarah England, Sarah Savery, Corinna Edwards-Colledge, Julia Tugwell, Jan Ruth, and last but never least, the lovely Rumer Haven. Huge thanks also to my editor Jeff Gardiner, he's always such a pleasure to work with, and Gina Dickerson, who designed the cover and formatted the books for print and e-book. Thanks also to you, the reader, so many of you have been a great support, right from the very first book. I hope you enjoy this one too.

Foreword

The Venetian is the first book in my new This Haunted World paranormal series – a set of books not connected by characters but by places in our big wide world that are considered haunted. Each book will be a standalone and seeks to mix fiction with fact – or at the very least the myth and legend that haunted places tend to be shrouded in. Like all my books, I try to find the 'human' story behind the ghosts, what they've suffered, why they're still grounded, and why some of them seem hell bent on revenge and destruction. My books aren't 'horrors' but sometimes, and inevitably, the boundaries blur. If you're reading at night, you might want to leave a light on…

Prologue

LOUISE took a deep breath. This was it. She couldn't put the moment off any longer. She had to know. She looked at Rob. He was as eager as she was.

"Just do it," he urged.

"Okay, I will. Wait there won't you?"

"Sweetheart, I'm going nowhere."

Louise hurried upstairs to the bathroom. After shutting the door she crossed to the mirror and looked in it, trying to steady her nerves, her hands too – she was shaking like a tree caught in a thunderstorm. Closing her eyes, she opened them again to stare at herself. In her mid-thirties, of medium build with brown shoulder-length hair, she could be considered attractive she supposed, but there were lines around her eyes, a careworn look to them. Would that disappear today? Would they glitter instead with happiness? For as long as she could remember she'd wanted a family. Growing up a single child with only her mother to look after her, her father on the scene but more off than on, the need for lineage ran deep. It was what she fantasised about – a child, two children, more than that, a brood – and she and Rob the perfect parents. And they would be... so many of their friends agreed, friends who were busy starting families of their own.

She picked up the pregnancy test and carefully unwrapped it. Something she'd done so many times before. Two lines, that's all she wanted, to show her dreams had taken root. Whilst squatting she prayed, reciting one word over and over. *Please, please, please.* There'd been other signs this time, a metallic taste in her mouth, sore breasts – signs that her body had changed, had responded.

Standing up, she flushed the toilet and yanked her knickers up, all with one hand. The other wouldn't let go of the stick, not until she knew. She stared at it, begged every deity there was for a positive result. A single line appeared, then... nothing.

As if the stick was molten, she threw it across the room. Her back against the door, she slid down, familiar pain engulfing her. It was always the same: there'd be hope and excitement at the possibility of a new life, the sheer miracle of it and then disappointment. *Crushing* disappointment. But far worse was the anger. It would rear up and consume her.

Oh, God, the anger...

PART ONE
Louise

Chapter One

TOUCHING down on Venetian soil, Louise grabbed her husband's arm.

"We're here, we're finally here!"

"I'm aware of that." There was a wry smile on Rob's face.

Louise leaned into him. "Oh come on, you must be excited!"

"I am, look at my face, I'm excited."

Louise laughed. She knew his feelings matched hers but they were on an aeroplane, a packed aeroplane, and he was a bloke; there was no way he'd be as effusive as her. Rob liked to play it cool. They'd known each other for fifteen years, been married for most of them, and it was here she'd wanted to come for their honeymoon – Venice with its gondola-strewn canals, its labyrinthine alleys and its sense of timelessness. But there'd been a house to buy, careers to forge, IVF to pay for when babies refused to come along. Recently, they'd come to a decision. They'd live life for each other, travel to all the places they wanted with Italian cities top of the hit list. They'd marvelled at the Coliseum in Rome, grown starry-eyed at art in Florence – she was still high from seeing Botticelli's *La Primavera* – and admired Milan's fashionistas. Now it was the turn of Venice, number one on her hit list but number four on his, and he'd got his way. No matter. They were here now.

There was movement all around them. Although they were still taxiing to their designated port, belts were being unclicked, mobiles turned on, and coats and scarves retrieved. Impatient to get off the plane too, to actually stand on Venetian soil, even if it was only the airport tarmac, Louise rubbed her hands together in anticipation. She could hardly contain herself. This 'carpe diem' ethos they'd devised after their fourth round of heartache was really doing the job. Their failure to conceive was neither his fault nor hers – it was simply unexplained. In a third of cases a clear cause is never established, and, incredibly, they'd fallen into that third, despite various tests. What a verdict! Modern medicine had come so far and yet still they couldn't find a reason? They could clone animals but not spark the flame of human life? 'Don't blame the doctors,' Rob tried to reason. 'They're not Gods.' No, but they were similar in a way. They'd both let her down.

A quick glance at Rob and she abandoned such thoughts, reminded herself to live in the present, to forget about the past and not dwell on a childless future – to remain in the here and now. Sound advice from her psychiatrist. And right here, right now life was good.

Finally they were able to follow a long line of others as they moved along the aisle and out into the open. It was mid-November. Not the ideal time to visit Venice, admittedly, it was going to be cold, but they'd been too busy to visit any earlier. Rob was an architect and she was in marketing.

Both self-employed, they had to commit whilst the work was there, travelling off-peak was the norm but it had a definite upside: there'd be fewer crowds. Where they lived, close to the centre of London, it was always crowded.

Not only cold outside, it was raining, coming down in sheets. Although it was only a few minutes past four, the sun had given up and retired for the night. Rob stood close to her as they waited at passport control, the cedar wood smell of his aftershave a familiar comfort.

"The weather will make Venice even more atmospheric," he said. "Honestly."

He'd visited the city before, when he was younger, a couple of years before they'd met, rode in with some friends of his on their motorbikes. He'd only stayed for the day and hadn't been that impressed. 'Then again,' he'd elaborated, 'we only really went to St Mark's Square. You'd never believe the price of a coffee there. Got to keep away from the tourist traps I think.'

As they exited customs and followed signs to the water taxi, Louise started talking about Poveglia, a small island in the Venetian lagoon with a very chequered history. Not only had it served as a temporary confinement station for plague victims throughout the centuries, but also, in the 1920s, buildings had been converted into an asylum for the mentally ill. Apparently, the practices carried out there had been dubious to say the least. Thankfully, the hospital had shut down in the late sixties and had since fallen into disrepair. The island was now privately owned, the anonymous investor deciding how best to develop it.

"I wonder who buys an island with that kind of history?" she mused. "They say about one hundred and fifty thousand people have died there. Really, it's one big graveyard."

"Who knows? Who cares?"

"I know, I know. It's just that when I was researching what sights to see, 'haunted' Poveglia kept coming up, there's tons written about it. You've got to admit, it's fascinating."

Rob shrugged, looked sideways at her. "The supernatural *is* fascinating, but let's stick close to the living this weekend."

"Not too close," Louise reminded. "You said off-the-beaten-track remember, although to be honest, the city looks as if it's fairly compact, everything's within walking distance. Rather than structure each day too much, shall we just go where the mood takes us?"

"Spontaneity's fine with me. We'll take a look at St Mark's Square, but we're not eating or drinking there!"

"Ha! You've never got over having to part with however many thousands of lira it was for a coffee have you? It must be the Scottish in you."

"Hey, don't knock my Scottish roots, I'm proud of them! I just think there are better, more authentic places to down an espresso. Besides which, I'm not *that* mean, I've paid for a private speedboat to get us to Venice, we don't have to rough it on the water bus."

"Shame you didn't hire a gondola."

"A gondola, how naff. There's no way you're getting me on a gondola!" He raised an eyebrow before adding cheekily, "Besides, they're bloody expensive too."

At the dock, their booking was taken and they were shown to their boat. The driver took their bags and, with his thumb, motioned for them to go into the cabin. The roof was so low she had to bend right down, as did Rob, both of them wary of banging their heads. He then positioned himself at the helm for the half-hour journey across the waters into the heart of Venice. Settling into their seats, Louise looked out of the window. This was what life was all about – new experiences, new sights and sounds, this was what made her feel alive. A miracle considering how low she'd sunk after finally realising they'd never start a family together. Black days they were; days when she'd acted... crazy. There was no other word for it, swinging between moods like some wild pendulum. She hadn't realised it was possible for one person to cry so much. 'Don't forget your hormones have been messed with,' Rob would say as one of his many attempts at consoling her. 'IVF plays havoc with everything.' Which is why they'd called it a day. There was only so much she could take; only so much *he* could take. Remembering that, she sighed.

"Everything all right?" Rob asked, noticing.

At first her smile was forced but gradually it relaxed and became more natural.

"Of course I'm all right, I'm happy," she replied, reaching over to squeeze his hand.

They might be travelling under cover of darkness but the journey was still impressive. The rain had let up slightly and the clouds must have parted because moonlight shimmered on the sea, lending it an almost ethereal touch. Acting as guides, wooden pilings rose upwards, looking to her like stick men, worn ragged by the constant wash of salt water. She pitied their loneliness. Out here, in the lagoon, you were so near to civilisation, and yet so far. You were stranded. Where was that island, she wondered? They'd passed several on their journey.

"Look, there's Venice, can you see it?"

Rob was talking again. She shunted closer, breathed in his smell, relishing that as much as the sight in front of her.

As they approached Venice the boat slowed, observing city speed limits. Quickly she became entranced as buildings rose like giants on either side of them, painted in faded shades of pastel. Far from humble, most were grand structures with arched doorways, balconies and shutters, as romantic as she'd hoped they'd be. In front of them various boats were moored, most of a practical nature. The canals were narrow at first, their driver negotiating them with impressive ease, but they turned a corner and it widened into a much bigger expanse. It was the Grand Canal, teeming with colour, with life, with the toing and froing of boats, taxies and buses, all of the aquatic variety and packed to bursting.

"Look, there's a couple on a gondola!" She couldn't help it, she was squealing again.

Rob rolled his eyes but he looked amused nonetheless. "Our hotel's a bit further down, I hope you like it. It's got rave reviews on-line."

"I'm sure I'll love it. I love everything about this place. Everything!"

"Everything?" queried Rob as the driver made a slight left so he could dock. "Even that weird island you were reading about, what's it called? Pov…"

"Poveglia," she replied, laughing about it. "It's called Poveglia. You don't pronounce the 'g' apparently, so phonetically it's Pov-el-ia."

"Ah, okay, Pov-el-ia," he repeated in an exaggerated manner.

Realising the driver had cut the engine she edged the short distance towards the deck, Rob close behind her. It felt good to be standing tall again, breathing the fresh air. She was about to thank the driver for a safe journey – *grazie mille*, thanks a million – but his expression rendered her mute. What was wrong with him? He looked… horrified.

"*Perché parli di questo posto?*"

Louise had no idea what he'd said. "I'm sorry, I…"

"*Poveglia, perché parli di questo?*"

The island – the one she'd researched, that Rob had just mentioned… correction, *she* had just mentioned – is that what he was referring to? In a string of alien words, she recognised that one at least. Not sure he'd understand her, she tried to explain.

"Look, it's just a joke, on Google when I—"

Surprising her further, the driver closed what little gap there was between them. When they'd climbed on-board, she hadn't really noticed him; she'd been too caught up in everything around her. But he hadn't set any alarm bells off; he'd been benign enough, a shadow figure; someone who'd transport them to Venice and be paid well to do it. But now she recoiled. He was no longer benign – he'd transformed into something menacing.

Panic ignited. "Look," she said, "we're only here for the weekend, we…"

Unsure what else to say, she looked at Rob for help, he seemed as confused as she was, his mind working overtime, trying to figure out what was going on.

"Hang on a minute, mate—" he began but the driver was having none of it.

A rush of words tumbled from his mouth and again it was just the one that stood out: *proibito*. When she'd been looking at images of Poveglia, there were a couple that had included a sign, located at the entrance to the island where the boats pull up, and on that had been inscribed the word '*Proibito*' in large red letters. The place was prohibited.

As Rob and the driver continued to square up to each other, the expressions on their faces growing increasingly fierce, she held up one hand in a conciliatory gesture and forced it between them, desperate to stop the situation from escalating. "*Capito, capito,*" she said, cursing her pigeon Italian, "*proibito, Poveglia proibito.*"

What had been in the driver's eyes – horror, anger and something else too – began to dissipate, but with a slowness that was excruciating. Even so, she waited patiently for him to speak and when he did she felt almost weak with relief to notice he was calmer.

"*Capito?*" he repeated.

"*Si,*" she hurriedly replied. "I understand." Making a wide arc with her hand she continued, "Just the city, we're visiting the city, that's all."

"*Proibito,*" he emphasised. And then in hesitant English, "Do not go. No tourists."

"We won't." Vigorously she shook her head to emphasise her words. Glancing again at a still startled Rob, she said, "Pay the man and let's get to our hotel."

As the driver stood by – thankfully letting them pass without further incident, she whispered to her husband. "And make sure you tip him."

Right now, all she wanted was to appease him and to escape.

Chapter Two

"WHAT the fuck was all that about?" said Rob, as he stood on the jetty, staring as the driver reversed his boat to disappear into the thick of the traffic.

Louise was shocked too. "It's because I mentioned Poveglia. It must be a bit of a sore point with the locals."

Rob stooped to get his bag. "Well don't mention it again then."

Watching him stride off, she couldn't believe it – he sounded annoyed with her now! She wanted to shout after him, defend herself. *You brought the subject up in the boat, not me!* But she made a conscious effort to hold back. They were here to have a good time not argue – certainly not over some bloody-minded taxi driver and an island with a dodgy history.

Making an effort to breathe evenly, she grabbed her bag and followed. In front of her, inscribed in gold lettering on glass double doors were the words *Venezia Palazzo Barocci*. As she pushed them open and stood in the lobby, she saw that the interior was as grand as the outside. It was nothing less than opulent, with a white marbled floor, and tasteful accents of gold, red and black in the décor. Paintings of Old Venice graced the walls – harking back to a time when it had been a trading port rather than a tourist destination. In the boat Rob had said he hoped she liked the hotel he'd chosen. She didn't – she loved it.

As they walked towards the reception desk, one of the paintings in particular caught her eye. Unlike the others it was of a house, set over an archway, a quiet lane beneath. It hadn't been romanticised, just the opposite; it was bleak, Dickensian in style she'd say. He'd been here too hadn't he, during his Grand Tour of Europe? That was something else that had come up when she'd researched Venice: Charles Dickens having visited, and how he'd described it as a dreamlike city, 'so decadent it confused the senses.' Had images of Italy inspired his books or had they been written before? Whichever way round, the scene in front of her looked more like nineteenth century London than London probably had. But it was Venice all right; a gold plaque underneath with the single word Venezia on it confirmed that fact. She was so looking forward to exploring, to immersing herself in its character and atmosphere.

About to turn from the painting and join Rob, something else about it captured her. In the window of the house was a shape. Taking a few steps closer, she peered at it. It was a figure, a woman perhaps, something white covering her head – a veil? The artist had made her hazy, as though you were looking at her through layers of gauze. Was she an afterthought, or the focal point? Were you meant to spot her straightaway or was she intended as a late 'surprise'? Quickly, her eyes scanned the rest of the windows, but they were empty, no one else loitering. Whoever the figure was, she stared back at Louise, taking advantage of having been noticed, mesmerising her.

"Darling, would you like a glass of champagne?"

Champagne? With some effort Louise managed to tear her gaze away. Rob already had a glass and the receptionist was holding the bottle, ready to pour another.

"Oh, erm… yes, please. That would be lovely."

"Welcome to Venice, Mr and Mrs Henderson," said the woman as Louise walked to the desk – Gisela from the name-tag – her voice only slightly accented. "Is it your first time?"

"It's my first time," Louise took the glass from her. "Thank you for this, how lovely."

"It is a pleasure," Gisela smiled. She was young and pretty, with dark hair in a chignon, red lips and kohl-rimmed eyes – the very epitome of chic. Louise noticed Rob gazing at her appreciatively and felt very dour, very English in comparison, dressed as she was in jeans, boots and a somewhat scruffy black jumper, her hair also untidy from the journey. Being gorgeous seemed so effortless for foreign women, whereas she couldn't remember the last time she'd felt that way. *Get a grip.* She raised the glass to her lips and sipped. *He's allowed to look.* As another young couple, clearly guests too, walked past them and out into the night, she found herself admiring the male half, tall and lean with a sharp suit on. *And you're allowed to look too.* The thought of which made her giggle.

"Cheers," said Rob, clinking his glass against hers.

"Cheers," Louise replied.

Her attention back on him, he looked relaxed. So easily he'd put that encounter with the taxi man behind him. His eyes were as lively as Gisela's, his smile wide. He was handsome, she realised – surprised at how often she 'forgot' that. Then again, when you lived with a person for so long, you tended to see the whole person, to focus on their essence rather than their looks. She was sure the same was true of him.

A shame really…

Catching her scrutinising him, his smile became a grin, a cheeky grin. There was a message in his eyes, she was sure of it: *hurry up and finish that drink, let's go upstairs.*

Much to the bemusement of the receptionist, she downed it in one, no longer feeling dour but sexy, and eager too, more so than she had in months, longer even.

The bubbles must have gone to her head. A few minutes later, when they were alone in the lift, she couldn't resist grinding her body against his. Rob's response was immediate. When they reached number 201, he opened the door and they practically fell into the room, their hands still busy exploring. Her eyes on him rather than the plushness of their surroundings, she dragged him towards the double bed and pushed him onto it before climbing swiftly on top. Meanwhile, he tugged at her jeans, fumbling with her belt.

"I can't undo the damned thing," he complained.

She batted his hands away. "Here, let me."

Standing again, she swiftly removed her jeans and jacket, indicating for him to copy her. He readily complied; clearly impressed with the way she was behaving. Semi-naked, she pulled him back onto the bed, taking the lead, riding him. In control of everything except her emotions, but this time *wanting* to give free rein to them. It felt good, so damned good, riding that wave, all the way to the top, higher and higher, further than she'd ridden it before. When she reached the summit, her cries of pleasure seemed to be torn from her. Rob couldn't help himself either. Despite being in a hotel room, his cries were loud too – guttural. Afterwards, she collapsed by him, her breathing as ragged as his.

"Bloody hell!" Rob said, when he was able to. "I should

whisk you away more often."

Louise took in his bemused expression. "I think it's *me* who brought you to Venice. You kept putting it off remember, and all because of that coffee."

"That damned coffee! Look what it's deprived me of all these years."

"Don't worry, we can make up for lost time."

"I hope so, but in a while perhaps. Once the little fella's had time to recover."

Seized by a new desire, Louise tapped him playfully on the stomach. "Nope, come on," she said, pushing herself away from him and rising to her feet. "It's getting late, it's nearly seven. I want to go and explore." In fact, she was almost as rabid about that as she'd been about seducing him. *Rabid?* She paused. What an odd way to describe it! But it was also apt. "Do you know what, I'm foaming at the mouth to get out there."

"Foaming at the mouth? Sweetie, how vulgar."

Retrieving her knickers from the floor, she threw them at him.

"If you don't want to put me to the test, move your lazy arse."

Artfully, he dodged them. "Me lazy? You cheeky cow." Pushing himself off the bed too, he chased her towards the bathroom, both of them shedding more clothes en route. In there, he trapped her against the doors of a very swanky shower, the cool of the glass a welcome contrast to the heat of his penis, which throbbed at the front of her. Clearly the 'little fella' had more than recovered. As Rob leant inwards to nuzzle her neck, she willingly succumbed – just one more time and she'd let him take the lead. She suspected Venice,

15

like so many cities, never really slept; they had hours to explore, there was no need to panic.

"I'll show you who's lazy," he murmured, his kisses showering her rather than the water.

Chapter Three

IT was gone eight by the time they made it out. The rain might have stopped but it was still wet, the damp in the air compounded by the water lapping at the sides of the embankment. A city built on water; it was, as Dickens described it, dreamlike.

Outside the hotel, in the Grand Canal, were several gondola mooring posts – red and white striped like giant candy canes and nothing less than iconic. Louise insisted Rob pose for a photo in front of them, Rob rolling his eyes at the prospect.

"Lou, you're being embarrassing again," he complained.

"Oh, shut up and smile," Louise admonished and he did, albeit reluctantly.

After she'd got the picture she wanted, they continued walking, inwards rather than along the main thoroughfare.

"We can go to St Mark's Square if you want. It's just west of here," Rob suggested, looking at the map Gisela had given him. "Look here it is, the *Piazza San Marco*."

Louise shrugged. "Maybe tomorrow. Let's walk the alleys around here tonight."

"Like a couple of tramps, you mean?"

"In your case, darling, not mine."

"Oh, I don't know, Lou, the way you were acting in the hotel room earlier."

Louise came to a halt. "Are you calling me a tramp?"

"Erm… I was joking."

"A joke's funny, right? That wasn't. It's perfectly okay for a woman to have a sexual appetite, to take the lead now and then. These are modern times, not the dark ages."

"No, I realise—"

"Then why say such a thing?"

Rob looked far from impressed by her outburst. "Louise, back off okay? It was a joke, just a joke. What happened up there, in the hotel room, I loved it. I hope there's more of it to come. It's… you know, it's been a while since it's been like that between us."

For the second time that evening Louise had to consider her reply. He was right, what had happened was a good thing, it had been a while, a long while, and she knew he was joking, of course he was. Why had she got so riled about it?

She decided to change tack. Adopting a coy smile, she asked, "So you loved it?"

"You know I did."

"And you want more?"

"Lots more. Please act like a tramp again when we get back."

With peace restored, Louise burst out laughing. "Buy me a posh dinner and I might."

As she fell into step beside him, Rob pulled a face. "Posh? No, no, no, Louise, real Italian cooking is honest; it's down-to-earth, it's real. We need to find where the locals go."

If there was one thing Rob was passionate about, besides architecture and sex, it was food. He adored cooking, often dominating the kitchen at home with his bold and brave recipes. Italian cookery was one of his favourites, if not his utmost favourite, and she agreed with him. It was more authentic dishes she wanted to eat too, not fodder for the masses. They'd managed to find some superb restaurants in the other cities they'd visited – she never knew a simple ragu could taste so good – and hopefully they'd manage to find more of the same here. But first the passages of Venice waited. They were more of a maze than she'd expected. They were dark too, only barely lit by ornate lanterns attached to the many and beautiful buildings that lined the waterways. Quiet was another way to describe them. Away from the Grand Canal, and despite their hotel being in the popular San Marco district, the silence on corner after empty corner was almost preternatural.

"It's as though Venice belongs to us and us alone," Rob marvelled.

"I know. Where is everyone? One minute you see them and the next you don't. It's like they've been spirited away, gone up in a puff of smoke."

As they continued to wander, their footsteps the only sound to accompany them, a thought struck her. "How are we going to find our way back? I'm lost already."

"Simple, we make our way to the Grand Canal and follow it home."

She stopped, took the map from him and began to study it. Between the lack of light and the tiny writing she couldn't read a thing. Unease shoved excitement aside. "We'd better not stray too far. It'll be easier to get our bearings tomorrow."

"Rubbish," Rob protested. "We're not going to get lost, besides which, I want to go over the Rialto Bridge, into the San Polo area that Gisela was telling me about. It's the most ancient part of Venice apparently, where the fish market is held during the day. She said there's some great restaurants over there, that we'd love it." He then went on to explain that Venice was divided into six districts, or *sestieri*. There was the district their hotel was in – San Marco; San Polo over the bridge; Cannaregio, which was apparently the Jewish district; Castello; Dorsoduro; and Santa Croce, the area immediately behind San Polo.

"How'd you remember all those names?"

Rob made a show of looking smug, but quickly he caved. "It's on the map, you idiot. Each area is a different colour and there's the legend for it in the bottom right hand corner."

She wished there was better lighting; she might have had half a chance of checking what he'd just said. All the research she'd done and the divisions of districts had passed her by. Too busy looking at tourist attractions she supposed, amongst other things.

Holding out the map, Louise asked Rob to point to the San Polo area, and to their hotel. He obliged and her unease increased. "There's quite a distance between the two—"

"But that's where Gisela said the best restaurants are, the most authentic."

"I don't want to go that far!"

"For God's sake, why not? What are you scared of?"

She looked around her, at the narrow alleys with no one in them. "What if... it's not safe at night in Venice? For tourists I mean."

"Not safe? Are you joking? Why wouldn't it be?"

"I don't know, I'm not sure..." But her unease refused to abate. That encounter with the taxi driver had really thrown her. Were all Venetians as aggressive as him? She shook her head, scrubbed the thought. He'd only got angry when she'd mentioned Poveglia. Even so, it hadn't got their weekend off to the best of starts. Exhaling, she rubbed her temples before pushing strands of hair away from her face. They were safe, of course they were safe, and it wasn't as if she was wandering an unknown city alone, she had Rob with her – he was tall as well as broad and more than capable of looking after them should they encounter any trouble. "Okay, okay," she relented, "lead the way to San Polo. You're right, it does sound good, but are you sure you'll remember the way back? Your sense of direction is a bit suspect at times."

"Hey, I'm not the one who got us lost in Rome, in Florence, in—"

"All right, all right, you don't have to go on. It's just… I'm relying on you, remember?"

Unlike in the guest room earlier, she didn't feel in control at all.

On the way to the Rialto Bridge, they found more bars, restaurants and people – passing some lovely shops too, selling a chic assortment of clothes, hats and gloves. Louise tried to remember the names of the ones she wanted to visit the next day but she was still finding the whole Venice experience bewildering. She could honestly say she'd never been anywhere like it before; it kept twisting and turning. Despite stopping to look at the map several times with Rob, she would never have worked out where to go if it hadn't been for signs on walls pointing the way to the Rialto Bridge and even those appeared to have been placed at haphazard intervals. Scurrying along, that's what they were doing, like mice in an experiment, veering this way and that, trying to find an exit. It started to get busier. She found the hustle and bustle around her comforting rather than annoying with couples, groups of friends and families passing by, some assured of their direction and others, like them, clearly confused. Suddenly Rob cried out, obvious relief in his voice.

"The bridge! There it is!"

"At last!" Louise replied before frowning again. "Oh… it's covered in billboards."

It was, and scaffolding too – not quite the thing of beauty she'd seen on the net. As the oldest bridge across the Grand Canal it needed to be maintained, she understood that, but staring at giant pictures of women modelling luxurious knit-wear instead of the intricate carvings of ancient stonework, she was disappointed. Rob was as enthusiastic as ever.

"Come on," he said, grabbing her hand and pulling her upwards.

They reached the middle plateau before descending to 'the dark side', as he described it. She was reminded of Florence's Ponte Vecchio. Shuttered windows either side of the bridge's expanse, most with graffiti scrawled over them, indicated that vendors sold goods here too, probably opening until late in the summer months but closing early in the depths of winter. The eastern banks of the Grand Canal's shores, however, were very different from Florence – rather than open into a wide expanse, she got a sense of being further enclosed. To the right was a market square, an ancient church at its helm, from which flowed a series of curved arches. Wine bars and restaurants nestled beneath them, silhouettes of people framed in the windows eating, drinking and laughing. And Rob was right, it was dark, so dark – the light from windows above the arches cast very little relief. Nonetheless, it was beautiful. She could see Rob thought so too; he was as wide-eyed as her at its antiquity. They steered forwards and gazed into the windows of one establishment – *Osteria Al Buso*. Louise suggested they go in but Rob was still reluctant.

"Let's see if we can find something a bit more special."

"*This* looks special enough."

"It's too close to the bridge, Lou."

"So?"

"Well, it's… touristy still."

"It's not though, the people in the window, they look like they're local."

Rob seemed amazed. "How exactly do they look local, Louise?"

"Erm…" She dug around for an answer. "It's the way they're talking, you know, fast, like Italians do, with lots of hand gestures."

"And that's proof enough is it?"

Instead of laughing she got annoyed. "I'm hungry, can't we just go inside?"

Rob looked fed up too. "Lou, we've only got three nights here, I don't want to waste one night eating at a place like this because you're too scared to explore further."

"I'm not scared!"

"Well, what are you then? Because you seem scared to me."

"I…" This was ridiculous, of course she wasn't scared, she was just wary of getting lost – how many times did she have to say it? Getting to know a city as complex as Venice in the dark was not ideal. She could imagine what would happen later when they'd had a few drinks, they'd take a wrong turn down a dark alley and end up in the canal, the thought of which succeeded in amusing her. She softened. Rob could be stubborn when he wanted to be, it was usually her that gave in and she did so this time, but not without compromise. "We'll give it ten minutes, if we haven't found somewhere by then, we come back here."

"It's a deal."

He hurried away from *Osteria Al Buso* as if he was worried she'd change her mind, but he needn't have, she was resigned to following him. Heading east, it wasn't long before it became quiet again, people falling away as if they'd never been there. There was definitely something about Venice, something *unsettling*. Without cars gliding by, without any green spaces, with very little in the way of modernity at all, it was an alien landscape.

Looking at her watch again, she couldn't believe it. They'd been walking for twenty minutes not ten. So quickly time had slipped by. Stopping in her tracks, she said, "Come on, I've done what you wanted, let's go to *Al Buso*."

"Yeah, yeah… oh, hang on a minute, what's that place there?"

She squinted. "What place?"

"There with the lights on. The restaurants in Venice, the good ones I mean, they don't look like the kind of restaurants we're used to, they're not that obvious. They're just doors in walls, you push it open and, hey presto, a whole range of gourmet delights await you."

"Okay, okay, we'll check it out, but if you're wrong—"

"I know, back to *Al Buso* we go."

A few minutes later, seating themselves opposite each

other, she hated to admit it, but Rob was right – this place was fantastic. The tables around them were packed to bursting with not an English accent to be heard. The liveliness of the place was such a contrast with the quiet alley the restaurant was located in, it was like a world within a world, which was an apt way to describe Venice too. The tension of earlier began to drain. Before food she wanted wine, and so did Rob. He ordered a particularly nice bottle of Barbaresco, which the waiter promptly brought over, filling their glasses and leaving them to savour the taste of it whilst they decided what food to eat. She drank hers quicker than Rob and he refilled her glass. Eventually they decided to opt for seafood, which was the speciality of the region, Louise wincing at Rob's exotic choice of spaghetti with cuttlefish ink.

Holding up a forkful, he tried to get her to eat some. "Go on, it's delicious."

Louise recoiled. "No thanks, I'll stick to clams."

"Scaredy-cat," he retorted.

"There you go again, insisting I'm scared all the time, I'm not."

"Really? You could have fooled me."

Although it was another throwaway remark, she bristled. She didn't like it when he put her down, even jokingly. Focussing on the dish before her, she took another mouthful of her own spaghetti. Their relationship was volatile at times, and in the past some rows had raised the roof; but she didn't want to argue anymore, she wanted her life to be calmer – *she* wanted to be calmer; for the turbulence inside, the constant churning, to stop. More wine was needed, it would mellow her, make her less sensitive. She used it as a crutch sometimes, but it suited them both. A calmer Louise equalled a happier Rob. Holding the now empty bottle aloft, she signalled to the waiter that they'd like another.

The evening flew by, rounded off by dessert, espressos and two rounds of liqueurs, limoncello for her and grappa for him – the latter, Rob told her, Italy's very own version of firewater. She had to admit, he looked extremely proud of himself for trying it, only his watery eyes hinting that he was finding it nothing less than a challenge! By the time they left the restaurant, they were, as she'd predicted, staggering.

Outside, Louise looked left and right. "Come on, Amerigo Vespucci, which way?"

"Amerigo who?"

"He was a famous Italian explorer, knew his way round, like you do – apparently."

Rob took the jibe in the spirit it was meant. "You think you're so clever don't you?"

"I'm just saying that's all. I'll tell you why I remember him; he's the man that the name America derived from. Incredible isn't it, to be born in one part of the world, *this* part, and to have another part of the world named after you. To be *remembered* like that."

"Yep, that's all we want I suppose, to be remembered." The way he said it surprised her. He'd looked wistful for a moment, sad even. Within a heartbeat he was back to his normal self. "Right, it's this way, follow me."

Leaning against each other, they started forwards, him giggling as much as she was.

"Who cares if we get lost," she declared after several steps, alcohol having upped her bravado levels. "We'll wander 'til dawn."

"No we won't, we'll find another bar to hole up in, get even more drunk."

"Lose the weekend entirely."

"There is that danger."

Venturing down another alley, all of which were beginning to look the same, she came to a standstill. This was not the same. This one she recognised.

"This is the alley in that painting!"

"What painting?"

"The one in the hotel lobby."

Rob shrugged. "Don't know what you mean."

To be fair he probably didn't. He'd been drinking champagne when she'd first noticed it and she hadn't pointed it out to him on their exit from the hotel that evening. She'd forgotten all about it in fact, until now. Although attempting to stand still, she was swaying slightly. "It's definitely the same place, I remember that archway and the house over it." She remembered the woman in the white veil as well, and how secretive she was, like the city itself.

Fishing about in her jacket pocket, she retrieved her mobile. "Hang on, hang on, I know, let me take a photo and we can compare them when we get back, see if I'm right."

"Whatever," Rob said. He started to walk on without her.

"Rob, wait!"

"Do what you have to do but hurry up," he called. "I want my bed."

She took some snaps and then caught up with him. Lascivious again, nothing less than a miracle considering how much she'd drunk, she wanted her bed too and him in it.

Chapter Four

DESPITE the pair of them hardly being able to walk in a straight line, once they hit the bed, energy surged from nowhere, empowering her again as she took the lead in another round of vigorous sex. From the look in his eyes, Rob couldn't believe his luck. After so many years, and despite whatever trials they'd faced, there was still chemistry between them but rarely was she free of all inhibition, as she'd been since setting foot in Venice. She felt like a different woman.

A couple of hours later, Rob was on his side, snoring softly but she was awake, wide-awake – adrenaline still coursing through her. She screwed her eyes shut and willed sleep to come, but the harder she pleaded, the more elusive it became.

"Damn," she whispered into the darkness. She'd be hungover *and* tired for their first real day of exploring Venice, both of which tended to make her grouchy – something she had to watch. There'd been enough grouchiness already, especially on her part. Over-sensitivity seemed to be a by-product of her failure to conceive; she could find the hidden dig in even the most innocuous of comments. Hard to believe her mother used to call her 'thick-skinned', albeit in an affectionate manner. She only wished she still was.

Opening her eyes, she wondered what to do. Wake Rob up? Fool around a little more. She was tempted. It was lovely to feel this close to him, to feel like she used to when they'd first met. God, how she'd fancied him, this friend of a friend who'd joined a whole group of them for a drink in a local pub one evening. She could barely take her eyes off the stranger in their midst; luckily he'd had the same trouble regarding her. She was the first one to say hello, incredible really, as usually she was shy in that department, preferring to let others make the first move. They'd talked all night, the crowd around them thinning, met the next day, and the next. So quickly they'd married, and what a perfect day it was, the sun shining down on them, and so many friends and relations in attendance. She thought she'd burst with happiness, a future with him such a thrilling prospect.

Her mother used to worry about her sometimes, whether a father who was by and large absent in her life would affect her trust in men – surprisingly that wasn't the case. There was something about Rob, something unquantifiable. He was just so *steady*; exactly what she needed, but not only that, dynamic too – an irresistible combination. Their first few years together had been a riot. Together they'd felt invincible – at least, she certainly had. Remembering such good times, *revelling* in them, one hand reached out, almost as though it had a will of its own, but she drew back. It wasn't fair to disturb him and besides, lack of sleep tended to make him grouchy too and one of them would be bad enough.

Turning onto her side, she grabbed her phone, which she'd left charging on the bedside table. Checking the time, it was 3.04 am, an ungodly hour if ever there was one. She sat up carefully, tapped in her passcode and went onto Facebook – it was quiet on there too, only a few posts capturing her interest. She sighed. What could she do to pass the time?

More research?

I've done enough.

What about restaurants? See if there are any more gems to discover.

I'd be happy going back to that restaurant we went to tonight to be honest.

No, no, you have to try other restaurants. He'll insist. Bars, what about them?

Okay, okay, I'll have a look.

She had no choice; her inner dialogue threatened to go on forever if not. Switching over to Google, she typed in *Venice Restaurants and Venice Bars* but there were so many of them it was overwhelming, all boasting a plethora of 5-star reviews. Perhaps they'd stumble on more excellent eateries, the way they'd done tonight. Some things were best left to chance. Charles Dickens sprang to mind again and the question she'd had earlier regarding whether the landscape of his most famous works had been inspired by Venice – researching that, she found that most had been written pre-Grand Tour. It was in 1844 he went to Italy, living in Genoa for two years and taking the opportunity to visit other cities whilst there, including Venice – the city he'd described as an 'Italian Dream'. Even though she'd been wrong, she'd bet he couldn't help but be struck by the 'similarity' of the landscape to that he'd described so vividly in his books. *Pictures from Italy* was the book that contained his memories of his time spent here, and she made a mental note to hunt down a copy back home. Where she lived had several antiquarian bookshops – she, and sometimes Rob, would browse in them on Saturday mornings – one was bound to have it.

Still wide-awake, still bored, she wondered what to research next. Almost lying in wait, one word sprang to mind:

Poveglia. Just what was that taxi driver's problem? He'd been angry, for sure, but there was also something else in his eyes – something, that in the quiet reaches of the night she thought she recognised – fear. Was that it? Was she right? The mention of Poveglia had frightened him? No longer bored, her mind went into overdrive. Why was he scared? Did he have some personal link to the island? Perhaps an ancestor had suffered there – been one of the plague victims or an asylum patient? Maybe it really was haunted, and those who lived in the city knew it. Maybe *all* Venetians were afraid of Poveglia?

Unable to resist, she typed Poveglia into the search engine. Most of what came up, she'd already read: The Independent's article for example, declaring it 'the world's most haunted island', sensationally describing it as a 'dumping ground' for plague victims and patients with mental health issues, and an 'island of madness'. Scanning it again, it told how, in the late 1930s/early 1940s, a doctor experimented on patients with lobotomies, only to throw himself from the hospital tower after claiming he'd been driven insane by the ghosts of his victims. The article included a reference to 'Little Maria' too, not just a plague victim but the stuff of legend; many visitors to the island having insisted they saw her at the edge of the lagoon as they rowed away, her hand pointing to the mainland and crying. Louise couldn't help but wonder at the story behind such a wretched being. Were her parents plague victims too? Were they with her when she was transported to Poveglia or was she, to all intents and purposes, alone? And if she was alone how awful, she couldn't imagine anything worse than a child being torn from its mother's arms.

Scrolling, she found another article, this one was heavily illustrated with photos of the abandoned buildings that the island was home to. The author of the article explained he had persuaded a boatman to take him there, not an easy task, as most refused to go, not least because it was against Italian law to visit – hence the *proibito* signs. Although a sanatorium in the fifteenth century, he stated, a stay there was not necessarily a death sentence. On the contrary, many people recovered from their ailments and left the island in a far healthier state than they'd arrived. But that had all changed during the sixteenth century, when plague hit Venice and panicked officials banished those struck down with disease to the island – that was when it became nothing less than hell.

Another picture – an illustration this time – of a doctor wearing a long-nosed mask and a long brown overcoat rowing the ill and the suffering to the island in a wooden boat, made her shudder. The nose of the mask was stuffed with herbs the author explained, meant to deter germs, but even so they made ghouls of the people wearing them.

Quickly, Poveglia was overrun with the dead and the dying. Soil, once used to grow produce, was now littered with bones. And then came the asylum, its location allowing for dubious practices to be carried out in splendid isolation. Louise scrolled through photo after photo that had been taken of buildings and rooms still in existence, some empty, others stuffed with bedframes and cabinets, mould on the walls and vines creeping in, their roots spreading everywhere. The floor of one room was covered entirely in pages torn out from books. Why? That photo in particular disturbed her. On the far wall was a window with bars across it; leaving no doubt that it was, in fact, similar to a prison. Scrolling further, she discovered there'd been a chapel, a huge industrial kitchen, a laundry room – huge mangles for wringing out wet sheets and clothes still in-situ – and a spiral staircase that appeared to lead nowhere. There were more detailed, artier shots of doors with paint flaking off them, various windows, none that were barred this time and a close up of another floor, this one with ornate terracotta tiles still intact. When it came to aesthetics, the Italians couldn't help themselves sometimes, even on an island like this.

Returning to the room with the barred window she studied it, fascinated again by the reason behind the torn pages. The window dominated the wall but the frame looked rotten, blue shutters either side hanging off their hinges. Some of the bars were missing as if they too had been torn off in fury. What was the view, she wondered? Green fields could be considered pleasant, but plague fields? Hardly. How awful to have nothing but that and four walls to stare at – to be locked in, hidden away, and all because you were ill. Madness – it was a horrifying concept and so easy to fall victim to, life itself hell-bent on driving you towards it sometimes, or rather life's myriad disappointments. Something she could identify with. As she stared at the photograph, she had to blink to suppress tears. So easily she could imagine herself in that room, trapped. She blinked again. Was that someone standing by the window, staring out of it – a figure? She focussed. It was a figure: hazy, barely an outline, but somehow familiar.

Where've I seen that before?

Her mind was aching with tiredness and the after-effects of sex and alcohol.

Come on, Lou, where?

It was no use, she couldn't think. She yawned widely and decided to turn off the phone; the light from it was beginning to irritate her. She needed sleep; deep, restorative and dreamless sleep – to purge from her mind all that she'd seen and the tragedy of it.

So familiar…

As she snuggled beside Rob, the heat from his body warming her, she remembered yesterday, standing in the lobby, and the painting on the wall.

Having closed her eyes, they sprang open.

That's where! It's the woman in the painting!

Just as quickly she dispelled the notion. Of course it wasn't. Why would it be? Frowning, she registered movement in the corner of the room, something white against the black. It was the curtains, a slight breeze from the window rustling them. But for a moment…

She closed her eyes again and this time kept them shut.

Chapter Five

HAVING set the alarm on her phone for eight o' clock, Louise woke feeling surprisingly refreshed, with no trace of a hangover. Her stomach rumbling, she realised she was famished, despite a large meal the night before.

"It's all that sex," Rob joked, as they left their room to go and find the dining room, where, according to the hotel website, a 'sumptuous buffet' awaited them.

"It must be," Louise replied; she could eat a horse. "Actually no, scrub that, I couldn't."

"Couldn't what? What are you talking about?"

Realising she hadn't voiced that last thought, she laughed. "Oh nothing, never mind. I'm being silly. Come on, hurry, the lift's here."

Setting foot in the lobby, what she'd seen during the night came rushing back – the 'veiled lady' as she'd dubbed her, standing in the window of one of the photographs taken by the journalist who'd visited Poveglia. Stopping Rob, she related what she'd seen.

"It's the same figure that's in this painting over here," she said, leading him to it.

She was watching his face rather than the painting and noticed him frown.

"I can't see any figure, Lou," he admitted.

"Look," she said, shifting her gaze and leaning forward too. "Oh," she blinked in disbelief, "she's not there anymore." The window was as empty as the others.

"There's a blob of white paint," Rob said, attempting to offer an explanation. "'There's the same in other parts of the painting too. It's clearly one of the artist's techniques, a highlighting effect, the sort of thing that's meant to be effective from a distance, I think."

"Yeah, but…" Retrieving her mobile, she started scrolling through on Google. "Here, this'll prove it."

"Shall we do this over breakfast?" suggested Rob, clearly hungry too.

"No, wait a minute. I want to show you."

It took another minute or so to load the right page and photograph. "It's this one," she declared before swearing under her breath. "Damn! She's not there either."

Rob looked amused as well as hungry. "She's elusive this woman of yours."

She was. Even so, there was no way she could have made the same mistake twice. Another thought occurred. Tapping her photo gallery icon she retrieved the images she'd taken after they'd left the restaurant last night, the ones that featured the same alley as that in the painting. *Maybe, just maybe…* But whatever she'd been expecting to see, she was disappointed.

"I'd been so sure …"

"Look, never mind," Rob put an arm around her shoulders. "From here, that blob does actually look like a woman, and it's only when you get close you can see it isn't."

But she *had* seen it close up, that was the point, and although hazy, it was defined.

"Come on," Rob cajoled, squeezing her briefly before removing his arm and turning in the direction of the breakfast room, "we can talk about it later."

She knew what 'later' meant to Rob – never. Like so many things, he'd just hope she'd forget about it and maybe she would. Maybe she should. She was getting too intense again, too dark, carried away on flights of fancy. Where was the girl she used to be? Was she gone forever or still lurking, deep inside? Would she ever be her again?

Stop with the questions, go and eat!

Once again she had to hurry to catch up with him.

Breakfast was indeed 'sumptuous', with an impressive range of hot and cold items, including a dazzling array of pastries, cheese, cured meats and panna cotta with fresh fruits. There was even prosecco available and some of the guests were indulging but for Louise and Rob it was too early to contemplate. After eating their fill, they returned to 201 to get their things, Rob making sure he had Gisela's map in his back pocket. As he sorted out some more euros to stuff in his wallet, Louise studied him: his expression as he concentrated, the thickness of his hair, the set of his shoulders. Desire stirred. She was amazed. Would it never cease this weekend? She was still aching from last night. Even so, she made her way towards him.

"Lou, what are you doing?" Rob asked, as her arms snaked around his waist.

"You need me to explain?"

"But I'm all dressed now, I'm washed, I don't want to have to get in the shower again."

She laughed, a low, throaty sound. "Stop being so practical!"

Her hands going lower, she began to tug at the buckle on

his belt, eager to undo it, to discard any barriers between them. So quickly her breathing grew heavy at the thought of what was to come, the sensual delights, his hands on her, her hands on him, his scent, earthy, enticing, intoxicating. Touching him made her feel alive; it sent electric currents into the heart of her, igniting her, waking something that had been sleeping for a long time, something that had lain dormant. She'd wanted to visit Venice for a long time, ever since she could remember, as a child even, looking at guide books that belonged to her mother, also a keen traveller, although Louise's arrival and her subsequent marriage breakdown had curtailed such wanderlust. This city built on water had always appealed, so why on earth she'd waited so long was beyond her. Despite this, she couldn't care less if they never set foot outside these hotel walls, if they stayed holed-up for the entire weekend, the two of them, in this room, behind closed doors, feeding off each other, vampiric almost, feasting – losing his identity, hers, becoming one. *But who is the veiled lady? I saw her. I know I did.*

Louise stopped what she was doing.

"What is it? What's the matter?" Rob, who had clearly got over the nuisance of having to shower and dress again, looked baffled. "Louise?" he prompted.

She turned away, needing to make sense of what had just happened before she could answer. One minute she had nothing on her mind but her husband, the next the veiled lady had encroached, striking, like a bolt of lightning, from nowhere and with just as much impact. The ardour in her had died at once; it had simply snuffed itself out.

It was Rob whose arms encircled her this time. "So what's happening?" he murmured his breath hot against her ear, scorching almost. "Am I doing my belt back up or what?"

She tried to laugh but couldn't. It was as if she'd been denied, something precious offered with one hand and then snatched back with the other. Quickly she tried to stop herself from getting upset. What was the big deal? It wasn't as if having sex ever led anywhere; it never resulted in anything.

"Louise?" Rob's voice had more urgency to it now. She had to answer.

"It's getting on actually, we should get going."

"So, I *am* doing my belt up?"

"Yeah, yeah, sorry."

Rob's arms fell away. "No, it's fine. You're right, I suppose, you know, about the time."

"We can always sneak in a cheeky one before we go out tonight," she returned, trying to soften the blow. "It's just... we need to make the most of the daylight."

Still clearly disappointed, Rob readjusted his clothes and they headed outdoors.

Chapter Six

"IT'S raining," Rob moaned, standing outside of the hotel. The water from the canal was high this morning, almost lapping at his feet.

"I wish I'd brought an umbrella, we'll get soaked," Louise replied.

"It's not a problem, we can buy one."

"Yeah, yeah, of course."

On their way through the lobby, Louise chose not to look at the painting. If the woman was in it or not, she didn't want to know. Besides which, she'd developed a theory: she'd been stressed after the incident with the taxi driver, not thinking straight. Captivated by the painting, she'd thought she'd seen something that clearly wasn't there, and then later on in bed, when she was reading about Poveglia, her mind – once again in a state of high alert but this time for more pleasant reasons – had conjured up the same figure. It was now stuck in her mind, hovering at the far reaches, which is why it had made a comeback in the midst of seduction. The not so far reaches actually, it had boldly pushed its way forward, but she wouldn't allow that to happen again. Wild imaginings were not welcome this weekend, she told herself as they endeavoured to find a stall or a shop that sold umbrellas. Wild sexual acts, however, she'd give the green light to. She was enjoying this whole other side to her that had reared up since arriving in Venice or rather she *had* been enjoying it until the veiled lady had interrupted. Well, she wouldn't fall prey again, because that's what it had felt like she realised – as if she'd fallen *prey*.

"It really is so strange here," she muttered, to herself as much as to Rob.

Not seeming to realise what she meant, Rob looked around him, at crumbling buildings that lined narrow passages, at alleys that led nowhere, at boats that rippled on lonely waters, some covered and some exposed to the elements. "I know. It's so different."

It was. Timeless too and full of… what was the word? Decay. That was it. "There's decay all around us."

Rob, who'd been admiring a church building – Chiesa di San Beneto, frowned. "You sound as if you don't like it here. It was your idea to come."

"I love it. It's… an observation that's all."

Rob returned his attention to the church. "I think it's fantastic, it's ancient and it feels like it, as though the modern world doesn't exist."

He was right about that. Everything outside city limits seemed insignificant. They started walking again, intent on finding an umbrella, happening upon a *supermercato*, squeezed in between residential buildings. Shaking off raindrops from their shoulders and hair, they decided they'd share one, Rob holding it, and being careful to cover them both.

Venice by daylight still had lonely alleys in abundance, but it was significantly easier to negotiate. Deciding to get the main tourist attractions over and done with, they headed to St Mark's Square first, only to find the basilica, like the Rialto Bridge, under scaffolding.

"Shall we queue to go in?" Rob asked, clearly not

impressed by a long line of people snaking outwards from the entrance.

"No. Seen one church, seen them all, although I do know an interesting snippet about this building too."

"Oh?" Rob inclined his head towards her. "Go on, enlighten me."

"Well…" she cleared her throat, enjoying the fact she *could* enlighten him. "Trying to tempt pilgrims to the city, two Venetian merchants went over to Alexandria in Egypt in the Middle Ages and stole St Mark's body from its tomb there, transporting it back by ship in a crate covered with pork."

"Pork?" Rob's face was a picture. "Why?"

"To stop the Muslim guards from discovering it of course. They won't go near pig meat."

"Ah, I see. But why go all that way? What about more 'local' saints?"

"They'd hardly be as appealing as St Mark would they? He was one of Christ's disciples, he wrote The Book of Mark too, one of the Gospels. He was a major player."

Rob stared at the building, at its majestic Italo-Byzantine façade and the five spires that surmounted it. "Do you think his body's still there?"

"Maybe, in a vault somewhere, a few precious bones on which an empire was built."

"Or a thriving tourist trade at least." Eyeing the queue again, he added, "I still don't fancy waiting an hour in the rain to find out. Maybe we'll come back tomorrow. The Bridge of Sighs is around the corner, let's go and see if that's covered in scaffolding too."

It wasn't, thankfully. And this time Rob was the one

telling her what he knew about such a famous landmark. "Some people think it's called the Bridge of Sighs because people sigh when they look at it. Its beauty moves them."

She had to admit, it was certainly moving her. Unlike other bridges in the city this one was high-up, connecting one building to another and made of limestone. Not an open bridge, it was closed, a glorified tunnel she supposed. Rob told her it led to the interrogation rooms in the Doge's Palace, which apparently once entered, very few left.

"And that's the other explanation for its name, the more romantic explanation if you like, that the view from the windows with their stone bars was often the last the convicts saw before they were imprisoned, the poor souls sighing at their pitiful fate."

"And that's supposed to be romantic is it?"

"I think it is, in a Gothic sort of way," Rob insisted before proceeding to inform her that, in actual fact, the days of inquisitions and executions were long over by the time the bridge was built. "So you see, that story, as so many are, is pure fabrication, just another way to tempt punters to come and have a look, to fuel their imaginations."

She looked around her. "This city certainly does that."

"Yep, whilst bleeding you dry of every last euro."

In a way, she was disappointed to learn the truth, to have her bubble burst – she actually preferred the romantic explanation. To illustrate that, she did indeed sigh at the iconic landmark before her, a protracted sound that made Rob laugh.

"Come on," he said, his arm around her, "let's get out of here."

They continued to walk, into the Castello sestiere, the

eastern part of Venice and mainly residential with lines of washing hung over the canals, which only added to the charm. Traipsing up and over bridges of all kinds, some rickety wooden ones, others more ornate, they veered away from the canals on occasions to encounter big stone squares instead – or 'campo's' as they were known. She still found the lack of green startling; there was no grass whatsoever to soften hard lines and edges. And children, where were the children? She expected to see some, certainly the offspring of those who lived here, but they were conspicuous by their absence too. '*Venice is closer to death than it's ever been*'. She'd not only read about Venice but watched a documentary about it too and that was something the presenter had said, referring to the fact that the age of the city's population was the highest in Europe. His words seemed pertinent on many levels.

Their legs growing weary, they decided to treat themselves to a pit stop at a bar in an empty square. There were only a few people sitting in its ill-lit interior and all locals by the looks of them. Rob chose his usual espresso, whilst she tried an Aperol Spritz – a drink she'd seen adverts for in the airport. Taking a sip, the taste was sharp and refreshing.

"Mmm," she informed Rob, "this is delicious."

"A new favourite?"

"Perhaps, whilst we're here anyway."

"Do you want another?"

She was surprised: not only that he was asking but also that she'd finished it – it had evaporated like air. Staring at the glass, she contemplated before shaking her head. "No, let's get going, we've still got loads to see." Besides which, the atmosphere in the bar was hardly scintillating, in fact, it seemed as though their presence was a hindrance. There were scowls on most of the occupants' faces; even the man who'd served them could barely raise a smile. There were cons as well as pros to venturing off-the-beaten-track.

It was whilst exploring another mainly residential area, Cannaregio, further north, that they decided to head back towards the Rialto Bridge and the more populated areas.

"We need shops," Louise decided. "Shelter basically. This rain is getting on my nerves."

The main shopping centre, if a series of shops clustered in ancient buildings could be called that, was close to the Rialto and, having reached it quite effortlessly, they wove in and out of doorways much as they'd weaved in previously empty lanes. There were brand names she recognised, including a clutch of designer boutiques, Italian of course, Prada, Gucci, Fendi, the wares on display sumptuous as well as very, very expensive. Giving them a wide berth, Louise stopped in front of a shop selling traditional Venetian masks, pulled in by their jewel-like colours and intricate designs. Some were light and pretty, able to make even the plainest of faces stunning, others much darker, with plumes of black feathers surrounding them and skull-like details. Studying them, she realised various materials were used to fashion the masks, including leather, glass and porcelain.

One mask, although tucked away in the corner of the otherwise busy window display, stood out – it was so different from the others. Not a thing of beauty, it looked to be made from bone, although that couldn't be, its ivory-coloured beak long and protruding, circles cut away for the eyes and rimmed in black. She knew what this was: a plague mask, the kind a medieval Venetian doctor would wear, the one she'd seen on that webpage she'd been looking at. Staring at it, she felt as cold as bone too.

"Rob," she called out. She was going to suggest they find another bar, one that was warm, dry *and* inviting this time, either that or go back to the hotel, have a hot shower and perhaps indulge in a little afternoon delight before heading out to eat. Whatever they decided to do, she just wanted to get away from this shop, from the masks on display in the window, and from one mask in particular. "Rob," she called again, turning her head to see an empty space beside her, and beyond that, just a sea of people.

Turning in a half circle, her eyes continued to seek Rob out. Where was he? Had he gone into the shop selling the masks? If so, why hadn't he told her? Despite not wanting to, she walked to the shop's entrance, pushed the door open and poked her head inside.

"*Ciao*, welcome, come in, come in," a voice beckoned.

"No, it's okay, I'm just seeing if my husband's in here." She hadn't a clue if she'd be understood or not, but rather than stare at the elderly assistant, she looked around her. Like the window display it was crammed with masks, hundreds and hundreds of them, thousands even – on walls, on tables, hanging from the ceiling. There were more plague masks too, not so apologetically on display, almost proudly presented, a centrepiece.

The man was standing behind a desk so big it swamped him. For some reason he agitated her as much as the masks did, with his wrinkled skin and eager eyes, black rimmed like the mask in the window. His nose was long and hooked too, but more than that it was his manner that disturbed her. He seemed greedy for her custom.

"Come in, come in," he repeated, bending his finger to entice her.

"I—"

"Masks, pretty masks, come in and choose one."

Did his eyes dart towards the plague masks as he said that? What on earth would she want with one of them? They weren't pretty, they were hideous, and not the kind of souvenir you'd want to proudly display on your return home – the damned thing would cause nightmares. The entire shop she found hideous as well as the concept of masks full stop, hiding what you really were – your true nature – *fooling* you.

She wouldn't go any further in. Rob wasn't here anyway.

"Sorry, excuse me."

Before he could answer her, try and persuade her to stay, to *lure* her in, she backed out, closed the door on his peculiar world and stepped into the rain once again.

"Rob!" she continued calling but he was nowhere.

Although it was cold and damp she began to feel hot and sweaty as the realisation hit that she was a stranger in a strange place.

Where the fuck are you?

Anger emerged – anger at life, and the unfairness of it. It was always there, simmering, waiting to boil over, but even she was surprised at how quickly it struck this time. Rather than fight it, she indulged it. She seemed to *need* to feel this way. She had everything, except what she wanted most. And Rob's solution was to travel, he thought that would appease that 'want', so much stronger in her than him, or at least it seemed that way, it would plaster over an otherwise suppurating wound. It was a pitiful solution, a weak solution; the solution that she'd come up with not even countenanced.

Whose fault was it anyway, their failure to conceive? The blame had to lie somewhere. Was it hers or was it his? It couldn't be hers, it couldn't. There was that time, just before she'd met Rob, when she'd been with someone else, a time when her period was late – and she was *never* late, she ran like clockwork – when she'd thought, as young as she was, eighteen, that she was pregnant, and if she was, that she'd keep it, cherish it, she'd find a way. But then the blood had come, much heavier than usual and much more painful, her stomach cramping in protest. A miscarriage? She suspected it. If so, she was definitely not the one to blame. He was. It was his fault, all of it – this whole sorry mess.

"*Scusa!*"

A man rushing by bumped into her, unbalancing her slightly. Straightening, she glared after him. *Bloody rude lot!*

Moving forward, she continued scanning the crowds, one half wanting Rob to disappear forever, the other half willing him to materialise. Her anger was beginning to scare her.

Rob, where are you?

He couldn't have gone far. Why would he have done? He wouldn't leave her. And these people, they were all dark shapes, all anonymous, and there were so many of them, such a contrast to the area they'd been in earlier. They seemed to meld into one, unmasked but still indefinable – a mass of people, rather than separate beings. And then there was one that was entirely separate – a flash of white. Her head jerked towards it. In amongst the crowd, perfectly still, was a woman, a veil covering her head and a dress to match, long and full. A strange vision but, as the rain continued to fall, what was strangest of all were her eyes – sightless eyes – staring at her, stealing her breath, holding her captive again.

Chapter Seven

"WHAT are you staring at?"

Louise spun round, aware she was still holding her breath and that her chest felt like it was going to burst. It was Rob. The air rushing from her lungs, she fell against him.

"What is it, Lou? What's the matter?"

He was solid, real, so unlike what she'd just seen. She lifted her head and looked into his amused but concerned eyes, tried to tell him what had happened, opened her mouth to speak, but couldn't. Of course she couldn't! She'd sound insane if she did. *Oh, Rob, there you are. Whilst you were gone, whilst you were hiding from me, I saw her. Yeah, that's right, the one I was telling you about, the one in the painting in the hotel lobby, in the photographer's picture on the net, the veiled lady, the woman in white, whatever you want to call her, I saw her, over there, in the distance, standing boldly amongst everyday people, but focused on me, just me. I half expected her to lift her finger, to point at me, like some kind of grim reaper only in white, not black. She was dressed in white.*

She gasped again, pushed herself slightly away from Rob and, with her fist, thumped him on the chest. "Where the bloody hell did you go? I looked for you everywhere!"

"I was looking at the watches."

"What watches? Where?"

"There," he said, pointing to a shop close by. "What's the matter, aren't I allowed to leave your side for a few seconds?"

"Seconds?" It had seemed much longer than that. She pursed her lips, still indignant. "You should have told me where you were going."

"You were looking at the masks, I was on my way back. I didn't think you'd notice."

Oh she'd noticed all right, much more than she'd wanted to.

She moved fully away from him, and threw her hands in the air, trying to get her point across. "Just… tell me okay, if you're going to disappear."

"Okay, okay," he replied, looking just as exasperated. "What's wrong with you lately? Ever since we've got here you've been really nervy."

"No I haven't!"

"Yes, you have, and in other ways you've been different too."

"In what other ways?" But she didn't need him to elaborate, not out here, in a busy Venetian street, she knew in what other ways. Instead she shook her head, whispered almost. "I can't believe you're complaining. Most men would be delighted."

"I *am* delighted."

"It doesn't sound like it."

He moved closer to her, tried to bridge the distance she'd put between them. "Don't get angry, Lou, don't spoil things. Let's go and get another drink."

"Me, spoil things? You've got a bloody cheek!"

"Louise!"

There was a warning in his voice; she was tempted to ignore it, to indulge her anger further. He'd changed too during their marriage – he'd become someone who dismissed her all too readily, who treated her like a child rather than an adult, who happily pointed out her flaws – *scaredy-cat*. The halcyon days she'd been reminiscing over last night in bed seemed a million miles away, especially now, standing here in the rain, in the gloom, so far from home. They were a dream she'd woken from too soon. Of course she knew when things had changed. She was under no illusion about that. Suddenly their glittering world felt cursed. *She* felt cursed. That's when the rot had set in – each one dealing with their disappointment in their own way, not together but alone.

Looking at him, into the face she'd loved, his features slightly more grizzled with time and stubble with a hint of grey in it covering his chin, defiance still stirred within her. There followed a tense few moments in which she couldn't judge which way the pendulum was going to swing. It went one way and then the other, the momentum equal. Eventually familiarity tempered the rebel within. As irritating as she found him sometimes, as *disappointing*, he was her man and she was tired of fighting. More than that, she was exhausted, as if her energy had been leeched from her. She slumped, not against him this time, but she could feel herself wilt, cave in – give up almost.

Rob's expression relaxed – she hadn't realised until now how hard his gaze had become. Evidently he could see the battle was over and that he'd triumphed.

"Lou, I know we're wet, we're cold, but let's not bother going back to the hotel. Let's cross the bridge, go over into San Polo, find a nice wine bar, *Al Buso* or something, you liked the look of that one didn't you, and it's not far. Five minutes if that."

Not go back to the hotel? Was he worried she'd try and

seduce him again? *Jump your bones.* Couldn't he bear the prospect? He'd rather stay here; stay cold.

LOUISE, STOP IT!

She screamed the words out loud – albeit in the confines of her head – unable to believe where her thoughts were taking her. As for what he'd done, it wasn't so bad; she was blowing it out of all proportion. It wasn't bad at all in fact – why was she so intent on condemning him? And what she'd seen, the veiled lady, that was her tired mind playing tricks on her, nothing more and nothing less. Perhaps she shouldn't go to *Al Buso*, as much as she wanted a drink, perhaps she should go to the hotel room and sleep – how she wanted to sleep, but Rob was nudging her again, waiting for an answer. He looked in need of a drink too.

Shoving her hands in her jacket pocket she trudged silently towards the bridge.

Al Buso was packed with so many, like them, seeking shelter from the rain. The atmosphere was jovial enough despite the weather as couples and groups of friends occupied the various seats, talking animatedly, their laughter carrying. Rob spied an empty table in a corner and pointed her in the direction of it. She didn't need to tell him what she wanted, he knew well enough by now, a cold glass of white wine, anything but Sauvignon Blanc.

It took a few minutes for him to return, minutes in which she forced her mind to remain as still as a millpond, refusing to let any more thoughts encroach, or any visions. Here at least, surrounded by so many living, breathing people, she felt safe – it was just so *alive*.

Finishing the first glass of wine, she asked for another,

desperate to benefit from its relaxing effect. Rob didn't even query it, he simply returned with two more drinks for them to down in record speed too. Not usually one to show his emotions, she sensed he was as tense as she was, her mood rubbing off on him.

Their conversation warmed up with the second round of drinks, but they still carefully avoided the subject of what had just happened. Graduating from stock phrases such as 'I can't believe how busy it is in here' and 'It's only late afternoon, yet the place is packed' to 'I know I've been a bit jumpy but this place, it takes some getting used to doesn't it?' and 'It does, it really does, like we said before, it's different to other cities but it's beautiful, Lou, you can't deny that.' No she couldn't, she wouldn't. They had a day and a half left – she wouldn't count Monday as they were leaving Venice early in order to catch the mid-morning plane – so they needed to enjoy what time they had left to the full, to enjoy each other. All too soon they'd return to their busy lives, working late, sometimes only catching up with each other at bedtime, too exhausted to even chat, just kiss each other goodnight. On some days she swore she talked to the postman more than Rob. *That's why this time is precious*, she reminded herself. *What you have is precious.* It wasn't lacking, not in any way.

The wine doing its job, she wanted to laugh at how she'd behaved earlier, at the eerie masks and the veiled lady. She'd have to stop watching so many horror films, switch to rom-coms instead, take notes and learn a little – remember what she'd clearly forgotten. One thing was certain; she'd be on her guard for such nonsense from now on. Pleased with her decision, she brightened considerably and they continued chatting, continued drinking, another glass of wine slipping down very nicely.

"We haven't had lunch!" Louise said suddenly.

"No, we haven't." Rob seemed surprised too. He looked over his shoulder, towards the bar. "They've got cicchetti at the bar, do you fancy some?"

"Cicchetti, what's that?"

"It's the Italian version of tapas, there's lots of different dishes. I'll get us a selection." He looked at his empty beer glass, "And another round as well."

Feasting on more alcohol, and the cicchetti, including marinated olives, calamari with garlic aioli and various cheeses, Louise had to admit it, she was drunk, but happily drunk, the events of earlier tucked away nicely, a door closed on them. *You're taking a leaf out of Rob's book there*, she thought, but not with anger.

Deciding they needed something more substantial than cicchetti to eat, they left the cosy confines of the bar and returned outside. The rain had stopped but night had really taken hold – the lights around them so dim it was much blacker than it should be.

"Where to?" she asked.

"Another bar?"

"More drinking? I'm not sure I can."

"Oh come on, that's not the Lou I know and love!"

She groaned. "The spirit is willing, but you know what they say about the flesh."

"The flesh is gorgeous," he said, reaching out to hug her, making her feel hungry again, but not for food.

"Shall we just go home," she whispered into his ear, breathing him in.

"Home? The hotel you mean?"

She nodded; he was tempted she could see.

"Erm… no come on, another bar, and then food, we need pasta, lots of it. Bruschetta too, or whatever they call it, undo the damage we've done and are about to do more of."

It was later, much later that they stumbled into a restaurant – the same one as last night despite Rob wanting to try somewhere new. It just so happened that the second bar they'd been lingering in, laughing, chatting, leaning into each other, behaving like the couple they'd once been, with no cares, no worries, was close to it. They could literally fall out of one door, walk down one or two alleyways, under the same archway as before, the one in the painting, and fall into another. Initially Rob protested that they should go somewhere else, but he could see the logic of the situation, besides which, the food had been good, really good; they knew they were in for a treat.

Pushing their way in, it was as packed as the previous night. They had to wait over ten minutes in the cold entrance for a table to become free, Louise enjoying the banter of the waiters as they hurried back and forth, and their good-natured gesticulating. Eventually they were shown to their table – not ideal, it was close to another couple – very close. Louise hated it when that happened, but it was too late to turn back, despite her casting a longing glance towards the door. *It's too late.* Even after she sat, those words kept repeating.

Chapter Eight

LEANING in towards Rob, Louise realised she was mirroring the woman beside her, as if they were each, in their own way, trying to mark their territory – this man is my man, this boundary is our boundary, don't overstep it – another fanciful notion that made her laugh.

"What's the matter?" Rob's voice was barely above a whisper.

"Nothing," she replied, feeling coquettish. "I want to be close to you that's all."

"You want to sit on my lap?"

"I do actually."

"I dare you."

Louise placed her menu on the table and made to rise, keeping her eyes trained on Rob all the time, loving the amusement in his eyes. When he didn't falter, she did, collapsing back down again, stifling her giggles, trying not to disturb the other couple – and failing.

They were looking at her, both of them. Similar in age, she guessed, to her and Rob, around their mid-thirties, both were dark haired, slim and well tailored. The man had aquiline features and dark eyes, his eyelashes so long any woman would envy them. She considered the woman attractive, her features just slightly too sharp to be considered pretty, her skin alabaster, and the nails on her hands manicured.

It was the man who smiled first. "*Ciao*," he said. "You look like you're having fun."

Although heavily accented, his English was perfect. Immediately Louise apologised, mortified that their drunken behaviour had interrupted their meal. Not interrupted exactly, as there were no plates set before them, just glasses of wine – they'd either finished or hadn't started yet. It turned out to be the latter, as starters were delivered to their table, a small round plate for each of them with round potato dumplings arranged in the middle. She knew what it was: gnocchi in a crab sauce, she'd been tempted to order the same. As they picked up their cutlery, she'd thought they'd concentrate on each other rather than them – she was wrong. Once they'd broken the ice, they were dead-set on continuing.

"English, yes?" the man continued, spearing a piece of gnocchi and lifting it to his mouth. "You are on holiday?"

"We're here for the weekend," Rob informed him. "What about you, do you live here?"

"Si, we live not far away, in the Cannaregio sestiere." His fork now empty, he gestured around him. "This is a good restaurant, good food. It is mainly the locals who eat here."

Rob glanced at Louise, a smug '*I told you*' expression on his face. "We came here last night, actually," he informed them. "It was so good we decided to come back."

Not strictly true but what the hell, they were only making small talk. The waiter came to take their food and wine order. "We'd like water too, please," added Louise, "a big jug of it." She'd better make an attempt at sobering up.

Leaning forward once again, making small talk with her

husband instead, she could feel his knees rub against hers, a smouldering look in his eyes. They'd decided against starters and there'd be no dessert either – they'd race back to the hotel, her yearning for him needing further satisfaction. She'd have been happy to dispense with the meal entirely, cancel their order, get out of there – was about to suggest it, when the man beside her started speaking again. He was holding out his hand and introducing himself.

"My name's Piero and this is my wife, Kristina. We're glad to meet you."

She was hesitant and so was Rob, but quickly she remedied it and took his hand. "Hi, I'm Louise, and this is Rob. We're pleased to meet you too."

The couple had finished their starters and, like them, were waiting for their mains. Pouring from his bottle of wine into Kristina's glass and his own, he offered them some.

"Oh, no thanks, we've got a bottle coming." The minute she said it, Louise wondered if she'd appeared rude – perhaps sharing bottles of wine on the continent with strangers in a restaurant was the norm. It was very unlikely that such a thing would happen in England.

The man – Piero – didn't seem to take offence, he smiled and placed his bottle back on the table, just as the waiter reappeared with theirs. Quickly, she filled their glasses, making an effort to 'join in'. As she did, Piero pulled his chair even closer to them, encouraging his smiling wife to do the same. Bewildered by their 'friendliness' she looked at Rob for confirmation that he was feeling the same. Rob, however, had a big smile on his face and looked only too pleased to be chatting to them. Trying to hide her disappointment, Louise smiled as well. They could still eat their meals quickly and be out in an hour or so – it wouldn't hurt to be friendly too.

The conversation at first revolved around local foods and wine, twin subjects she knew from experience were close to Italian hearts. They'd got chatting to local people in other Italian cities they'd been to and conversation usually started off in the same way. Very soon though, and just as their main dishes arrived, talk turned to more cultural matters, Piero, in particular, wanting to know what sights they'd seen in Venice so far. It turned out, that like Rob, he was an architect too. After some time discussing the merits of the city's Gothic style architecture with its Byzantine and Moorish influences, Rob admitted that the only 'official' sightseeing they'd done had been in St Mark's Square.

"Ah, the coffee, tell me you didn't have coffee there." It was the woman who said it, Kristina, the first time she'd really spoken apart from murmuring a few agreements here and there. She couldn't have said a better thing – Rob roared with laughter, Louise did too – the damage to your purse caused by having coffee in St Mark's Square seemed to be widely recognised. As they began eating, Louise explained they preferred to get a feel for the 'real' Venice rather than focus on tourist routes.

"Have you been for a ride on a gondola yet?" Kristina asked.

"No, it's not really for us, again it's too touristy," Louise explained. "We arrived by speedboat though. Rob booked a private taxi, so that's our trip on the waters sorted I guess." Talking about the taxi ride reminded her of the taxi driver and his reaction when she'd mentioned Poveglia. Rob must have noticed her frown, making the connection in his mind too. *Don't mention the island.* She could hardly say the words out loud but she hoped her look said it all. She needn't have worried. He didn't bring the subject up. Piero did.

"If you're looking for different attractions, I know one. Have you heard of Poveglia?"

Rob looked as stunned as she felt. The island, it was never far away.

"Funnily enough," Rob replied, reaching for his glass of wine and taking a sip, "we have. Well, Louise knows all about it, she read loads about it before we came here."

"Not loads," Louise denied, "just a bit. I'm by no means an expert."

"You'll know all about the *fantasma* then?" Piero continued. "Sorry, the ghosts." Lifting his hands and jiggling his fingers, he accompanied his question with a "woo, woo."

Kristina laughed and shook her head. "Maybe no *fantasma*, but certainly, it is interesting."

In Louise's opinion, what was interesting was finding two Venetians who didn't flare up when talking about it. Considering the taxi man's reaction, she had to ask, "Is Poveglia a sensitive subject? I know it's got a tragic history, what with the plague and the asylum."

It was Kristina who answered. She pushed her plate aside, having hardly touched the food on it, and was quiet for a moment, obviously giving the question some thought. All three stared at her, as if she were an authority on the subject.

"It is known as the world's most haunted island," she started, her voice slow, her tone deliberate. "Many people have died there over the centuries, the diseased, the murderous and the insane. The atmosphere, it's bound to be... tainted. I have been several times, when I was younger. I think we Venetians may have a little fascination with it. I felt

60

uncomfortable there but not frightened. What happened, the people who suffered, I feel sorry for them. I have respect, although there are many who haven't." Frowning, it was as though a shadow had darkened her features. "The walls are covered in graffiti, people consider it a fun place to be. They want to scare each other, return with lots of silly stories, trying to impress others with their bravery. I work in commerce but I have a deep love of history, like I said, a respect. That is the only reason I ever went there... to *understand*."

Whilst Kristina was speaking, Louise and Rob nodded their heads solemnly. Once she'd stopped, the air of earnestness continued, becoming slightly awkward.

Louise was about to speak, perhaps even change the subject, when Piero, addressing Rob mainly, started talking about the architecture of Poveglia's asylum and its combination of civil, religious and military influences, referring to it as an 'architectural mongrel' but one that was unique. "I don't know if you are aware, but there are plans to regenerate the island," he added. "How much longer it will stand I don't know."

"Yes, I'd read—" answered Louise but Rob interrupted.

"I'd love to go."

Louise stared at him; it was the last thing she expected to hear. "Rob—"

"I mean, like you say, not only has it got a fascinating history, it's a fascinating building too, and one that's in danger of being knocked down. We should see it whilst we can."

"I really don't think—"

"Have you been there, Piero?" he asked.

"I went there as a teenager too. It's forbidden by law to visit, but people still do. Nowadays I think it's mainly tourists, people like you who have read about it and become intrigued. In Italy, if you pay the boatman enough, he will take you."

"I wouldn't dream of going…" Once again Louise attempted to speak but Rob had got the bit between the teeth and he wasn't going to let it go. For what felt like the umpteenth time he spoke over her, causing her temper to catch alight, as easily as taking a match to paper. Forming her mouth into a tight line, she did her utmost to conceal it.

"How far is it from where we are? How much do you think it'll cost?"

Piero shrugged. "It's not far at all, not even an hour. As for the cost, it could be anything." He paused. "Do you really want to go?"

"Yes," Rob replied, at the same time that Louise answered 'No'.

"There is nothing to be scared of," said Kristina, focussing on her.

"I'm *not* scared." Now they were at it, as well as Rob. "We have a busy day tomorrow."

"Oh come on," Rob cajoled, "we've seen loads already. Why don't we do something different, see if we can find someone to take us? Don't pretend you're not fascinated."

"I'm not!"

"You are! You're the one who told me about it."

"So what? Being fascinated is not a good enough reason to go."

"Why not?"

"It's… macabre."

"Macabre?" Piero quizzed.

"So many people died there," Louise explained.

"It's history," he replied, shrugging again. "The Venetians try to brush under the carpet what happened, to make light of it. But I disagree, it shouldn't be forgotten."

"It shouldn't be treated with disrespect either."

"Louise," Rob seemed annoyed with her again, "nobody said anything about disrespecting the place!"

"I know, but—"

"I'll take you." Piero said the words so quietly that Louise thought she'd imagined them.

"Sorry?" she said.

"I'll take you." His offer was clearer this time, more confident.

Rob's eyes widened. "Really? How much?"

Piero let loose a burst of laughter, waved his hand in the air. "No cost. We are friends. You're here tomorrow, so let's go then, mid-morning perhaps? We're free. One thing though, there is no lighting on the island so we need to leave before sundown."

"Thank you, it's very kind but—"

Again Rob cut her off. "You're serious? That would be brilliant! Absolutely brilliant! Are you sure though? It seems like one hell of a cheek." When Piero frowned in confusion, Rob added, "An imposition, it seems like an imposition to take up your time."

"No, I offered. I'm happy to take you. *We* are happy, aren't we, Kristina?"

Kristina looked as puzzled as Louise felt by his offer but she agreed nonetheless. "Perhaps one more time it would be good to visit. Where's the harm?"

Feeling as though she were caught in a vice, Louise tried to appeal to Rob. "The thing is, I'd really like to see more of the actual city before we fly home. Maybe we could talk about this, between us I mean, take a number or something and let Piero know."

"Sure, sure, take my number," Piero said, retrieving a business card from his wallet. *Piero Benvenuti, Architetto.* "It's no problem. Call me tomorrow, but early, let me know."

"Well, I'd love to accept," Rob said, taking the business card and handing it to Louise to put in her bag. "As for my wife, don't worry, I'll work on her."

Chapter Nine

"HOW bloody dare you!" Louise yelled. "What do you mean 'you'll work on me'? Like I'm some sort of doll without a mind of my own."

How she'd kept from exploding after Rob had delivered that particular gem, she'd never know. But she'd sat there, a smile plastered on her face, as the conversation had continued over coffee and liqueurs, the waiter serving a round of grappa on the house, clutching at her glass so tightly she'd been amazed it hadn't shattered in her hands. Around them the restaurant had emptied and finally they'd called it a night, their newfound friends kissing them on both cheeks, as was the Italian custom, before disappearing from sight. They had walked a short way too, to where the archway was, when she came to a grinding halt, unable to keep a lid on her fury anymore.

"The things I said, my reasons for not wanting to go to the island, you just dismissed them completely. You talked over me at every opportunity—"

"I didn't, I—"

"There you go again, let me bloody speak!"

"All right, all right, go on then," he replied meekly.

"That couple seem very nice, I'm not denying that, but we don't know them. It's a bit odd that they want to take us to Poveglia isn't it?"

Laughing, Rob put one finger to his mouth. "Shush, I

wouldn't say the 'P' word too loudly around here."

"This isn't funny!" Besides which, there was no one to hear them, the lane was empty.

She walked a few more paces and then stopped again, determined to have her say, right here, right now. "Look, you go if you want to, but there's no way I am."

"Why not? It'll be fun." His voice was slurred; he was definitely drunk, little wonder given what they'd consumed.

"Because… it doesn't feel right, that's why."

"'Cos you're scared they might be axe murderers?" His laughter was such a maddening sound. "Or is it the island itself that terrifies you, the *fantasma*?"

She drew closer to him, hissed under her breath. "I am *not* scared."

"Then let's go, it'll be an adventure, something unusual."

She was stunned. "So what we do, going away for weekends, working so hard, it's all a bit 'usual' for you is it? You need a few cheap thrills to spice things up."

He turned deliberately coy. "You're offering me cheap thrills now are you, Lou, in this alleyway, a bunk-up against the wall? Don't mind if I do!"

She slapped him around the face – hard.

"Hey!" he yelled, one hand cradling his cheek. "What did you do that for?"

"Don't cheapen me!"

"What… when… I was joking for God's sake!"

"Yet another one that's not funny."

No longer laughing, he was almost growling. "What the fuck's wrong with you? Sometimes I really do wonder."

Exhaling dramatically he started to walk, but she wasn't done with him yet. She grabbed his arm and threw him against the hard stonework of the wall. He started to laugh again, unable to help himself it seemed, finding her oh so amusing.

"Louise, stop it. Let's just go to the hotel and get some sleep."

"You never listen to me, do you?"

He held his hands up in submission. "All right, all right, we won't go."

"I'm not talking about that."

"Look he's an architect, like me, not a mad man."

"I said I'm not talking about that."

Rob looked puzzled. "What are you talking about then?"

"About the fact you don't listen to me, ever."

Any amusement in his eyes – whether genuine or forced – fled. He had cottoned on to the true meaning of her words and his expression held a warning: *Don't go off on one; don't get hysterical.* He never actually said it but the intimation was there – always. Even if there had been people around, the lane packed, she doubted she'd be able to stay calm. Perhaps he was right: she *was* mad. Certainly, standing there, underneath the archway, madness blinded her.

"I know we can't have children—"

"Oh for God's sake, Lou—"

"Just listen to me! I know we can't have children, that IVF hasn't worked for us, but there are other ways."

"We could steal one you mean?" His eyes were steely as he said it.

"We could adopt." The last word she spat at him.

"You know my feelings on that."

"*Your* feelings, not mine!"

"Louise, I'm not doing this here." As he pushed away from

the wall, she blocked him.

"It doesn't matter where we are, you won't talk about it. 'Not now' you say, and come up with some excuse: you're busy at work, the phone's ringing, there's a programme on TV you're dying to watch, anything to fob me off. Not anymore. I want to adopt."

Settling against the wall, he uttered one word. "No."

"Why not, why the hell not?"

"Louise," – anger was rising in him too she could tell – "we either have a kid of our own, or we… accept the situation. And I thought that's what we'd done: accepted it. Decided to live a great life, just the two of us, pursue our careers, travel, have fun—"

"We can't spend our lives running!"

"We're not running, we're taking back control. What's wrong with that?"

Everything, she wanted to scream. *Everything's wrong with it!* Instead she forced herself to speak steadily. "Tell me why you won't adopt."

"I…" He shook his head, faltered.

"Tell me!"

Still there was silence, he wasn't even looking at her – he was looking away.

"Rob!"

"Because… I'm happy with the way things are, I'm happy with it just being us."

And there it was: the truth. *He* was happy. Who cared about anyone else?

Her voice when she spoke was venomous. "I hate you sometimes, do you know that, Rob Henderson? I hate you with every bone in my body! I wish we'd never come here, I wish we were back in England, or I was back in England, you can do what the hell you like. I don't care anymore. You're an emotional coward, a selfish bastard. You bury things instead of facing them, and you want me to do the same, put on a happy face, smile and be content. But I can't, I'm not content. I'm not the one who's infertile either. I got pregnant once, before I met you, but I miscarried. I kept it secret from you, but not any longer, you need to know, you're to blame for everything. It's all your fault."

So many emotions, from anger and disbelief to deep, deep hurt, played across his face as she spoke. And the words, once spoken, couldn't be retracted. She didn't want to retract them, did she? She didn't know. Her mind felt so clouded, as if time really had slipped away, reality too, as if they were on some dark but dramatic stage, and any minute the audience was going to clap at a fine portrayal of a marital breakup, were going to roar in fact, to stand and cheer their performance. The sound would be deafening, it would bring the house down around them, the house... the one over the archway. She didn't want to look. Had carefully avoided looking on their way here tonight. But now she couldn't resist.

Who are you? The words formed in her mind of their own volition. *What do you want with me?* Her gaze was drawn upwards. She hadn't noticed a curtain at the window the first time she'd seen it, but there were curtains now – they looked like lace, the fabric thin, so delicate and swaying slightly. Was there someone behind them, reaching out, parting them? If she continued to look would she see a hand – more than that, a figure?

She looked away. "Rob?" He was gone again, but where?

She hadn't seen him leave. "Rob!" She turned on her heel, scanned the distance in front of her. It was empty.

Nonetheless, she darted forward, propelled herself underneath the archway, frantic to be away from there. Where was he? Was she the only one left on the stage? No. She wasn't alone. She knew that. She hadn't been since arriving in Venice.

"Rob!" Her throat was starting to hurt from all the shouting she'd done. How come she hadn't seen him go? Too busy looking upwards, that's why; entranced.

A flash of someone in the distance, not dressed in white – thank God – but tall and dark, someone she knew. And she *did* know him, his flaws and his attributes. And he knew her flaws too. Yet still he was happy. He'd said so.

Breaking into a run, she forced herself to go faster. "Wait! Wait for me!"

He didn't wait, he kept on walking but she noticed his pace slowed slightly. Even so, he was in no mood for talking. That was fine, she accepted that. It was enough just to be by his side as he led them away from the archway, towards the hotel and safety.

Chapter Ten

EVEN though the lobby lights were glaring, they were a huge comfort – such a contrast to the dark alleyway they'd been in twenty minutes before. So different... except for one thing – the painting – an all too vivid reminder of what had just taken place. Still refusing to speak to her, Rob made his way to the lift and got in. She could have followed him, *should* have followed him, but she had to face what was happening. Steeling herself she went over to the painting. Its execution was cruder than she remembered, the artist having wielded his brush in a slightly random manner. But it was a style of sorts, as Rob had said, the blobs of white meant to be effective from a distance but not close up. Not meant to be defined at all...

"I've noticed you looking at that painting. You like it, yes?"

Surprised to hear a voice behind her, she spun round. It was Gisela, the receptionist who'd greeted them with a glass of champagne on arrival. She'd spotted her at the desk when Rob had glided by, but hadn't heard her come over. Almost involuntarily, her eyes travelled to Gisela's feet – no longer in high heels, she had black ballet pumps on in the softest of leathers. Perhaps they were allowed to relax the uniform a little so late at night. The woman had asked a question, she had to answer. Did she like the painting?

"It's... interesting," Louise said at last. "That particular house, is it significant at all?"

Gisela looked bemused. "Significant? In what way?"

"Because of who lived there?"

Gisela laughed, a pleasant sound, reminding her of the tinkling of bells. "I don't know who lived there. Venetian street scenes are popular with artists."

"I know that," Louise replied, she'd seen many of them in shops around the city, "but this one…" How on earth could she even hope to explain it? "I've been there."

"Yes, it is in the San Polo area, near to some good restaurants. I pointed out several to your husband. Did you go there to eat?"

"Yes, yes, we did." She told her about the restaurant they'd visited, twice in two nights.

"One of my favourites," Gisela declared smiling, her red lipstick immaculate. Even dressed down, she looked so elegant. *What does Rob see in me?* Tears pricked at her eyes. She was far from elegant. She was mad at times. Barren. Despite having blamed him, it could be her fault – a suspected miscarriage, especially so long ago, didn't mean a thing. *None* of it meant a thing.

Gisela placed a hand on Louise's arm, her touch as light as her tread. "Madam, you are upset, why?"

It would take too long to explain and thankfully Gisela didn't press her. After a few moments of silence she asked if Louise would like some water.

"No, thanks, I'll be all right."

"A glass of champagne?"

"I think I've had enough to drink."

Gisela turned back towards the wall. "What is it about the painting that troubles you?"

Louise was surprised at how astute Gisela was. Should she tell her what she'd seen? Why not? What did she have to lose?

Lifting her hand, she pointed to the window of the house over the archway. "When I first saw this painting I thought I saw a woman standing in the window, staring at me." There was a slight frown on Gisela's face but she didn't interrupt. "That same woman – she's got some sort of white veil on, a white dress as well – I've seen her in the town too, as if she's following me. And just now, coming home from the restaurant, I was standing below that archway, I looked up and there were curtains at the window where there hadn't been any before, lace curtains, and they were moving, as if someone was behind them, getting ready to look out. To look at *me*."

"Maybe the curtains are new."

It was an explanation – a valid explanation – but still Louise didn't think so. The curtains weren't modern in any sense. And they weren't clean either, you'd expect curtains that had just been put up to be clean but these were slightly grubby. She shook her head. Grubby wasn't the right word. Like so much in this city, they had an air of decay about them; they *were* decayed. "But the woman," Louise continued, "what about her?"

Gisela averted her gaze and Louise winced, she really shouldn't have said anything, but then the receptionist surprised her by taking her arm and steering her away from the painting, back to the desk, a deliberate gesture, as if she wanted to remove her from its influence. Focussing on Louise again, she seemed to think carefully before replying. "Venice has a reputation. It's supposed to be the most haunted city in the world."

Louise nodded. "Yes, I saw something about that on the net. Do you believe it?"

"I have lived here all my life and I have never seen a ghost." She looked so solemn as she said it. "All I will say is, it is a city to inspire the imagination."

Yes, that was a conclusion she'd come to several times this weekend – her imagination playing havoc with her. Stress too. She'd been under a lot of stress before she'd arrived in Venice, the usual kind, to do with work and clients wanting everything done yesterday, not realising she was only human, that she only had one pair of hands. And the other stress – the stress she'd been under for a few years now. They were proving a lethal combination.

"Poveglia, have you been?" She could hardly believe she'd dared to ask.

Gisela's eyes widened. "Poveglia? I don't understand…"

"It's just, we were talking about Venice being haunted and Poveglia seems to be."

"I don't believe in ghosts," Gisela repeated her sentiment of earlier. *Almost as if she's trying to convince herself.* But she was right. Of course she was right. Ghosts didn't exist, there was no need to be afraid, no need at all. As for the Benvenutis, they were professional people, cultured and responsible, with no motive other than to show two English tourists something unusual, *historic* even. And they'd only be there in daylight – Piero had said so. They'd arrive back in Venice in time to find a restaurant somewhere, just the two of them, settle in, discuss what they'd seen – laugh over it, tease each other even, insist they'd glimpsed something when they hadn't. It would detract from what had happened tonight;

the things that she'd said and done – hitting him... actually hitting him. They could put it behind them and pretend it never happened; *bury* it.

Looking at Gisela, a shadow across her face despite the glare of the lights overhead, Louise decided to agree with her. "I don't believe in ghosts either." There she'd said it. A bold statement made and believed in. Making a show of looking at her watch, she added, "It's late, I'd better go to my room. It's our last full day tomorrow."

Gisela didn't reply, she just smiled at her, her face a mask again, a perfect Venetian mask. Backing away from her, Louise turned in the direction of the lift.

The hour was past midnight, but she'd still text Piero, that way he'd get the message when he woke up, nice and early as he'd requested.

Hi, Piero, I hope you're well. It's Rob and Louise from the restaurant. We'd love to go to Poveglia with you if that's still okay. Let me know what time to be ready and where to meet. We're looking forward to spending time with you and Kristina again.

If Rob wanted adventure, she'd give it to him. As the doors closed and the lift travelled upwards, she continued to convince herself it was the *only* way to make amends.

PART TWO
Charlotte

Chapter Eleven

Late August 1938

SO what do I call you, sister dear, now you are a resident of a land far away? Still Charlotte? Carlotta perhaps? Isn't that how the Italians would say it? Or the Venetian, should I call you that? Ah – the Venetian – it's grand, it's majestic. It rather suits you. My sister, the Venetian – it makes me sound grand too, by association!

More seriously, how are you? Did you enjoy every minute of your honeymoon? I miss you. As do Mother and Father and all your friends of course but Enrico, the handsome doctor, who could resist him? They say the Italians have a way about them…

I wish we could visit – I should love to meet the rest of the Sanuto family. I know he's an only child but does he have a cousin as pretty as he is handsome? Perhaps he has several and I

*shall be spoilt for choice. Ah, Charlotte, you cannot blame a
man for dreaming!*

*I hope the overseas part of your journey was bearable. I know
you are not keen on the water, strange then that you have ended
up in a city surrounded by it. I wonder if you shall move away,
further south, as Enrico has promised. Venice is sinking you
know, or that is the rumour that abounds, so you may have to,
sooner rather than later. Perhaps you shall return home to England. How wonderful if you did. Mother and Father should love
it. They send you their love by the way, Father is still suffering
with his chest and Mother is still insisting he rests but you know
what he's like, he tells her not to fuss, that there is nothing wrong
with him. Some things never change do they?*

*I must away now but write soon. I am so looking forward to
hearing about your new life.*

Your loving brother,

Albert.

Charlotte sat in the window of her new home, a suite of
rooms perched over the top of an archway in a quiet alley,
her brother's letter in her hands. *The Venetian* – it did sound
grand, romantic even – like the city she'd found herself in,
her husband's place of birth. She fidgeted, uncomfortable
suddenly. The sun streaming in through the window didn't
just feel warm, as it did in England; it was hot, too hot.
Would she ever get used to it? At least when they'd travelled
they'd been beside the sea. Here, in Venice, they still were,
but in such a different way. There were no beaches, not close
by, nowhere to dip your feet.

Not that she'd dip more than that. Albert was right, she
wasn't keen on the sea, had a lifelong fear of it. It certainly
was ironic she'd come to live in a city built on an archipelago

of so many tiny islands. There was no rationale behind her fear. She hadn't nearly drowned like her cousin Martha had when they were children, cut off from the tides on a Cornish coast, discovered in the nick of time. It was just... the sea had a hidden quality. Beneath the waves lay a different world. She didn't like what she couldn't see.

She shook her head, laughed at such imaginings and placed Albert's letter on the table. Leaning forwards, she pulled the curtains slightly apart. They were made of white lace, purchased from the nearby island of Burano, her mother-in-law had proudly informed her. The alley below held a certain charm, but it was bereft of passers-by. She'd only been in her new home for a few days. They'd been on something of a Grand Tour before, she and Enrico, that's what it had felt like, similar to the lords and ladies of old, and Dickens too, in the nineteenth century – her fellow Englishman. She'd brought a collection of his novels with her, intending to finally read them. His stories might help her feel closer to home.

Closer to home? This was home now, her *marital* home. She must dispense with such thoughts, and get used to it. Her mother had been so worried she'd feel homesick.

"Darling, I know how enamoured you are with Enrico, but... should you want to return home at any point let us know. Nothing is beyond reparation."

Reparation – *amends*. What an unusual word to use!

"Enrico is a good man," she'd insisted.

"I know but you are so young and he is—"

"Foreign, Mother. You can say it. It isn't a crime you know."

She was angry at her mother's attitude although she knew

there was no malice in it.

Her father had taken her aside later. Obviously her mother had been talking to him too. "Look here, darling, it's not just because this fellow's foreign. Your mother is not biased, nor am I. But there is unrest abroad, considerable unrest. No one knows what to make of Mussolini. I want you to be happy but think twice before marrying this chap of yours and if you must go ahead, suggest living here. As a doctor, Enrico's skills shall be in demand."

She and Albert had been blessed with liberal parents. Albert was older: twenty-four to her twenty-two and education had been provided for both of them, embracing the arts, the classics, maths and science. 'I want you to have a good grounding,' her father had said. They'd been encouraged to stand on their own two feet and she had, leaving her home in Somerset and securing a position in London, at the British Museum, not as a curator, nothing as fancy as that, she was a clerk to the curators, a secretary.

But that's where she'd met Enrico. She'd spied him in the Egyptian rooms, whilst visiting during her lunch hour. The history of that particular race fascinated her; she remembered enjoying studying it whilst at school and now took every opportunity to increase her knowledge, still eager to learn. The look of concentration on his face as he read the information board appealed. He was both intelligent and endearing. She guessed he was 'foreign' as her mother put it. He was dressed differently to an English gentleman, in a cream linen suit, striped shirt and colourful tie. Because he wasn't wearing a hat, she could see his hair, which was greased back; making it look very black and his swarthy skin was such a contrast to her own fair colouring. Their eyes met – his dark brown, hers the palest of blues – their gaze holding much longer than was decent. Even so, she refused to look away; she wanted him to *know* she found him attractive. Seizing her chance, fearing she wouldn't get another, she'd walked over and introduced herself. Charlotte Evans. He was Enrico Sanuto, from Venice, spending time in London, studying medicine.

"Mr Sanuto, I have work to return to, but this afternoon, say around five thirty, would you like to meet me for some tea? I should love to hear more about your… studies."

She wondered if Italian women were as forward. Whether a look of horror would temporarily mar his handsome features, and he'd turn tail and run. That didn't happen. He seemed surprised, but there was also delight on his face. Breaking into a smile, he bestowed a kiss on her hand whilst whispering he'd love to meet her. How she'd concentrated that afternoon at work was beyond her, although looking back there'd been more typing errors made than usual.

His English was impressive, better even than the boys she'd grown up with, their thick West Country burr sometimes difficult to understand. She and Albert had received elocution lessons from a young age. Her mother, having hailed from the southeast coast and the daughter of an army captain, couldn't abide the Somerset accent. 'First impressions count,' she used to say. 'As soon as you open your mouth people will judge you.' Clearly, in her view, the judgment passed on those residing west of Southampton wasn't entirely favourable! As Enrico continued to enlighten her about his studies, including his interest in psychiatric medicine, over cups of tea and delicate scones with strawberry jam, she committed details about him to memory, the glint in his eyes as he laughed, the perfection of his teeth, the strength of his jaw, and the lively gestures he made with his hands. He could have been reciting the alphabet and she'd have found it fascinating. When he asked about her, she hesitated. She enjoyed her job but wasn't sure it could be considered impressive. To her surprise he hung on every word she uttered too. Instead of feeling hot and flustered she bloomed under such scrutiny.

"Where in Italy are you from, Mr Sanuto?"

"Venezia. You have heard of it?"

"Venice! Sorry, that's how we pronounce it here."

He'd laughed again, a sound she already adored. "I know that. Have you been?"

"To Venice? Goodness, no!" Her family could be considered comfortable but they had never travelled internationally. "Although, I have studied it in picture books and certainly I should love to one day." Was that again too forward? "Is this your first time abroad?"

It was and he loved it. "I find you English… charming."

Tea was over too soon but a second meeting was arranged, and a third, leading to many more, to a low-key marriage in the village where she'd grown up, less than a year later, with just her parents and brother in attendance. Enrico's mother had been unwell at the time but Charlotte had gleaned his parents wouldn't have contemplated such a journey anyway. She'd also worked out he couldn't bear the thought of a ceremony back in Italy and the fuss and pomp it would create – he was terribly shy at heart. The day was perfect and, despite her mother's misgivings, she'd never been so sure of anything. She wanted to spend the rest of her life with this man, only three years her senior, had known from the minute she'd spotted him. There'd never be another for her, ever. She *craved* him.

Against her father's advice too, she wouldn't insist he stay in England, how could she? She'd follow him to the ends of the earth. It was Venice he wanted to return to after their honeymoon, to his home, also occupied by his mother and father – Stefania and Luigi – just whilst he completed his studies. It wasn't ideal she had to admit. Living with them they couldn't be as free as they wanted, and the way his mother looked at her sometimes, Charlotte knew she was still fuming over her son's decision to tie the knot in England. Not only that, Charlotte felt she was disappointed he'd married an English girl; bitterly disappointed. She took a deep breath, reined in her thoughts. She was getting carried away! Stefania didn't hate her; she was simply being protective. And she could sympathise – if she had a son she should like to attend his wedding too.

Perhaps… perhaps she was missing home more than she admitted, letting such notions fill her head. She had loved her job in London, had felt proud to occupy such a post. Was it possible to find something similar here? Without something to fill her time she could imagine the hours whilst Enrico was studying quickly becoming lonely. They'd be hours she'd have to spend with Stefania…

Taking hold of Albert's letter again, she kissed it before folding it into a neat square, ready to take to her room, to be stowed away – a treasure almost. She got up, her figure slight but causing the heavy chair to scrape against the dark floorboards nonetheless. Working in Venice – what a prospect! She'd certainly be 'The Venetian' then.

Chapter Twelve

"NO! It is not right."

"Mamma, she is a woman who knows her own mind—"

"She is a doctor's wife! Her role is to support you."

"I want her to be happy, Mamma."

"I am concerned with your happiness. And a wife – a *proper* wife – would be too."

"Oh, Mamma!"

Opening the door of her bedroom slightly so she could watch the exchange between her husband and her mother-in-law as well as listen to it, it was only later, when Enrico had translated for her, that Charlotte would understand what was being said. Although she knew Enrico wasn't telling her the entire truth, she'd already concluded that the idea of getting a job – even for a short while – was abhorrent to Stefania.

"Mamma is perhaps a little old-fashioned," Enrico had said. "She believes you should support me rather than get a job... I am not sure, in a shop or something."

"A shop? Enrico, I was thinking about a post similar to the one I held back home, a clerk or a secretary, and just for a few hours in the week."

"But you cannot speak the language!"

She didn't need telling. How she wished she'd spent more time learning from him prior to travelling. But she'd been lazy in that respect. "Surely you agree a job would help me to speak more fluently and besides, like you, there must be plenty in Venice who can speak English too. This is a major city, not an outpost. There has to be something to suit me."

Enrico had shrugged and looked away from her. His dark eyes seemed genuinely conflicted – pulled between the demands of his wife and that of his mother. Seeing him that way, she relented. He was still feeling so guilty about having denied his mother her son's big wedding. In turn, she felt guilty too. Thankful they were in the privacy of their bedroom, she threw her arms around his neck and started to kiss the skin there.

"Darling, when can we get a place of our own?"

"When I am earning enough, *tesoro*." Already he was stirring against her.

"It's just... won't it be wonderful when it's the two of us again?"

In England, home for Enrico had been lodgings in a guesthouse, similar to the ones she'd occupied. Impossible to spend time at either – it would be unseemly – they'd signed into a variety of anonymous London hotels already as man and wife to spend days and nights together – the only accessories she'd taken with her sometimes a packet of Lucky Strike cigarettes and a favourite red lipstick. The sheer illicitness of it had been thrilling. She hadn't been a virgin when she met him; she'd had a brief love affair before, and saw no need to pretend otherwise. She wanted to be 'real' with him, herself, a woman who enjoyed sex and wasn't shy to admit it. So many of her friends acted coy with men, but that wasn't her way. The first time they'd been intimate, she'd dared to take the lead, just as she'd done when she'd introduced herself. He'd been surprised again, had faltered, clearly not used to it. He'd grown used to it, however, meeting her passion with equal ardour. Their honeymoon had only served to heighten the passion between them, culminating in their first night in Venice, spent not at his parents but at *Venezia Palazzo Barocci*, a hotel his father managed. Despite incessant rain, it was everything she'd hoped a first night in such a romantic city would be. Behind the doors of room 201 she hadn't held back. But now it was different. In this suite of rooms over the archway, with its thin walls, she had to stifle the cries that wanted to burst from her.

"Enrico," she said again, her hands beginning to unbutton his shirt, pulling it open to reveal his chest. Her breath, as it always did, hitched at the sight of him – at the tautness of his tanned skin and the muscles that lay beneath. Her mouth parting, she ran her tongue down the centre of his torso, unbuttoning his trousers too, tugging at them, his hands helping her, as eager. Down she went, until her lips closed firmly around him, her tongue still working, swirling the tip of his penis in gentle circles, teasing, tantalising. She heard him gasp, his hands grab at her hair, pulling her closer until he filled her mouth entirely. Oh, this was power! In this position he was at her mercy. She could play him any way she liked. *Is that what appeals about sex? The power?* Maybe, but combine power with love and it was even more intoxicating. She *loved* him, this exotic man, who loved her too.

Before the point of release she let him go and worked at the patterned dress she wore, peeling back her stockings and discarding them. Lying back on the bed, her hands either side of her curled blonde hair, she played the role of a wanton wife, waiting.

"Enrico," she breathed.

"ENRICO!"

Her whole body jerked. That wasn't her voice; it was Stefania's, close, too close. Her head snapped to the side. In the doorway – her bulk filling it – stood his mother, her eyes not on her son, but on her daughter-in-law – abject disgust in them.

"Oh God!" Her hands tearing at the thin sheet beneath her, she tried desperately to cover herself. When it refused to give, she jumped off the bed and hid behind it. "Stefania, please, you should knock before entering!"

Enrico, who was also busy trying to cover himself, glanced only briefly at his mother. Instead, his eyes were trained on her. "Charlotte, do not speak to my mother like that!"

She couldn't believe it. He was telling *her* off? "She barged into our bedroom!"

Still he was furious. "In my mother's house you will respect her."

She stared at him with wide eyes, lost for words. She could see he was embarrassed too, acutely so – his cheeks were suffused with colour – but she was unyielding in her view. Stefania should have knocked! Besides which, they weren't doing anything wrong, they were married and therefore entitled to have sex.

"*Enrico, vieni con me!*"

Hearing Stefania's voice again, Charlotte managed to tear her gaze from him and back to the doorway. The older woman wasn't looking at her now; she was *refusing* to. His head bowed, Enrico started forward, responding immediately to his mother's summons. He looked much younger suddenly, like a little boy scolded; what self-assuredness he possessed gone. *We have done nothing wrong!* She wanted to scream it, but refrained – fearing it would make him angrier still. As the door closed behind them, she felt imprisoned, despite the fact there was no lock on it. Feelings of shame rose in her for the first time ever. She looked down at her own nakedness, at the creamy flesh of her thighs and the dark patch that nestled between her legs. The female form was something to be celebrated; she'd never been led to believe anything less. But right now, in this bedroom with its heavy furniture and rug-covered floorboards – her pride had been trampled.

She could hear Stefania and Enrico talking in the living room. A fortnight had passed since Stefania had caught them in flagrante, and ever since then the older woman had ignored her, uttering sentences only when absolutely necessary. His father too, although kindlier than Stefania, hardly conversed either, but then his English was very poor. Things had been strained between her and Enrico too, she could barely forgive him for siding with his mother and he knew it, withdrawing from her rather than giving her his reasons why. As for sex, there hadn't been any. Only once, in the dead of night, had his hand reached out in an attempt to caress her. She'd refused to reciprocate. Not until he apologised, which he hadn't. Although in the past day or two he'd looked more sheepish than normal.

Enrico and Stefania's conversations, always in Italian, angered her too. His mother was able to speak some English, and had done so when she'd first arrived, making a semblance of effort. But she was making an effort no longer. It was mid-September and, in England, the leaves would be changing from verdant green to tan and gold. There were so many trees where she came from, the land with its undulating hills and pastures, lush. Here there was nothing but stone, and water where there should be roads. It wasn't exotic, as she first thought, or romantic. Rather, it seemed harsh. Attitudes were different too. In England, women were beginning to work outside of the home, even married women, at least before having children. In Italy, married women dominated in one area and one area only – the home. Enrico would never say it but clearly his choice to spend time studying in England was a chance to escape such tyranny. Whether consciously or sub-consciously, he'd been seeking a respite.

As she continued to listen to the exchange between mother and son she blinked back tears. Sitting on their bed, she lifted her head to look at the room's only decoration – a painting of the alley they lived in, of the suite of rooms that sat over the archway.

It upset her further, that painting. It reminded her of how lonely she was, sitting behind the window depicted, day after day, looking at such emptiness below, waiting for someone to pass by, to look up, to notice her. She needed solace and so reread her brother's letters. She had a total of three now and she longed for his enthusiasm and lightness of being. Here it seemed as if the darkness encroached too readily. Like the maze of lanes that surrounded them, there were too many secrets. A maze she hadn't fully explored yet and certainly not with Enrico, not since their first night. He'd been too busy at the local hospital, learning his profession in a more hands-on fashion, under the tutelage of his uncle, Fabrizio Gritti, a brilliant surgeon or so she was led to believe by the way his sister, Stefania, talked of him – no, not talked, she gushed. Charlotte wondered how acceptable it would be for a woman to explore alone and guessed it wouldn't be. No matter, the thought didn't really appeal. Venice was a city for lovers to lose themselves in, not for solitary meanderings. Finding work was the only way to break the monotony of her days and she was determined to do that, despite Stefania.

Distracting herself from the conversation she was not included in, she started to read, only half smiling at the envelope addressed not to Charlotte Sanuto but to 'The Venetian'.

September 1938

So, Enrico has no cousins that you know of? I am surprised. I imagined scores of them! Ah, well, you know best but how you dash my hopes, Charlotte. And he's beloved of his mother is he? Do I detect a hint of jealousy in your writing? Does his mother not like to share? From all you've said I imagine her to be big and blousy, forever dressed in black and hovering like some dark angel over her son. Bad luck if that is the kind of mother-in-law you've landed yourself with.

Her reading was interrupted by the voices from the living room again. Enrico's voice had raised slightly, enough to let her know he was agitated. Was he actually arguing with his mother, daring to? As for the kind of mother-in-law she'd landed herself with, she was the kind who came barging in on you during intimate moments; that seemed to abhor the fact you even had intimate moments.

To my news now, I have applied to join the army! I can just imagine you frowning, but I will be fine, I promise. Besides, if there is a war coming I want to stand up for my king and country, to do the right thing just as you and I have always been taught. Father is all for it, surprisingly Mother is reticent, but I am bored, Charlotte. The life of an accountant is suffocating, labouring in an office all day, trapped within four walls. I want something different. You did too, and so you find yourself in Venice.

She was surprised to note a tear landing on the letter. She hadn't realised she was crying. Wiping at it, she smudged the ink slightly and so let it dry naturally. Yes, she'd wanted something different, she'd had expectations, but they weren't being met. She hadn't even made love in two weeks. *It's not all about the sex!* Yes, yes, she knew that, she wasn't obsessed, but she missed the closeness that came with intimacy. She missed Enrico. Never mind a life abroad, it was him she wanted, still wanted, despite everything.

If I do join the army, then of course I shan't be able to visit, not for a long while. I'm sorry, old girl, I know that isn't what you want to hear but time off might be a problem — even with good behaviour! I'm worried about Father still; his chest infec-tion is proving stubborn. Mother has been trying to persuade him to see a doctor and, can you believe it, finally he agrees! That is a relief at least. Father is made of stern stuff and I'm sure he will be his old self soon. Look, I will keep on writing and you must write back. Let's try and write as often as we can. And stay safe, Charlotte. The world is so unstable right now. But all will be well. We will be well. You and I are made of stern stuff too.

More tears fell, one after the other. Quickly, she folded the letter and put it back in the envelope; afraid she'd ruin it completely if she didn't. Like the books she'd brought with her, they were all she had of home — souvenirs of a life left behind. She thought of her brother's words: 'The world is so unstable right now', and yet a few short weeks ago it had been full of promise. Now her brother was joining the army and her father was seeing a doctor — the latter significant news given the type of man he was. As for her, her heart was wrenched in two. She folded her arms across her stomach. She couldn't stop her brother, and besides, she'd half suspected he'd join the army. He had talked before about 'wanting to do his bit'. Regarding her father, it was, as Albert said, a good thing he was seeing a doctor, with medication he'd be well again in no time. Which only left her situation.

She heard movement and swung round half expecting to see the looming figure of Stefania framed in the doorway, her eyes wide and glaring — disapproval oozing from every pore. It wasn't her — it was Enrico, a cigarette in his mouth but which he stubbed out in an ashtray on their bedside table as he came hurrying forward.

"*Amore*, my love, you are crying."

She was stiff at first as his arms encircled her, but as he pulled her closer, she relaxed, the smell of him stirring familiar desire.

"Enrico," the word came out as a sob.

"*Amore*," he repeated. "I know you have been sad lately but do not cry, I hate to see you sad." He hesitated, but only briefly. "I have been talking to Mamma. We have an idea."

"We?"

"*Si*," he replied. "I think together we have found the solution to your unhappiness."

Chapter Thirteen

SHE needed a cigarette. Taking one from her silver cigarette case – one of the many presents Enrico had showered her with during their honeymoon and monogrammed with the word '*amore*' – she lit it and took a deep drag. Closing her eyes for a moment to savour the hit, she opened them again to fix her gaze on him.

"That is your solution, your answer to my unhappiness?"

She'd thought he was going to suggest they move at last. That would have been the answer! She should have known better – *they'd* concocted this idea between them, he and his mother. Not just an idea, she suspected it was set in stone. She could rail as much as she liked but it would do no good. They were to accompany his uncle, Fabrizio Gritti, to the island of Poveglia, where he and Enrico would tend to those that were mentally ill and she'd be an auxiliary. They'd live on the island. Immersed in the madness.

"I refuse to go!" she declared, slamming the door shut with her free hand.

"Charlotte, I have agreed we will."

"Without asking me?"

"Yes, without asking you. This is my career!"

She placed the cigarette to her lips, inhaled again before deciding it was a hindrance and also stubbed it out. "What about my career? It's over thanks to you!"

Enrico's eyes flitted nervously to the door, but then

returned to her – a steely glint in them she hadn't seen before.

"Charlotte, you are humiliating me as well as my family. The decision has been made."

She grew more stubborn. "No, I won't go. You can't make me."

"Then tell me, what will you do? Where will you go?"

"I will go home!" How she regretted having left. This strange land and the people in it, they were not for her. The ache that was constant in her intensified, for her friends, her brother and her parents as well as a landscape that she was used to. She wanted it as much as she used to want Enrico. *Used to?* The words – the sentiment – startled her. Was this it, her marriage was crumbling? Before she'd even had a chance to build it? Perhaps Albert was wrong: she wasn't made of stern stuff, not if she caved so easily.

Confused, she turned away but he grabbed her arm.

"Let go of me—"

"Charlotte, please, keep you voice down!"

"Why, because of *mamma*?" She spat the word at him, knew that Stefania would hear all too well, her ear pressed against the door, a satisfied smile on her face. Knew what she'd be thinking too, that her 'rival' was getting what she deserved.

"Not because of Mamma, because of us. This is a very good opportunity for me. It is not always that someone of my age can experience such a thing. My uncle is held in high regard, he is offering to be my…" He faltered, struggled for the right word. "*Mentore.*"

"Mentor, you mean a mentor? I understand that, but what about me?" She tried so hard to keep the pleading note from her voice but it was obvious.

His grip relaxed slightly. The steeliness had gone from his eyes and he looked hurt instead. "I thought when you married me you understood the role you would take."

"That of an equal."

"Charlotte," if anyone was pleading it was him. "I am a doctor. I want... I *need* you to support me. Why... what are you so scared of?"

"Scared?" Why would he think that? "I am not scared!"

Releasing her entirely, he stood before her, thoroughly perplexed. "Since we arrived in Venice, you have been different. Not yourself."

Her mouth dropped open. "And you blame me for that do you? For the way I was after your mother walked in on us, after you took her side?"

"I did not take her side."

"You failed to stand up for me!"

"She is my mother."

"I am your *wife*!"

"I know, I know." Again there was that sheepish look, "I am sorry. Mamma still thinks I am a little boy, certainly she treats me like one at times." He smiled, but there was no humour in it, rather she saw a flash of pain, deeply ingrained. "She has never knocked before coming into my bedroom, although I have asked her to so many times. Since... what happened, I have made her promise not to do that again, to respect our privacy."

"She will never respect our privacy."

Again his hands reached out to hold her. "Then we leave, Charlotte, seize our chance."

"To go to this island." She shook her head. "I can't even

recall its name."

"Poveglia."

"Poveglia," she repeated, testing the word on her lips. "Where is it?"

"In the lagoon, a short boat ride away."

They'd entered Venice via the lagoon, a friend transporting them via his motorboat. She remembered seeing several islands in the distance as they'd travelled and had wondered about them. "How big is this... island?"

"It is not big, but, Charlotte, the waters around it are still."

Despite his reassuring words, she found herself shivering. She'd be cut off from civilisation, even more than she was now. Trapped in a world within a world. She blinked hard, asked more questions, tried to think straight, to think like a wife. "On this island, there is just the hospital?" What else could she call it, an asylum – a *lunatic* asylum? She gulped as he nodded. "And as an auxiliary, what would my duties be?"

"You would help care for the patients," after a moment adding, "you wished for a job."

"Yes, I did, but not as a skivvy, someone to clean up after others! I wanted to work in an office as I did before."

"*Tesoro*," – she was sure the desperation on his face matched her own – "please, I ask you one thing, to do this for me, not forever. I do not mean forever. But for a short while and then after I have gained the experience I need, we will move on, go somewhere else."

A ray of hope dared to surge. "Where will we go?"

"Somewhere different."

"Leave Venice entirely?"

"If that is what you want."

It was, more than anything, and not to go further into Italy either, as much as she'd loved it whilst they were travelling. She wanted to go home. And she would, she'd go home. She couldn't bear the thought of not returning. But first... she owed it to her husband to go to Poveglia with him. Looking around her, at the bedroom that they stood in, at the painting on the wall, imagining his mother listening at the door, treating him like a little boy, and her like the enemy, it might even be an improvement. A laugh escaped her, surprising Enrico at first but then delighting him – he dared to look hopeful too.

"I will come with you, Enrico, but after that, allow me a say in our future."

"*Si, si, amore*, of course."

His arms tightened round her as he drew her towards him. She relaxed into his kiss, deepened it, defiantly so and, if 'Mamma' burst in, let her.

Chapter Fourteen

A local boatman ferried them across to the island, his expression solemn as he sat at the wheel flicking ash into the sea whilst steering through deep waters. Sitting away from the boat's edge, close to Enrico, his arm around her shoulders, Charlotte wished the sun would shine, but it was raining, and it was cold; colder than she thought October would be.

"Not long," Enrico whispered, sensing her discomfort. "We will be there soon."

One hand reaching up to adjust her hat, she smiled at him, then continued to stare outwards. It was easy to spot where they were heading, the ancient bell tower offering a landmark to guide them.

Since asking Charlotte to come to Poveglia with him, there'd been strained silence in the suite of rooms over the archway, his mother wanting rid of her but aware she was losing her son again. Certainly she'd been pleased Enrico was advancing in his career, but she also wanted to hold onto him, to be the main woman in his life as she'd been since his conception. Perhaps she might feel the same. Like Stefania, she'd think no woman was good enough for her male offspring. Or maybe they'd only have daughters: reared as she was, to be strong and clever, to be vital, contributing to society in some way and not just an appendage. And what she was doing, going to Poveglia to help those who were unwell, was vital. She'd come to see it that way. Felt happier about it, especially when she'd learnt a small cottage on the island had been prepared for them – the home that she'd longed for, and just the two of them in it – Doctor and Mrs Enrico Sanuto.

The bell tower loomed closer. Any minute she'd be off the boat and onto dry land. Something she was both grateful for and wary of. For the first time in her life, she had the notion she'd be safer on the water. That she should turn full circle and return to Venice, a city she could have loved if every night had been like their first night there, if they could have explored it together, at their leisure, and admired its sights. But it was growing misty too, white tendrils of vapour solidifying to form a shield wall, one that couldn't be breached.

Stop it! The island is full of people, not monsters. People just like you. Just like her? Perhaps. Right now she felt a little mad too.

"Charlotte, we are here."

Pulled from her reverie, she frowned. "Where is your uncle? Isn't he going to greet us?"

Enrico held out both his hands and glanced upwards. "The rain," he said, as if that explained his absence.

The boatman tied the boat to a strut with a length of rope, stepped onto the ledge and helped her out first and then Enrico. He then jumped back into the boat and handed them their luggage, frowning as he lifted the suitcase with all her clothes and books in it.

"*Grazie,*" she said as it was placed before her.

Meanwhile, Enrico took his wallet out and withdrew some notes. "*Grazie,*" he said too. "*Grazie mille.*"

Taking the money from Enrico and stuffing it in his jacket pocket, the boatman turned to go, leaving them to stare after him.

"What a grim man," Charlotte remarked, pulling her woollen coat tighter.

"He is just doing his job."

"As you are, bringing us to this island?"

Enrico looked at her. "*Scusa?*"

"Nothing," she dismissed. Instead she pointed to what looked like battlement buildings, a few feet across the water, forming a kind of channel as they came in. "What is that?"

"The Octagon," Enrico informed her. "It was built during the fourteenth century to repel Genoese invaders and then in the Napoleonic wars to ambush the French commandos."

She was impressed. "This island has a lot of history."

"It does. Come and I will introduce you to Fabrizio."

The man who wouldn't brave the rain to greet us? I can hardly wait.

She turned in the direction of the hospital to get her first real look at it. It was not what she'd expected: something austere and grey, crouching menacingly before them – a version of Dickens' bedlam. It was actually quite attractive. Divided into three separate buildings, each one was stepped slightly back from the other, the bell tower at the far right end. The main building comprised three storeys and the two either side were on two floors – how deep they were it was impossible to see from this angle. Boasting a natural sandstone façade, there was also an edge of grass, which served to soften the building further. There were trees too; it was lovely to see a glimpse of nature again, some colour. Intrigued, despite herself, she asked Enrico to tell her more about the island's history.

"It dates back to Roman times. So many islands in these

waters were used as an initial means of defence. In the eighteenth century it was also a checkpoint for all goods and people going to and from Venice by ship. And the bell tower is what remains of a church."

"Why would they have a church on an island this small?"

Enrico laughed. "This is Italy. Where there are people, there are churches."

Whilst they talked they made their way to the main entrance, rows and rows of windows looking down on them – *like* eyes, she thought, *sightless eyes*. "And now it is home to an asylum," she mused, listening out for cries and shrieks from within.

Enrico was quick to correct her. "It is a hospital and the people inside are our patients."

She noted the emphasis on the word 'our'.

"Come on then. Do we knock on the door, yank the bell pull or go straight in?"

Enrico shrugged, tugged at the bell pull and then stood back. He shuffled slightly and cleared his throat. She was about to ask him if he was nervous when the door opened, creaking as it did so – the first sound she'd heard on the island aside from their voices. She looked up, wondered if she might see sea birds circling overhead. There were none.

It was a woman who answered; petite, like Charlotte, but with dark hair and wearing a white, starched dress and nurse's cap.

Enrico extended his hand. "*Buon pomeriggio.*"

"*Dottore Sanuto, ben arrivata, entra.*"

"*Grazie.*" Motioning for Charlotte to step forward, he introduced her as his wife. The woman shook Charlotte's hand too, her grasp limp.

Without any further exchange they were led along a lengthy, narrow corridor; walls painted cream but peeling in places, particularly around the top where the pipes ran. There were several doors either side, but they were all closed. She guessed they were recreation rooms as the wards would be on the upper levels. There'd be a kitchen too, a dining hall, a laundry room. *A world within a world* – a thought that kept recurring.

At the far end, behind another closed door was Enrico's uncle's office – his name emblazoned on the door's glass inset in fancy gold lettering. Finally they'd found him. The nurse knocked confidently and opened it when a voice from within gave the order.

So, this was Fabrizio Gritti, the eminent surgeon and Stefania's brother. She wasn't quite sure what she'd been expecting – a larger-than-life figure, rotund too with eyes that glared. But he wasn't like his sister. He was tall, slim and, if not handsome, authoritative in his well-pressed suit, his dark hair thick and his features neat. Older than Stefania by a few years, Enrico had already told her he wasn't married, 'only to his work'. He had a presence about him, a charisma, so she could understand Stefania's pride in him. It was only a shame she couldn't apply that same level of respect to her husband. When she spoke to Luigi – a mere hotelier in comparison – it was almost always with derision.

"Enrico, Enrico." Taking the cigarette from his mouth, Dr Gritti came rushing towards him, kissing him on both cheeks. "*Sono contenta che tu sia qui.*" He then turned to Charlotte and kissed her on both cheeks. "Welcome, I have heard much about you."

Charlotte's smile was tight as she wondered who had told

him, Stefania or Enrico? If the former, she dreaded to think what had been said. The doctor held her gaze as if assessing her and then clapped his hands together, the sudden noise making her jump.

"Your suitcases, where are they?"

"At the door, Uncle, they are heavy."

"Yes, yes, of course, I will send for one of the orderlies to take them to your living quarters." Looking specifically at Charlotte, he added, "We do not have many auxiliary staff on the island, not many staff at all. It is not easy to persuade people to work here."

Convenient you can make good use of me then. It was a thought she didn't dare voice.

"Please, follow me and I will show you around."

Charlotte widened her smile in an attempt to show she was grateful the doctor was speaking in English. The matron, who was standing beside the open door, stepped aside for Dr Gritti to go first and then gestured for Enrico and Charlotte to follow him. In the corridor they turned towards the staircase, holding onto the bannister as they climbed to the second floor. She'd guessed correctly. This was where the wards were. Entering the closest, it was clean and warm if sparse, the smell of disinfectant making her eyes water but masking other, perhaps more offensive, smells. Only a few of the metal-railed beds were occupied and all by women, lying prone, a thin blanket to cover each one.

As they walked, Dr Gritti talked about the hospital – lapsing into Italian only now and again. He informed them of the types of conditions patients suffered from, including manic-depressive psychosis, anxiety and obsession. At the end of one patient's bed – an elderly woman, who appeared dead if it were not for the gentle rise and fall of her chest – he declared that 'delusion' was at the heart of such illnesses.

"They imagine so much," he said, his eyes trained on Charlotte. "They think they hear things, see things, they insist they can touch what is not there. Fantasy and reality blurs, they begin not to realise there is a difference. My treatments could be considered…" he averted his gaze now, looked almost imperiously into the distance, "revolutionary. I believe no matter how entrenched the madness there is a way back. And if not a way back, there is a way to subdue it so that patients are no longer a danger to themselves or society."

After delivering his speech he was silent, giving them time to absorb his ethos. Charlotte saw no reason to disagree. She knew very little about mental illness, never having been exposed to anyone with problems of that kind. He was the expert and her husband was to learn from him and become an expert too. Keen to appear as interested, she asked, "Only some beds are occupied, where are the rest of the patients?"

"They are either at recreation or receiving treatment," was the reply.

With one hand, she gestured around her. "Are there only women here?"

"In this wing yes. The men's wing is further away. It is wise to keep them separate, you understand? But," he paused briefly, "I have to say that it *is* mainly women on the island, because they are the most prone to the conditions I have described."

"I see," replied Charlotte, but in truth she was surprised. Could that really be true?

They continued on their journey, leaving the wards and

venturing deeper into the building. Like Venice, it was a maze. They didn't travel every corridor; the building would take time to explore fully but, returning to the ground floor, they were shown the recreation rooms, where she noticed significantly more patients milling about and various staff to administer to them. Again the rooms were sparse, tables and chairs in them and little else, certainly nothing that could be considered frivolous such as a vase of flowers or a painting; no homely touches at all. The number of 'ill' outnumbered the 'sane' but remembering Dr Gritti's words about subduing them, she felt comforted. Nobody looked particularly menacing and the atmosphere was quiet enough, a few murmurings here and there. Perhaps their time on the island wouldn't be so bad. It'd be bearable. Despite the institutionalised feel of the place, it was functional and she'd have to function within it.

Having decided he'd shown them enough, Dr Gritti asked a nurse to fetch an orderly to take the couple to their lodgings. Enrico wasn't starting work until the next day, and they had been assured that a fire had been lit and some food prepared.

"You will find it comfortable," he said, leaving no room for doubt.

It was dark as they were led across the grounds to their cottage – the only one of its kind it seemed, so perhaps the rest of the staff lived in quarters in the main building – and the mist hadn't abated. There was a sound in the distance, the tolling of bells, not coming from this island but from another, perhaps even Venice itself – St Mark's Basilica. When at last it came to an end she questioned if she'd really heard it. It truly felt as if there was nothing nearby, that they were cast adrift, to float aimlessly forevermore, she, Enrico and so many mad strangers. She looked at the bell tower. Before the asylum, how many had had to call this place home because of their occupation? Had they formed a successful community or had living together in such close proximity proved trying? Lost in thought, she failed to notice a rock jutting out of the ground. Caught off guard, she stumbled and fell, landing heavily.

"*Tesoro!*" Enrico rushed to her side to help her but before he could, her hands sunk further into the rain-drenched soil; she was surprised at how quickly they disappeared, as if the earth was ravenous. Desperate to get a hold, convinced her whole body would be devoured if she didn't, her hand at last closed around something solid. As Enrico hauled her upwards, what was in her hand came up with her. Before she could examine it, Enrico was hugging her, fussing over her, wiping the mud from her coat.

"I'm not hurt," she assured him, keen to see what she'd retrieved.

Pushing him away slightly with her free hand, she got a good look. The object was long, thin and white. *It looks like a bone, a human bone.* Could it be? If anyone would know, it would be her husband. She decided to ask him.

"Enrico—"

She didn't get any further; he'd also noticed what was in her hand. Taking it from her, he examined it too, but only briefly, then threw it back into the mud. Surprised by this, she watched as it returned to the depths, helped on its way by his foot stamping on it.

"Why did you do that?" she asked.

"It belongs there."

"Was it a bone?"

"It is nothing, it is gone."

"But, darling, if it was a bone—"

Again he interrupted her, "Let's go to the house. It is not fair to keep the orderly waiting whilst you interrogate me."

Interrogate him? She was doing no such thing. She was curious that's all.

As Enrico continued on his way, all concern for her gone it seemed, she looked at the orderly, an old man with a wizened face. He was staring at the space where she'd fallen, the same look on his face as on Stefania's when she'd barged in on them – disgust. Should she ask him if what she'd discovered was a human bone? Or should she leave it? Perhaps it was best to leave it. Not 'bother' either man. Even so, she shuddered. Like Enrico, she wanted to reach the cottage too, get out of the rain, and close the door. And, unlike her bedroom door at Stefania's, it would have a lock. She'd make sure to use it.

Chapter Fifteen

ENRICO started work the very next day, which he was excited about. She, however, had bagged herself a couple of days' grace, time in which to unpack, write to her brother, enquiring after their father, and even read a few pages of one of her novels. She'd chosen *A Tale of Two Cities*, set between London and another foreign land, France. The opening sentences resonated with her: *It was the best of times, it was the worst of times... it was the season of Light, it was the season of Darkness... it was the spring of hope, it was the winter of despair... we were all going direct to Heaven, we were all going the other way.*

It was the best of times for her too, she was young, married, in love with her husband, a brilliant doctor, and soon they'd plan to start a family. But it was the worst of times in other ways. She was resident of a tiny island in the Venetian lagoon – surrounded by water – the other residents, in the main, the mentally ill. She had no friends, no family; she was about to start work as an auxiliary, cleaning, feeding, fetching and carrying. It was a far cry from how she'd imagined life to pan out. Before meeting Enrico she'd loved the hustle and bustle of London life, the to and fro, the hubbub.

Even so, any regret she'd felt at marrying him had vanished. They'd bonded again since that debacle with his mother. Last night the sex had been fast and furious, then slow and tender, the way she loved it, the pair of them giving free rein to a passion that had recently been subdued. It was a true celebration of being together. Odd then that her mother's words kept repeating. '*Should you want to return home at any point let us know. Nothing is beyond reparation.*' Charlotte decided to write to her as well as Albert and let them know she was fine. She'd held off mentioning anything about the island just in case there'd been a change of plan. Now she was here, she must attend to it, making sure to call the asylum a hospital. What was her address exactly? Charlotte Sanuto ('The Venetian' in brackets just for fun), Poveglia, Venice, Italy? Would that be enough to receive a letter in return? Certainly, it was accurate.

Informing Enrico this morning about her intent to write to her family, he'd told her that letters were sent as a batch twice weekly from the island and were to be handed into the post room. He said that he too was looking forward to hearing Albert's news and hoped her father was better. He also asked her to send them his warmest regards. She'd smiled at that. Family was so important to Enrico; he was typically Italian in that respect. Glancing at her stomach, she wondered if last night's lovemaking might bear fruit. If not, she wouldn't be too disappointed. It was strange but she'd rather conceive when they were off the island, maybe even on home ground. How perfect to conceive in England! When quizzed, Enrico had said they'd be on the island for a few months only. To her, that meant they'd be gone before springtime. Meantime, she wouldn't try *not* to conceive but she wouldn't worry about it either, she'd relax, in her own cottage, no mother-in-law in sight, read a bit more of her book, look forward to the parts set in London...

The hiatus was over and Charlotte was 'put to work', Enrico

leading her over to the main building and introducing her to Elisabetta, a nurse younger than the one who had greeted them on arrival, not much older than herself. She was going to take her under her wing and show her the ropes – working predominantly on the women's wards. It was another dull morning, the patients as she came across them as solemn as the weather.

As soon as she'd been handed over, Enrico disappeared, hurrying to his uncle's office, as though concerned he'd be late and therefore admonished. Only briefly she wondered if that would be the case. Perhaps she'd see him later, when he was on his rounds. She hoped so. The working day was long and there'd been talk of nightshifts too, which she supposed would be peaceful at least. That was the thing: it was *peaceful* on the island.

After changing into her uniform – a starched white dress similar to the ones the nurses wore – and securing her hair, already in a short style, with clips, she followed Elisabetta, administering pills to the patients and feeding those who required help with their breakfast, a porridge-like mixture that hardly looked appetising but which none complained about. Rather, as she lifted the spoon, mouths opened eagerly, reminding her of baby birds being fed by their mother. One by one they lapped it up. A plus point certainly, but it saddened her, that they should *enjoy* bland food so much. As she knew she'd have to, it was time to help empty and clean bedpans. Carrying them through to the wash rooms, she tried not to heave as contents were washed away, knew she'd be scrubbing at her hands afterwards until they were raw in an attempt to feel clean again. Washing the patients was also part of an auxiliary's duties. She noted

Elisabetta's precise no-nonsense approach to this. The woman neither interacted with the patients nor treated them roughly but performed her duties as economically as possible.

Whilst attending to one woman, she attempted to ask Elisabetta if she lived on the island too. "*Abita a Poveglia?*"

Elisabetta frowned. Had what she said been complete nonsense?

She decided to repeat her question in English this time, annunciating each word exactly whilst using hand gestures to point towards the floor. "Do you live on Poveglia?"

"Do I live here?" Her English was broken but understandable. "On Poveglia? No."

"Do you live in Venice?" With her hands she indicated a boat crossing water.

"We must work," was Elisabetta's curt response.

About to protest, to say she realised that but it was nice to talk at the same time – for someone to talk around here, for a conversation to be had – she stopped. Elisabetta had returned her focus to the woman she was dealing with, her expression pinched, angry even. Why, Charlotte didn't know. They finished the rest of their rounds in silence.

Just before dark, Elisabetta rushed off, her departure abrupt. Ward nurse, Roberta, told Charlotte she could go too – back to her cottage. Hopefully Enrico wouldn't be far behind. She wanted to ask what he'd done today, what he'd done for the past few days. She already had, but he'd been vague. 'I am learning so much' was all he'd said, but learning what precisely? And did he do the rounds of the female wards? She'd been expecting to see him but no doctor had come by, it had just been nurses and other auxiliary staff.

As she trudged across the hospital grounds, she picked up

pace. It was cold and the mist was closing in again, edging ever closer. It was still muddy underfoot, so she'd be quick but careful, she didn't want to fall – to *sink*. The ground was certainly softer in some places and again she had a sensation it might cave in beneath her. She welcomed the sight of her cottage, resolved to leave a light on in future. And in the next few days, if Elisabetta still refused to converse, she'd make more of an effort to speak to the patients. Some of them had made eye contact today and one – an elderly woman, Catarina Castelli, had even smiled at her, which is more than Elisabetta had done. She wouldn't have to shadow the nurse once she'd learnt the routine. There'd be time to sit and talk, which was as essential in the caring process in her opinion as more perfunctory duties. She could take her books along to read aloud, and even though it would be in English, it would break the silence. *The fearful silence*. The thought formed of its own accord.

Chapter Sixteen

AT last Roberta deemed Charlotte proficient enough to be assigned certain patients, and certain duties, Catarina amongst them. She'd been here just over two weeks and despite her reservations, she was, if not enjoying her work, finding a degree of satisfaction in it. She pitied how imprisoned some of the patients seemed to be – not just within these walls but also within their minds – and found it a privilege to help them, to relieve the burden of their various conditions in some small way. She supposed many people would find what she saw on a daily basis alarming, the constant rocking back and forth, the hushed but incessant muttering, mouths opening in silent screams, the catatonic stares, but Charlotte surprised herself and empathised instead, wondering what had happened to make them the way they were. Were such illnesses inherited or the result of terrible events?

Enrico was pleased she was happier. He too found his work fascinating.

"My uncle is a genius, who is not afraid to take risks,' he said one night as they lay entwined, taking it in turns to draw on just one cigarette, the smoke encircling them like the mist. "His practices may appear controversial but do you see any violence on Poveglia, any unrest? Some of these patients have inflicted terrible damage upon others and themselves but that behaviour is under control. Some may even be returned to their families, eventually."

"They escape?" she replied, tongue-in-cheek.

He turned his head to look at her, not amused. "Why do you use the word 'escape'? They are not prisoners, Charlotte. They are in need of help. We are not prisoners either."

Although tempted to snap back, she didn't want to argue, she was enjoying herself too much lying in his arms, and wasn't yet satiated. She took the cigarette from him and inhaled one last time. "Tell me more about the hospital. When was it founded?"

"According to my uncle fifteen years ago, dealing with severe cases as well as mild."

"So it is where the mad of Venice were packed off to?"

"Charlotte!" Again he was reprimanding her. "Please, respect my profession."

Pushing herself up onto one arm, her breasts brushed lightly against his chest. "*Why* do you want to specialise in mental illness, darling? You have told me but only briefly."

He looked into her eyes. "Why should I not specialise?"

"That's no answer. Do you have a mad relative? Someone you encountered as a small child? Someone who left a lasting impression?"

Enrico laughed. "What an imagination you have! No, I do not!"

What about your mother, she wanted to say. In Charlotte's opinion she was mad enough. But of course she didn't. Besides which, he was speaking again.

"It interests me, that is why. Treating the body is one thing, we can do so much nowadays, but treating the mind, that is something else entirely. The mind *controls* everything, Charlotte, including disease. If we can find a way to switch off negative impulses in the brain, the world will be a better place for it."

"So the mind controls the human, but you and your uncle want to control the mind?"

"We want to *understand* the mind, the way it works, for the greater good."

She mulled over his words. "And you would do this through more refined medication?"

He shook his head. "Medicine is too expensive, it has side effects, so continually administering it to patients is not an option. We would do it via an operation. But first we need to know which part of the brain to operate on, so we do not lose the entire person."

"The way that medication sometimes does?"

"Exactly," he seemed pleased she'd 'got it'. "That is where we differ from other surgeons, or rather where my uncle differs. He wants to retain what is best in a person, their essence. He is at the forefront of this idea, a leader in his field, and if he can get it right he will be remembered." Warming to his subject, he added, "It is only a small part of the brain that needs to be worked on, the skill is in finding which part and isolating it."

"But what if it is unique to every person?"

"No… we do not think so."

"But what if it is? It seems perfectly feasible to me. Each person is unique after all."

"*Amore*, please, you should not concern yourself."

"Enrico! I'm not a child. I'm entitled to an opinion."

"Charlotte," the skin around his eyes crinkled, "you are so passionate about everything."

"Is that such a bad thing?"

"No, of course not."

Still she was concerned about what he'd said. "It would be wonderful if what you are trying to achieve can be done but I'm not sure. I still think the mind is as unique as the person itself, and if you fail to acknowledge that, you run the risk of switching everything off. Turning people into... mere shadows. So many people here are like that already."

"Because of the medication, Charlotte, as you have said – it shuts them down."

She grew even more curious. "How much success have you had, Enrico?"

He shifted slightly, looked away. "It is true to say we are in our infancy, but success will come." Returning his gaze, becoming animated even, he added, "We may make mistakes but think, if we find a way, if we succeed, madness will no longer exist, we would have cured it, Dr Fabrizio Gritti and Dr Enrico Sanuto!"

Cured madness? What an interesting concept.

"If you succeed there will be no more wars," she said. After all, what was war but madness? She thought of Albert and what was happening in Europe. Hopefully he'd got the letter she sent, and she looked forward to receiving his.

Whilst she contemplated, Enrico reached out a hand and stroked her hair. "Maybe there will be no more wars, but I think somehow that is a long way off – madness exists in many forms, not all of it is obvious. Meanwhile, there is much to learn. I am lucky to be here."

"*We* are lucky. There are two of us, remember."

"I know. I know there is." He lifted his head to kiss her, an appeasement at having just forgotten her maybe. "You are settling, *amore*?"

"More than I imagined I would, but perhaps that is

because I know an end is in sight."

"Of course."

"And there is isn't there?"

"What?"

"An end?"

"As I have said, a few more months we will be here."

"England," she blurted out, surprising herself as much as him. "I want to go back."

He drew back slightly. "We must go where the work is."

"But there will be plenty of work in England. They'll need doctors, good doctors, especially if another war is coming. And they will need auxiliaries, people to help in hospitals. If I can't find office work I simply carry on. Put to use all I have learnt here."

"Charlotte—"

"Promise me you'll consider England! You said you loved it."

Enrico closed his eyes but only briefly. "How could I not love it, it is where I met you."

As he continued to nuzzle against her, she reached downwards, took hold of him in her hand and began rubbing rhythmically, noticing his breath catch in his throat.

"Promise me," she repeated, whispered like words of seduction.

Catarina Castelli was not as old as she looked. On first meeting her Charlotte presumed she was in her seventies, but, managing to take a look at her notes, she could see her birth year was 1875, which made her only sixty-three. The *diagnosi* was *isterismo*. When she'd asked Enrico later what that meant, he'd answered 'hysteria'.

"What does that mean?" she queried.

"Women are emotional beings," he'd replied, "some are perhaps *over* emotional."

Catarina was just one of the patients in Charlotte's care. She had up to twenty to see to on a daily basis, all concentrated in the eastern wing of the main building – the female only section. She had no clue about patients elsewhere, except those who frequented the mixed recreation rooms. Apart from the tour that she and Enrico had received on their first day – which hadn't included all parts of the asylum, by any stretch – she hadn't had time to explore. But she was happy with her lot, and by and large her patients were compliant, allowing her to feed and bathe them without any fuss or even concern. Were any of them guilty of heinous crimes? Enrico had mentioned some patients having 'inflicted damage', but she simply couldn't imagine it. In a way they were as docile as children.

It was Catarina whom she first started reading to. It was hard to carry on a one-way conversation, even if there were smiles involved, which is why she'd had the idea of reading to her patients in the first place, especially during the nightshifts – of which she'd done a couple so far. Her voice might sound comforting in the stillness of the night, she hoped, lulling them to sleep. Enrico had laughed when she'd told him what she was doing but good-naturedly so. She even thought she saw a hint of pride in his eyes, as not only was she making the best of their situation, *supporting* him, she was coming up with ideas.

As Charlotte read, Catarina would lie against the pillow, her eyes half-closed. Charlotte wondered if she understood any of what she was saying, even just a word here or there.

The book she was reading from was *A Tale of Two Cities*, which she'd only got halfway through on her own.

Patients in the surrounding beds gradually began to listen too, their heads turning towards the sound of her voice, the expressions on their faces different to usual, Charlotte noticed – not as vacant, more focussed. So often she'd felt left out at the Sanuto family home when Enrico and his parents would insist on speaking in Italian, but here language didn't seem to be a barrier. Just being together, in the same place, united them.

She found herself preferring the night shifts to the day, requesting more of them. It was easier to connect at night. The day was just too busy. She was more in charge – other staff close by to call on if she needed them but not *too* close. When her patients finally slept she would write to her parents and to Albert, asking how they were and when they were going to write back, telling them about life on Poveglia, which was not as she'd feared it would be. She could even forget about the sea that surrounded her, most of her life was spent within the walls of the asylum anyway. Enrico hadn't been keen on her volunteering to work nights at first. 'What about us?' he'd asked, his expression telling her he was worried she might have tired of him. 'I'll be back before you go on duty,' she'd answered, 'to ensure your day gets off to the best possible start.' And she'd done that, sending him to work with a smile on his face, a smile playing on her lips too.

The walk from the hospital to the cottage at dawn took minutes only, but often she'd stop and admire the setting she'd found herself in. Like Venice, it had its own beauty. The days on the run up to Christmas were unseasonably warm; it had stopped raining and the sun had returned. So often the early morning sky took her breath away – it was such a contrast to the dark confines of the ward. Gold and red would hold sway, at least for a short while, pushing aside deepest black before blue dominated once more.

She'd finished *A Tale of Two Cities* and was planning to read *A Christmas Carol* to the patients, although, having finished a round of night shifts, she was back on days. This morning, another bright offering, she hurried to her ward, nodding courteously at other members of staff. She hardly saw Elizabetta anymore, who'd gone to work in another part of the hospital, but she was no loss, not on a personal scale. It was the patients she'd befriended. As she entered the ward, some would get excited at the sight of her, start clapping their hands in quick succession, rocking back and forth – and she was excited to see them too. *My children*, she thought again. Mad perhaps but not evil – surely not evil?

There'd be no time for reading, not until the afternoon. She got stuck in, fetching bowls of porridge and feeding those who weren't capable. Not all the patients were old, far from it. There were young women on the ward too, a varied mix of ages, and she'd greet everyone individually, even those who didn't respond to her, like Leda, a woman of middling years who looked at no one, and Luigina, no more than thirty she'd wager, who was also very insular. Having fed several patients, it was Luigina's turn, and so, after tucking in her bib, she started lifting the spoon to her mouth, telling her as she did about the book she was going to start reading to them next – how 'seasonal' it was.

"I'm also going to see if I can arrange a trip into Venice tomorrow, I should love to choose some decorations, not just for the ward, but for the dining room too, it looks so cheerless." She also wanted some ribbon for her hair – it had been an age since she'd worn anything as frivolous – as well as hand cream; hers had become so chapped. Still spooning in mouthfuls she continued chatting, telling Luigina about Christmas in England and the ancient tradition of wassailing, still popular in Somerset where she hailed from, and traditionally held on Old Christmas Eve, January the fifth. "Almost every farm in Somerset has an apple orchard," she explained. "They use the apples to make cider, which is a drink many English people like, an alcoholic drink. To go wassailing means to go from door-to-door, singing and offering cider from the wassail bowl in exchange for a small gift. Everyone in the village does it, we all know each other you see." *Much like we do here*, she thought. "Some also go into the orchards, and this is where it can get a little odd, they recite incantations and sing to the trees in order to produce a good harvest for the coming year. The ritual is designed to see off evil spirits—"

She didn't get any further. With almost lightning speed Luigina knocked the bowl from her hand, its lumpy contents flying everywhere. As Charlotte looked in horror at the mess she'd made, she didn't notice her lunging forwards, or her hands as they closed around her neck. Surprise gave way to shock. Luigina was one of the most docile patients on the ward. What was wrong with her? Why was she so upset? Reaching upwards, she tried to loosen the woman's almost superhuman grip whilst at the same time staring into her eyes, in a bid to understand what was happening, to make a connection. The change in her was dramatic. Normally smooth features were contorted – her thin lips scraped back and chipped yellow teeth bared. She simply didn't look like the Luigina she knew – she looked… Charlotte struggled to think of the right word, struggled to think at all. *Terrified* – that was it! Luigina was terrified! As the choking continued she registered something else – Luigina wasn't looking at her, meeting her equally terrified gaze, she was looking at something in the distance and gibbering manically all the while.

Chapter Seventeen

"CHARLOTTE, breathe, just breathe. We are here now. You are safe."

We? What... who was he talking about?

As her mind swam back into focus, she sat up – aware that Luigina had been wrenched off her. She looked wildly around. "Where is she? What have you done with her?"

There was no sign of Luigina but several other patients were in obvious distress at what had just happened. Having grown used to peace and quiet, she couldn't believe the din they were capable of, jumping up and down some of them, bashing the metal rails of their beds against the wall. Others were screaming, one was wailing, the noise as sharp as any blade. Her eyes sought Catarina. She wasn't making a sound but her hands were pressed to her ears, her eyes screwed shut, clearly finding it intolerable too.

A voice roared behind her.

"*FERMARE QUESTO!*"

The harshness of it sent shock waves through her all over again. It was Dr Gritti, standing dead centre in the room, at last showing a resemblance to Stefania as he glared at the debacle he was presented with. Very rarely did she see him or Enrico during the day, the two senior doctors occupied themselves elsewhere, chasing that elusive cure for madness she presumed. Seeing him here now was an added trauma.

"*FERMARE QUESTO,*" he roared again, "*QUESTO*

ISTANTE!"

Still clutching onto Enrico, she asked, "I can't understand. What is he saying?"

"He wants them to be quiet."

As though he'd waved a magic wand, the room did indeed fall quiet, going from mayhem to familiar silence in just a few minutes.

Satisfied, he turned his attention towards Charlotte. "Are you hurt?" he asked, his voice still something of a bark.

With the help of Enrico, she was on her feet now. "No, I… I seem to be all right. I'm not sure what I said to upset Luigina, one minute she was quietly eating her breakfast and the next she was frantic." She looked around her. "Where is she? I can't see her."

"She is being taken care of," Dr Gritti replied, scrutinising her, as though unsure she was telling him the truth when she'd said she was fine.

Immediately she started worrying. "I should hate for her to be punished on my behalf. Maybe what I said upset her."

Dr Gritti narrowed his eyes and peered closer. "What was it you said?"

She had to work hard to keep meeting his gaze. Despite the fact she'd been at the asylum for a number of weeks now, she barely knew the man standing before her. When work was done for the day there was no socialising with him or any other member of staff for that matter, no cosy dinners during which more personal issues might be discussed. Life was all about work on the island. The fact that it was Christmas made no difference. There was still no social interaction. She loved this time ordinarily; it was a time spent with friends and family, *her* family. Not spent here, being attacked.

"Charlotte," Dr Gritti prompted.

"I... mentioned Christmas," a sob escaped her as she said it – impossible to stifle she was feeling so upset. "I was talking about an ancient tradition in my village at this time of year, wassailing. It's a ritual carried out to protect apple crops, to keep evil spirits away."

The look on his face changed, went from one of curiosity to fury. "Evil...? Enough! We cannot talk about such matters here. Enrico, remove her, take her home."

"Wh—?"

"I said no more! It is little wonder the patient got upset with you talking such nonsense."

"I had no idea she could understand me!"

"These people are not here to be talked to! And now I must deal with the consequences of your actions. Get out of my sight!"

Fresh tears erupted as Enrico led her away, what his uncle had done, how he'd admonished her, made her feel so ashamed. *These people are not here to be talked to?* But surely it wasn't a crime to treat them as human beings? And yet she'd upset Luigina. Her words, whether understood or not, had had an effect, a terrible one. Glancing at Enrico, noting how grave his expression was, she registered how he'd kept his eyes averted when Dr Gritti had banished her from the ward. Yet again he'd failed to defend her, but right now she didn't have the energy to blame him. She only blamed herself.

As they exited the hospital building and walked the short distance to their cottage, she was more homesick than ever.

It was Christmas Eve when Charlotte returned to work, two

days later. It wasn't ideal working over Christmas but day staff had apparently refused to accept extra hours. In Italy, Enrico explained, spending time with family during the festive season was of paramount importance. 'We could insist they work,' he'd said, 'but why cause anger and upset? It is hard enough to retain staff as it is.'

Seeing his logic she'd asked him if they were seeing his parents at any point soon.

Enrico had said no. "My parents understand I have to work, that the patients need to be looked after. They realise the importance of my job."

A flash of irritation rose up in her – was he trying to say that she didn't? Perhaps he'd like to acknowledge the importance of *her* job for a change? "*Personal* matters need addressing, Enrico, I agree, feeding the patients, tending to them, cleaning the ward. Are you going to do that, get your hands dirty, like I do every day?"

Enrico pulled her to him. "Yes, *amore*, I am. I intend to help you on the wards."

His answer nonplussed her. "You will? You're going to help me instead of your uncle?"

"Yes."

"And he's agreed?"

"He is happy with the arrangement."

"I… " She was lost for words.

Enrico wrapped his arms tighter around her. "Of course I am going to help you, it is Christmas, it would be unfair not to."

Her earlier irritation quashed, she breathed him in, caught a hint of musk from the balm he used after shaving. This wasn't their first Christmas together. Their first was spent in

England, with her parents, who, she supposed, on retrospect, were as suspicious of him as Enrico's mother was of her, although certainly not as obtrusive. Nonetheless there'd been a slight abrasiveness to them, which he'd met with good humour. In the end, seeing how much their daughter adored him, they'd relaxed and an enjoyable time had been had.

She would love to spend this Christmas with her family too, but part of her was torn over the matter. Even if it were possible to leave, how could she knowing that so few staff remained? The patients deserved to have a nice time as much as anyone, even Luigina, whom she held no grudge against. Perhaps her talk of Christmas cheer *had* been insensitive. Who knew what she'd suffered in her life prior to Poveglia, memories concerning the festive season might have triggered something. When she saw her today she'd apologise, just say it, one word, one simple word, keep it short and sweet and then move on. If Enrico was helping, he could feed her at least and perhaps whoever else was on duty would tend to her hygiene. Before she went to the ward she'd make her usual detour to the post room. Mail could take some time to travel between countries – especially if the world outside was preoccupied with the threat of war – but she was surprised she hadn't received even one letter from Albert yet. She longed for his humour.

As she returned Enrico's hug, an idea formed. Dr Gritti had a telephone in his office, could she use it to call home? Not her parents, they didn't have a telephone, but her previous place of work – a colleague might be able to pass on a message, and, in turn, get one back to her. She knew transatlantic calls were possible via an operator, also that they were expensive, but she worked hard, didn't receive an individual wage and perhaps if the doctor was tactfully reminded of that, he might be persuaded. Enrico could at least ask on her behalf. How she wished her parents had a telephone. She'd love to wish them a happy Christmas and find out what the political situation was; she was so removed from it all here. How ironic if Albert *wasn't* at home, if, like her, he'd already taken up a post abroad. If so, that would explain his lack of correspondence. But her parents could have written, they knew where she was, she'd told them.

Her mind was made up. If there were no letter waiting for her when she had time to check, not even a Christmas greeting card, she'd ask Enrico to ask his uncle about the telephone. How wonderful if he did permit her to use it! It would make up for the way he'd admonished her in front of everyone. She'd forgive him.

Pleased with her plan, she kissed Enrico on the lips before declaring she'd better hurry – she'd be late for her shift if she didn't.

"I will be along soon," Enrico called out. "After I have met with my uncle."

There was no post for her and, when she got to the ward, there was no Luigina either. Her bed was empty. Disappointed on both counts, she walked over to Roberta, the ward nurse, and asked where Luigina was.

"With Dr Gritti," Roberta replied.

"*Where* with Dr Gritti? Has she been transferred to another ward?"

Roberta held up both hands. "*Non capisco*," she said – *I don't understand* – before returning to her paperwork, effectively dismissing Charlotte.

127

Sighing in frustration, she decided to get on with her duties, trying hard not to mind how bleak it all looked with no festive decorations. She'd been too upset to visit Venice after what had happened with Luigina, but she should have made the effort – not hidden away. After much deliberation, she'd brought *A Christmas Carol* with her onto the ward, she wanted at least a nod towards the time of the year and the book was the only way in which she could achieve that. She wasn't going against Dr Gritti's will, not really, she wasn't communicating directly with the patients, but she was still communicating – something she refused to think of as wrong. Regarding the ghosts of Christmas past, present and future, she'd play them down of course, skip any paragraphs she deemed too dark or frightening and concentrate on the more benign content, in particular the descriptions of Old London – although she acknowledged that was for her own sake more than theirs. Looking at the amount of work that needed to be done, she wondered if she'd even get a chance to read. If Enrico hurried and they worked efficiently as a team, she might find time this afternoon. Luigina's case was isolated, no one had ever attacked her before and she doubted it would happen again. You had to have trust and she did, she *trusted* these people, almost more than she trusted the staff.

An hour passed, then another and another. She kept glancing at the clock that hung over the entrance to the ward, noticing the minutes, the seconds, passing. *Where was he? He said he'd come and help. It's Christmas Eve!* Was he becoming unreliable? Did his promises mean nothing? Was his uncle to blame, changing his mind about allowing Enrico to help, and insisting he help him instead? Clearly that was the case.

Despair threatened to overwhelm her – she felt *abandoned* – but before it could take over she forced herself to look at her patients; either lying in their beds, or sitting up and staring ahead, eyes wide and hardly blinking. One was pacing backwards and forwards – Gabriela – a habit of hers she'd carry on all day if you let her, the tiles beneath her feet becoming worn. Their obvious plight moved her. Only rarely had she seen post delivered to them too, and, as for relatives visiting, she'd not caught sight of any. Admittedly she was not with her patients all the time, only during certain shifts but if anyone did visit, surely she'd notice them arriving by boat. Their very presence would inject a new energy. She fancied she'd be able to *feel* such energy. Instead it was all so... stale, days fading into one another with nothing to mark them as different, not even Christmas.

No, the only people to visit the island were those who had to, those who delivered correspondence and provisions, and they made sure not to linger. They'd turn their boats around and disappear, the ever-present mist swallowing them as the ground once wanted to swallow her. The day staff would follow suit, downing tools the minute their shifts were over. They were the forgotten, her patients. Out of sight and out of mind, with mothers, fathers, brothers, sisters, and offspring shunning them. She might tend towards gloom on occasion but it was nothing in comparison. Their despair consumed them.

Squaring her shoulders, her hands brushing imaginary creases from her dress, she resolved not to lose herself in self-pity but to do what she'd intended, which was to read to them, her way of showing she cared. And, because it was Christmas Eve, she'd stay until every last one of them was asleep.

As she approached Catarina's bed, the old woman smiled. It seemed like such a gift – precious – and her heart lifted. Others might be content to abandon these poor souls but she wouldn't stoop so low. They *needed* her. She was only glad someone did.

Chapter Eighteen

PULLING up one of the chairs to sit beside Catarina, Charlotte opened her book and started to read. As she did her earlier upset diminished. Already she'd set the scene: turning off the main lights and switching on sidelights. She knew if she were outside she'd be able to hear church bells calling devoted parishioners to prayer. There was a chapel here too but as far as she knew it was never used, certainly no priest had been asked to come and say mass on Christmas morning – religion all but forgotten as well, surprisingly.

As she always did whilst reading, she spoke slowly, annunciating each word clearly – using her voice as a calming tool. Turning the pages it wasn't just Catarina that was enraptured. As they'd done before – even Luigina when she'd been here – other patients relaxed too. Gabriela stopped pacing and stood still for a while before padding silently to her bed. There was a slight chill in the air, but inside she felt warmth. Not only that, but a relevance. There was meaning in what she was doing, she was sure of it. It helped.

As she continued to turn the pages, the light from outside gradually faded. The patients had been given an early supper of cheese and bread so that the day staff could leave in good time, and now nothing waited for them but a sleep she could ease them towards. Feeling tired from all the work she'd done earlier, she had to stifle a yawn on several occasions, but she persevered.

Unlike *A Tale of Two Cities*, this Dickens had a purely English setting and she was enjoying it immensely. This was the third novel she'd read of his; the first had been *Pictures from Italy*, a travelogue of sorts, documenting his time spent in Italy and which she'd read prior to travelling here herself. In it he'd described Venice as an 'Italian dream'. Not only that but a 'ghostly city' and 'strange'. She'd agree with the last two sentiments perhaps but regarding the dream reference she might seek to correct him – although certainly what had happened to her since she'd arrived in the city had been dreamlike.

Pausing, she looked around her – night had fallen in earnest and the ward was deathly quiet. What was it like on other wards? Had whoever was in charge managed to lull their patients too? And those residing in other parts of the hospital, parts as yet unexplored, were they at peace? Was Luigina being attended to, given the help she so clearly needed? She hoped so. Most of her patients had indeed fallen asleep. Studying those close to her, the rise and fall of their chests was even. It was peaceful, so peaceful. Even her anger at Enrico's non-appearance dissolved. There'd be a reason. Perhaps several patients had fallen ill and he and his uncle were treating them. He might even be in theatre. She'd find out later. The patients had to come first. She wouldn't argue with that.

Catarina was quiet too, her rheumy eyes closed. Deciding to call it a night, Charlotte rose. She'd go to the cottage and wait for Enrico there. She wouldn't be angry on greeting him; she'd kiss him instead and take his breath away. Doing her utmost to stop her chair from scraping against the tiled floor, she heard a voice, seemingly disembodied.

"Thank you."

In its way it startled her as much as when Luigina had lunged. Having been reading about ghosts, she wondered if she'd conjured one. Her eyes wide, she looked towards the night nurse's desk. It was empty, no doubt she'd taken the opportunity to go outside and have a cigarette, certainly she reeked of them. If it wasn't her, who was it? When the words came again, they were more of a whisper.

"Thank you."

She looked towards Catarina. "Is that you?"

The old woman opened her eyes and nodded, an almost imperceptible gesture.

"But… You can speak?" She berated herself. Of course she could speak! She'd just proved it. But there was something else, more bewildering. "You can speak in English?"

Slowly, very slowly, Catarina raised a hand and beckoned Charlotte to come forward. "Please… help me… sit up," she instructed, her voice low and with a scratchy quality to it. Only briefly hesitating, Charlotte obeyed, too curious not to.

The older woman looked so small in the bed, as if life had shrunk her. Charlotte wished she had a blanket to place over her thin shoulders so she might keep her warm, but they were in a cupboard too far away. If she left, this moment of lucidness might pass.

Instead she sat as close as she deemed safe. She sensed that Catarina spoke only because all the others were asleep, and so kept her voice low too.

"You can speak in English?" Charlotte repeated. "You can understand me?"

Catarina nodded again. "Growing up I had an English governess." She paused before adding, "I enjoy that you read to me."

"I… I'm glad." There were so many questions she wanted to ask but she forced herself to remain still, to listen. Catarina's next words surprised her further.

"You should not be here."

"I'm here because—"

Catarina shook her head. "You should go."

This time Charlotte did reply quickly. "I am going, soon, back to the cottage, my living quarters on the island, *our* living quarters. I'm married to Dr Gritti's nephew—"

Agitation crept into Catarina's voice. "To stay is dangerous."

"Dangerous?" She found it anything but. "How is it dangerous?"

Catarina closed her eyes, but only briefly. "It is not easy to speak."

"No, of course, I realise that—"

"But I must. The history of the island, you know it?"

The history? Only what Enrico had told her, that it had been used as a means of repelling invaders, hence the Octagon just across the water. Also that it had been a sort of checkpoint for people coming in and out of Venice in the eighteenth century.

Before she could answer, Catarina held up a hand, a surprisingly abrupt gesture. "You read to us of ghosts, but this place, it is full of them."

Ghosts? She was talking about ghosts? Charlotte remembered Catarina's diagnosis – hysteria. Should she try and calm her or go and find the night nurse? Enrico and Dr Gritti even? It seemed Catarina guessed what was on her mind.

"I speak the truth! Poveglia is haunted, it always has been, ever since the plague victims."

"Plague victims? What plague victims?"

Clearly Catarina was bewildered. "You have not been told?"

"Told what?"

"Do you know where Luigina is? Do you even have an idea?"

"I... erm... yes. She's being looked after."

"She has been murdered!" Again, Catarina hissed at her, as though frustrated by her ignorance. "So many have been murdered here, first those who were sick physically, confined in the lazzaretto, quarantined, and then us," she raised her hand, tapped at her skull. "Those they consider sick in our heads. But why is grief a sickness?"

Grief? "Catarina, what happened to you?"

If she thought Catarina might divulge any more personal information, she was wrong. Instead, her agitation increased. "My concern is for you."

She should call the nurse. Catarina was definitely having an episode. She tensed, made to move but Catarina's next words stopped her.

"Have you noticed the soil is soft on the island? It is because you are walking on graves. There are bones under your feet, countless bones, all of us mixed together, buried and forgotten, or so they like to think. But they are wrong. The dead do not forget. They are still here. They want revenge and they will get it. Somehow they will get it."

Tempted though she was to dismiss Catarina's words, the memory of her first day surfaced. How she'd fallen, her hands sinking into soil as soft as Catarina said it was, one hand closing around something long and smooth but hard to

135

the touch – something Enrico had thrown from him, as if it were still contaminated – a human bone? She remembered thinking it was, but only initially, forgetting about it soon after. But if it was – if she were right, if *Catarina* was right, then to whom did it belong? A soldier from long ago? A patient from the asylum? A plague victim? There were green fields edging the island; she'd planned to walk in them when she had time. That prospect didn't seem so appealing now.

She swallowed – what had been revealed was bad enough but more worrying was the issue of Luigina. It was too fantastical to be true.

"Luigina is alive. Patients are not murdered here."

Catarina was unfazed by her stringent denial. "They are. Luigina is not the first to disappear. There are others. If you make a fuss, if you show that the opiates are not working, then they silence you in other ways. Everyone knows, but no one will say. Dr Gritti has too much power."

"Dr Gritti is trying to help." And subsequently her husband: trying to find a way to cure their madness.

"But he does not help! He fails, over and over. Yet still he keeps on experimenting. Once you are on this island no one cares. You are dead from the moment you arrive."

"That isn't true."

"It is! There are other parts to this hospital, secret parts. You are aware of that? That is where they experiment. Open your eyes, girl, and see where it is you really are. You are in hell. If you can, if it is not too late, leave." She paused, her eyes glistening. "You are different. You do care. But it will do you no good. Listen to me and leave Poveglia."

"But my husband, Enrico…" She could feel her eyes moistening too, if what Catarina was saying was true, it was awful. But surely they were the ramblings of a mad woman?

"If he refuses to come, leave him. As I have said, Dr Gritti has too much power."

She closed her eyes, tried to process all she'd been told: Poveglia was once where plague victims were quarantined, where they were sent to die? And now it was home to an asylum, where patients were experimented on. And when the experiment went wrong, they died, murdered in other words and no one stopped it. All were complicit, or looked the other way. *She* had looked the other way, ignored paths she didn't have to tread, concerned herself only with what she had to do; dampened any curiosity. After all, she was leaving soon; she was simply biding her time. But now... now it was different.

If she were to believe Catarina, she needed to find proof. The ground outside was a starting point, she could dig where she'd fallen, see if she could find the bone she'd grabbed hold of, other bones perhaps. She could explore less common areas, and if someone stopped her, she'd pretend she was lost. Enrico was another port of call, he was her husband, she'd quiz him; he'd tell her the truth, put her mind at rest. Catarina was prone to hysteria, she reminded herself of that. As for claims the island was haunted, she'd never been unsettled by anything supernatural, not even the stillness of it.

"Catarina, there are no ghosts—"

"There *are* ghosts. Look and you will see."

"But it is so peaceful here."

"There is no peace."

Engrossed in their conversation, she didn't register initially that Catarina had begun to shake. She'd also turned her head to the side to look at something. Compelled to look too,

Charlotte took a deep breath and turned her head slowly, so slowly, her nerves getting the better of her. She exhaled in relief. It was only the night nurse. She'd returned and she was staring at them; her eyes narrowed and lips pursed.

Trying to shield Catarina from view with her body, Charlotte leant forward. "You are not to worry, I won't say anything, or tell her we've even talked. You are safe, perfectly safe."

Her reassuring words fell short as Catarina continued to shake.

Chapter Nineteen

AS she'd planned to do, Charlotte greeted Enrico with a kiss that night. He'd come rushing through the door only a short while after she'd arrived home, a thousand apologies on his lips, there'd been several emergencies apparently and it'd been impossible to get away. As he continued to make a fuss of her, she asked what type of emergencies they'd been.

"One patient started having hallucinations, he had to be restrained," Enrico explained, surprising her by offering to open a bottle of red wine, so rarely did he drink. "Another started to convulse. *Amore*, it is all very boring for you but what happened today, it is standard for us. I had to stay to assist my uncle, I had no choice."

Pouring the wine, which he'd ordered in at the beginning of their stay, she studied his demeanour. The tremors running through him were in no way as noticeable as Catarina's but the glass shook slightly in his hand as he held it. He also lit a cigarette and puffed at it in rapid succession. Was he nervous? He seemed so. Or was she being fanciful again? Fired up by Catarina and what she'd said? There was only one way to find out.

"Darling, Luigina wasn't on the ward today."

Again the glass shook as he lifted it to his lips. "Luigina?" he repeated. "No, she... erm... will not be returning any time soon."

"Why not?"

"The relapse she has suffered is significant. She needs to be... tended to."

She drank from her glass too but refused the cigarette he offered her. "Enrico, this cure you are trying to find for madness, the operations you carry out, it's all within the limits of the law isn't it?" She couldn't believe she'd asked, that she'd ploughed straight in.

To her relief, Enrico laughed. "Of course! You think I would break my code of ethics?"

"No... I..."

Enrico drained his glass. "*Amore*, I cannot believe you doubt my integrity!"

"I don't, not at all, but, Luigina, *how* is she being tended to? Please, Enrico, just tell me."

Enrico had been sitting but now he rose abruptly and walked over to the window, taking her silver cigarette case with him and lighting another from it. He stared in the direction of the asylum, before looking back at her. "We have a high security wing, Charlotte, it is not in the main building it is in the building to the right of it. You have not been there and nor should you. It is, or rather it can be, very distressing, home to only our most disturbed patients. She has been placed in a cell there."

"A *cell*?"

Enrico sighed at her reaction, rolled his eyes. "A padded cell, for her own safety. She will hurt herself otherwise."

"A high security wing?" Again she repeated his words, trying to make sense of them.

A cloud of smoke surrounding him, he looked slightly feverish, she thought. Twin spots of colour glowed on his cheeks. "You must realise there is one here?"

"Yes, yes, of course." And yet it had never crossed her mind, not until Catarina had spoken of it. "Luigina will be all right?"

"She is in my uncle's care."

"But she will be all right?"

She could sense his impatience. "Charlotte, what is this all about?"

How could she tell him what it was all about? The last thing she wanted was to get Catarina in trouble too. "I feel responsible," she answered.

He walked back over, but not to offer a reassuring hug, to pour another glass of wine. Soon he'd finish the bottle. "You are not to blame. Luigina will be treated appropriately."

"Operated on you mean?"

He paused briefly before drinking again, wiping at his mouth afterwards. "Charlotte, I have explained what we are trying to do, the purpose of it, and you understand, yes?"

"Yes," she supposed she did. Taking a sip from her glass, she decided to probe him about the history of the island – the *plague* history – explaining that she was talking to a nurse instead of a patient who'd mentioned something about it.

Enrico dismissed that too. "It is history, *amore*, ancient history. Venice had no choice but to quarantine victims that had fallen ill, all around the world they did the same."

"Were they left to die here?"

"Some died, some survived, but most importantly *Venice* survived."

That was true, she couldn't deny it. Disease had to be contained and the healthy protected. Of those that had died, there was every chance at least some of them had been buried too, their bodies burnt to 'cleanse' them and what remained pushed into soft earth to lie unmarked – the ground just as secretive as the sea.

Enrico was talking again.

"*Amore*, it is Christmas, we have both worked hard all day, please, let us forget about work, about the history of the island, just for a little while. Try and make the best of it."

Make the best of it? He spoke as if he was finding it difficult too. He was right though. They had both worked hard today, her husband especially. She reminded herself how much responsibility his position carried, and the decisions he had to make, he must feel weighed down by them sometimes. Certainly, he seemed more care worn; he had done since they'd arrived on the island, since he'd arrived back home even. At his parents' he'd been on edge as much as her at times. They both had to report for duty in the morning, but tonight was theirs. She wouldn't worry about Luigina anymore – she was in the best place for her. And she'd try to forget Catarina's dramatic words too. As for the island's history, although unpleasant, it was, as Enrico said, over. Placing her glass back down, she fixed him with one of her looks, a look he returned, knowing full well what she wanted.

Christmas passed peacefully enough, Enrico helping on the ward on Christmas Day, making up for the day before. They spent the evening together amiably as well, Charlotte putting the disappointment of not hearing from her family on hold, remembering that Enrico was her family now, her *immediate* family. She'd tackle the issue regarding her parents and Albert as soon as the New Year began. Nothing more untoward happened on the ward following Christmas, Catarina didn't speak to her again, didn't even try and make contact. She'd retreated into herself, couldn't even raise a smile. Charlotte did try on occasion to coax her into speaking when the ward nurse was busy, but without success.

The New Year came and went, not the riotous celebration she'd always been used to but exciting in its own way – it meant their stint on Poveglia was to come to a close.

Since Catarina's words, she'd explored the ground close to where she'd fallen, but not found anything. To corroborate Catarina's theory of 'shallow graves' she'd have to take a shovel to the ground, but she was in no hurry to do that, squirming at the thought. Besides, would she be the unethical one for disturbing the dead? As for corridors yet unexplored, she ventured down a few but doors leading off them had been locked and, listening carefully for signs of activity from within, she'd found none. Once, whilst exploring, she'd almost got caught by none other than Dr Gritti himself and had had to pick up pace to avoid him. She'd heard him talking. Not to Enrico, it was a woman who'd answered him. Not wanting to explain herself, she'd thanked God for her keen hearing.

It was raining again. She missed crisp, cold December mornings as January settled in. It was miserable on the island when it rained and she was sure that the boatman didn't deliver provisions as often as he normally did, food rations seemed to be less than normal, for everyone. The postman too was conspicuous by his absence, and she was growing further agitated at the lack of correspondence from home, having noticed that Europe was indeed on the brink of war from a newspaper left lying about. It was even more essential to get in touch with her parents, with Albert, to find out how they all were, whether her father had recovered from his chest infection, if her brother had been stationed and where. The need to return home was also becoming more pressing, lest travel soon became impossible.

In-between her work on the ward, she kept regular watches on Dr Gritti's office, making whatever excuses she could throughout the day to keep popping down to the ground floor, to try and find a pattern of when he did and didn't occupy it. She'd asked Enrico to ask his uncle if she could use the telephone but he'd been fobbed off with Dr Gritti saying that he 'doubted very much a connection to London could be made from the island at this time.' Wanting to put the international exchange to the test herself, she'd decided she'd go in there when he and Enrico were on their rounds. She remembered the number to quote well enough, as she had spent enough time typing it onto correspondence.

The opportunity to do so came quite suddenly. It was a Monday morning and she knew for a fact that Dr Gritti and Enrico would be in the high security wing, tending to patients, Enrico had told her that much the previous evening. She'd been concerned about him going into work at all. He'd appeared feverish again, his dark eyes glittering strangely, but he'd said there was nothing wrong with him. Torn between insisting he take a day off and seizing her chance, she'd decided on the latter.

Poised at the door of the doctor's office, she hesitated, feeling like a thief who was breaking and entering. The door wasn't locked, so there was no breaking at least – Dr Gritti perhaps a little too arrogant in thinking no one would dare to go in there during his absence. Checking there was no one around her, she slipped inside.

The only time she'd been in here before was on the day

they'd first arrived. It was exactly the same; as neat, as order-ly, as precise – reflecting his personality she thought. He was a *precise* man, cold too, despite being charismatic. This hos-pital was his kingdom, he ruled it, but maybe it was with fear rather than respect. Did she respect him? His obvious medi-cal skills perhaps, but his bedside manner, his insistence on doping the patients so they were barely more than vegetables, his dismissal of her when she'd been attacked; those were qualities she didn't favour. Did Enrico respect him? Enor-mously. She could never voice her true opinion of his uncle, he'd never agree. Little matter it all was, they'd be off the island soon, they'd be home, she'd focus on what she came here to do – make contact – and then she'd start insisting they leave for good.

Crossing over to the telephone, she lifted the receiver and waited to be connected to the operator. When a female voice answered, she spoke in low clear tones. The operator was speaking back to her, her voice so faint, that even if they'd both been speaking English, she doubted she'd be under-stood.

"London," Charlotte kept saying. "Can you connect me to an office in London?"

"*Numero, per favore?*"

Numbers, the operator was asking for numbers. Charlotte recited it only to be greeted with what sounded like '*scusa*' – pardon me? She recited them again, loud and clear, hoping the operator's grasp of a foreign language surpassed hers. As her voice rang out, she glanced nervously at the door, pray-ing she wouldn't attract anyone.

There was silence on the other end – only for a few moments but it seemed longer. Time was so different on the island. It lingered, minutes melting into each other and stretching into eternity. A shiver danced along her spine. She had a sudden premonition: that's how long she'd be here – for an eternity, if she couldn't get through to London, if she couldn't persuade Enrico to leave... There was a ringing tone! She'd been patched through! She could hardly believe her luck. She'd find out news of what was happening in London, be able to pass a message to Albert and her parents. She'd speak to someone English. She'd be *understood*. The deceit of her actions was worth it if this was the result.

Hurry! Hurry! Please hurry.

More time passed.

Someone answer the telephone!

Still it rang.

Please!

It went dead; no more ringing tone, no crackling even. "Hello! Hello!" she cried but received no reply.

She dared to sink into the doctor's chair, and, having to steady her fingers, tried again. This time even getting through to the operator was impossible making her wonder if she'd imagined it before. Tears filled her eyes. *So near and yet so far... like this damned island.*

Reluctantly she replaced the receiver. As much as she cared for the patients here, she'd have to insist to Enrico that they leave sooner rather than later – she simply had to be out in the real world again, be a part of it. If he didn't agree, she'd leave anyway, go back to England and wait for him there. Maybe she could even pave the way for him, source what vacancies there were in the medical world. As she'd said, in London, especially in the current time, there'd be plenty of opportunities.

Trying to find solace in that plan, she started to rise from the desk when something caught her eye. A desk drawer to the right was slightly ajar. She sat back down, and, unable to resist, reached out to pull it further open. It was a mishmash of papers, not neat at all, but haphazard. Curious, she pulled open the drawer to the left too, again it was stuffed, this time with a jumble of office necessities, pens, scissors, rulers, a stapler, staples. Pulling open another drawer, and another, it was the same with each of them. She stood up and went to a filing cabinet located on the far wall; there was no system to anything, no attempt whatsoever at order. Was this a more honest reflection of Dr Gritti's personality: composed on the outside but inside a mess.

You've been living too long in a mental asylum! Despite her despair, the thought made her laugh. She most certainly had! She was getting jumpy about everything. About to close the drawer, something else stood out. One of the letters lying amidst so many others at the bottom of the filing cabinet looked familiar. The more she stared at it, the more recognisable it became. Stooping, she grabbed it. No wonder – it was her handwriting! This was the first letter she'd written on Poveglia, the one informing Albert and her parents of her new address. What was it doing here? Why hadn't it been sent? Holding it in one hand, she sifted through more of the drawer's contents, her hands seizing upon another of her letters, then a third and a fourth – none had been sent!

Snatching them up in a bundle she stood, swaying with a mixture of emotions – anger but something else too, the first real stirrings of fear. Had Dr Gritti intercepted them? If so, why? Enrico would be horrified when she told him. She'd take them with her, thrust them under his nose, and then he'd have no choice but to agree that they leave. His uncle couldn't be trusted, not if he could do this: withhold correspondence. That was why Albert or her parents hadn't written to her, they didn't know where she was! But surely they'd have written to Enrico's home address in Venice, why hadn't Stefania forwarded them? Or had she, and they'd been intercepted too, in which case they'd be here. She'd have more evidence to condemn him with.

Placing the letters on top of the filing cabinet she started working her way through the drawers again, this time more carefully, determined to find them. There *were* more letters, but who'd written them or whom they were addressed to remained a mystery, she could barely speak Italian, let alone read it. And notes, there was a copious amount of loose notes, some with diagrams attached to them, hand-crafted, crude drawings – the head, the brain, the torso, arrows pointing to various points, the writing beneath each arrow not neat but barely legible; a scrawl only discernible to its owner. Dr Gritti? It had to be.

She could find nothing more that related to her, nothing she could understand anyway. Straightening, she looked in the top drawer again; here there were notebooks in amongst papers and news articles, all it seemed, medically inclined. The limitations of her linguistic ability frustrated her but at least she'd found her own property – it was enough to start building a case with. There was no way the letters had been 'accidentally' detained. Dr Gritti had stolen them. Or he'd given someone the order to steal them.

"Damn him!"

How dare he do such a thing! Her parents must be worried sick, her brother too. And the feeling was reciprocal.

God, she hoped they were safe.

Not knowing whether to scream or cry, she resolved to get out of his office and find her husband. As she took deep breaths to calm herself, she noticed she still had one of the notebooks in her hand. Not a notebook as such, it was more of a ledger, thin with a dark blue cover. Curiosity getting the better of her, she opened it. Inside, words were scrawled in a series of columns, of which there were four to a page. Delaying her plan to take flight, she tried to decipher the words in front of her. Each column looked to contain a name and beside each name, in the second column, was more detailed writing comprising at least three or four sentences. The third column contained a date – the ledger was first started on 23rd October 1936 – and in the fourth column there was a single word only – *morto*.

Her eyes ran down the length of the fourth column where that word was repeated over and over – *morto* – dead. That's what that word meant, that the person named in the first column had died. She turned the pages, not all of them were filled in the same way. Some pages had notes scrawled all over them before the user returned to its intended use – diligently filling out the columns again – one page even had a huge black X marked on it, the paper torn slightly as if it had been drawn in temper. Again there were columns filled out, again the word '*morto*'. Her eyes flicked to the names of the people who'd died – tried to decipher them – Renata Cantu, Violetta Fabbri, Agnolo Piovene. Dispensing with their surnames, she continued – Adaline, Guido, Domenica, Jacopo, Marzia, Stefano... So many people, such lyrical names, all dead, but how, and by whose hand?

Her heart pounding, she flicked to the back pages, to

more recent dates, and ran her gaze down the length of the columns – searching. When she found what she was looking for, what she suspected, her heart seemed to stop. Luigina Morosini, the date 24th December 1938. There were some words in the third column and then a word in the fourth column – *morto*. She was dead, had died the day before Christmas, Luigina, who, although disturbed, appeared well enough physically. *Murdered* – at the doctor's hand, and perhaps… she could barely bring herself to think it, at her husband's too. That's why he hadn't come to help her; he and his uncle had been dealing with Luigina, treating her 'appropriately'. She was no longer subdued and they were taking further action.

Catarina!

She was no longer subdued either, and the ward nurse had noticed. Had she gone running to Dr Gritti, informed him?

She'd seen enough. Throwing the notebook back in the drawer and slamming it shut, Charlotte grabbed her letters and turned towards the door, determined to go to the ward first and make sure that Catarina was all right, that she hadn't been taken away. She'd be there. She had to be there. And there'd be an explanation for Luigina's death, one that was tolerable. The man she loved was not a murderer and nor would he collude with one.

About to bolt forward, she stopped. There was movement outside the door! Through the glass panel she could see an outline, small, neat, and feminine. The woman – one of the nurses – had been passing but came to a standstill and was looking towards the office. Had it been the slamming of the cabinet drawer that had alerted her? Charlotte berated herself. *You've drawn attention to yourself!* Small mercy that it wasn't Dr Gritti but even so she'd have to explain why she was in his office, what she had in her hands, and it would get back to him – *everything* got back to him – the man with too much power.

The nurse walked towards the door, slowly, tentatively, began to turn the handle and, as she did, Charlotte could only stand and stare, her mind having gone blank, refusing to even think of a reason. She was caught, as helpless as the patients, as Luigina, as all the names she'd just read, as Catarina. She screwed her eyes shut – a childish ploy she knew: if she couldn't see them, they couldn't see her – and waited.

"*Agata, Agata, vieni immediatamente in sala da prarizo, c'e un problema.*"

She opened her eyes; someone was calling the nurse! The handle stopped turning, the door didn't open and the figure retreated. She hadn't realised she was holding her breath until it burst from her. She had to get out of here, check on Catarina – and then she'd find her husband, tell him about the letters, ask about Luigina, make plans to leave, to return to her family she loved and missed more than ever. Folding the letters, she stuffed them into her pocket, opened the door, checked the way was clear and then softly closed it behind her.

Impatient, she took the stairs to the second floor two at a time, noticing as she did just how shabby the paintwork was, the cobwebs that had been allowed to gather and the dirt congealing in dark corners. She'd always thought of the wards as sparse but now, as she stood in the doorway to the one she worked in, they seemed cruelly so. Even flowers would have been a gesture, some simple flowers. But then where would they have come from? She'd seen none on the

151

island. Flowers wouldn't grow here. The scales were dropping from her eyes; it was as though she could see properly for the first time since arriving. She focused on Catarina's bed – Catarina's *empty* bed, and her breathing quickened. Catarina rarely left her bed; it was her world, her place of safety – the case with so many patients. Even their 'business' was performed on a bedpan. She *should* be in her bed.

She walked over to one of the nurses and asked about her whereabouts.

The nurse didn't even bother to look at her as she replied. "Gone."

"*Where* has she gone?"

"Gone," the nurse repeated before she turned and walked away.

Chapter Twenty

HURRYING from the ward, Charlotte almost knocked another auxiliary down.

"Sorry, so sorry," she blustered before hurrying onwards. She needed to find the high security wing. That's where Dr Gritti and Enrico were and where Catarina had been taken.

Weaving in and out of corridors, all identical to one another, venturing deeper into the building, the only thing different was the atmosphere. On her ward it was peaceful, even if it was an enforced peace, here she could feel something in the air: emotions swirled furiously around. There were so many, some she could identify with: confusion, grief, upset, and others that were so dark, so alien, she couldn't understand them at all – *extreme* emotions. What had happened since her last shift? Had Catarina drawn even more attention to herself, become violent even, like Luigina had? She couldn't imagine it, not Catarina, not her friend. The night nurse had obviously reported her, but she still couldn't understand why. What was so wrong with one of the patients having a moment of lucidity? Also, a couple of weeks had passed since the incident. If it concerned them so much, why not take her sooner? Questions, questions, so many reared up in her mind, all demanding answers. She had to find out what had happened, confront Enrico further *and* his uncle.

As she walked, the lighting above failed slightly, began to flicker, like a warning almost – *turn back, turn back* – but she couldn't, not until she knew her charge was safe.

A sound brought her up short. It was high-pitched, coming from further up. The hair on her arms stood to attention, even the hair on her scalp tingled as she broke into a run again, her feet carrying her along, into the heart of the hospital. *The heart?* No. If Catarina was right, this part of the asylum didn't have a heart, or if it did, it was rotten to the core.

Almost stumbling she was running so fast, she started calling out Catarina's name. If they were doing something to her they had to stop. They couldn't use people in such a way. It didn't matter that they were ill they were *still* people.

"Catarina! Catarina! Where are you?"

Up ahead there was a pair of double doors, the only doors on an otherwise blank wall. Was that where the scream had come from? She hurled herself towards them, expecting them to be locked but they yielded easily to her touch. Standing still, she found herself in a large sterile looking room, the walls covered in light blue tiles. There were shelves too, rows and rows of them, filled with all manner of medical equipment. In one corner a wheelchair lay abandoned, whilst overhead the light flickered as it had done in the corridor, as if it too was agitated. The room wasn't as sterile as she first thought; there was blood on the floor, not a huge amount but spots of it, trailing into a room beyond, which was hidden from view by a curtain. From behind it she could hear the shuffling of feet, more cries but muffled this time, dying out.

She moved forwards, determined to see what was happening, but, as she did, the curtains parted and Dr Gritti appeared, Enrico behind him, both wearing surgical gowns and masks covering the lower half of their faces. Her eyes travelling to Dr Gritti's gloved hands, she saw there was blood on them too. This was a theatre, an operating theatre

— a silent, secret place, hidden in the centre of that rotten heart.

"I... I heard someone screaming. Who is it?"

"You should not be here." It was Dr Gritti who replied, Enrico seemed unable to speak — he just stared at her in disbelief — either that or horror, she couldn't quite tell.

"I won't leave, not until you tell me who is behind that curtain."

"Turn around and go." There was a definite threat in his voice.

"Where is Catarina Castelli? Have you taken her?"

"It is not your business."

"She *is* my business!" Anger was rising in her now, not just because of Dr Gritti but because of Enrico, who was standing by him, not saying a word, just as he'd stood when his mother had burst in on them — doing nothing. She trained her gaze on him instead of his uncle, tried to provoke some sort of reaction. His eyes were glittering still, feverish — the same feverishness that was in Dr Gritti's eyes. Not the result of illness, could it be excitement?

She strived to keep her voice steady. "I heard someone screaming, a woman I think. The sound came from here. Catarina isn't in her bed. Is she behind the curtains? Let me see her."

Even though she couldn't see Dr Gritti's face behind his mask, she had a feeling he was smiling. "Ah, Catarina has been talking, filling your head with nonsense. Delusions and hysterics are all part of Catarina's condition. A condition I will try and eliminate."

"Eliminate?" What a strange choice of word to use. "Eliminate *her* you mean?"

Dr Gritti growled, glanced at Enrico. "Like Catarina, your wife is becoming a danger."

A danger? Why was Enrico standing by, accepting what his uncle was saying? Why wasn't he defending her? Now would be the perfect time for him to step up. He wasn't even looking at her anymore; he was looking away, staring at the ground. Instead, *she* was the one defending a woman that she barely knew.

"I believe that Catarina is through there, Dr Gritti. She was screaming just a short while ago but now she is silent, probably because you've sedated her. Are you planning to operate too, to *experiment?*"

As she said the words she made to dart round them but they easily blocked her. Fuming, she turned to her husband, "Enrico, what is wrong with you? It feels like you're siding with your uncle against me. Surely that isn't true."

"There is no side to take," Enrico said, his voice muffled, his gaze still averted.

"There is… this man… your uncle, there is something wrong with him." She had to come clean and tell him what she knew. "I went to his office, Enrico, to use the telephone. I wanted to try and contact someone at home, I was tired of being fobbed off."

"You went to my office?" Dr Gritti raised an eyebrow.

Charlotte nodded defiantly. "I failed to make a connection but nonetheless my time there proved fruitful. I found things." Retrieving the letters from her pocket, she waved them in front of them both. "These are letters I wrote to my parents, to my brother. They were never sent; they were in a filing cabinet instead, just tossed in there. And," she had difficulty swallowing, her throat was so dry, "in that same cabinet, I found a ledger, a list of people, I have no idea if they were all patients of Poveglia but they had one thing in common, they're dead. That is what it was you see, a ledger of the dead and Luigina was in it – her death recorded as the 24th December 1938, Christmas Eve. The day," – oh, God, she could hardly bring herself to say it – "the day that you didn't come to help me, the day you and your uncle were busy," she glanced at the hidden room, "operating."

Beneath his mask, Enrico was breathing heavily. "You failed to make a connection?"

"Yes... I just said that." Why had he singled out that fact, hadn't he heard what else she'd said. What she'd *implied?* "Enrico, we need to make sure Catarina is safe and then leave, your uncle might have stopped my letters from leaving the island but he can't stop me, stop *us.*"

"Your parents don't know you are here," Enrico continued to mutter, his eyes darting between her and his uncle. "No one knows you are here."

"Enrico, listen, what's happening on the island, the work that your uncle is undertaking, it isn't right." Catarina's words about the plague victims and the shallow graves came flooding back. "There has been so much death here and yet still it continues." Her voice hardened as she stared back at Dr Gritti. "Being mentally ill does not make a person bad and nor does it make them worthless. There are other ways to help people who suffer, *effective* ways – what I was doing for example, the simple act of communication. How can we even begin to treat the problem if we can't talk to our patients, if we don't allow them to talk back? That's the only way to understand madness, to be able to stand a chance of curing it – we need to find out what's at the root of it, what caused it in the first place, if it really is madness, or if it's something else, grief for example, loss. There could be so many reasons. Your way, your methods, all it results in is death."

There was a groan from behind the curtain. Catarina was still alive! She hadn't gone the way of other 'lost' patients – yet.

Hope surged within Charlotte. "Catarina, I'm coming."

Dr Gritti closed the gap between them and seized her arms. "You are going nowhere."

"TAKE YOUR HANDS OFF ME."

When he began to laugh, she wanted to cry. He turned his head to Enrico. "She will make an interesting experiment, your wilful wife."

He couldn't possibly mean it. "ENRICO!"

"Enrico won't help you," Dr Gritti continued to taunt. "He is too ambitious."

Too ambitious? Yes, of course he was, but he was good. Ultimately he was good. She wouldn't have fallen in love with him otherwise.

"Enrico, help me!" When she got no reply, she tried again. "Please!"

"We must get her into another room, Enrico."

Another room? What other room? "Enrico, we have to go home."

"Impossible," Dr Gritti said, abruptly releasing her before walking over to where the shelves were and reaching up to grab something: a syringe. "You know too much."

Ice-cold beads of moisture began to erupt on her forehead. She had to try a different tack, not scream and shout, not goad him anymore. "I promise, you can continue, Dr Gritti,

I won't breathe a word. Just let my husband and I go. There will be no more fuss."

The doctor didn't even deign to reply; he simply carried on doing what he was doing, calmly, casually – such arrogance in his stance. Flying to Enrico, her hands grabbed his face. "Darling, look at me, please. We can go. We can leave. He can't make us stay."

Enrico brought his hands up to cover hers. "*Amore* – we are close, so close."

"Listen to me, please. I am your wife!" It was the second time she'd had to remind him of this.

"I know."

"Then help me!"

He screwed his eyes shut, looked physically pained.

"Don't you love me anymore?" she asked.

"I do."

"Help me," she repeated. Strangely their voices had lowered, become whispers – two lovers, a husband and wife with words only for each other. "We can put this behind us, we can pretend it never happened. Be happy again. I make you happy, don't I?"

"*Amore...*"

Dr Gritti returned and, with one hand yanked her away from Enrico; the other hand held a syringe. "You do keep him happy, *amore*, in the bedroom particularly, but any woman can do that. There are many here as loose as you."

She was more stunned by his words than the sight of the syringe. "As loose as me, I... how dare you! What do you mean?"

Releasing her, Dr Gritti removed his mask, revealing an expression that was wolfish. His nose seemed much longer than before, his eyes more beadlike, his mouth a cavern. "You are a whore," he said simply. "Enrico tells me how wanton you are. He enjoys it, any man would. You are an attractive girl. But it is the strings attached that I tell him are no good, the demands you make, the attention you crave, how you use sex to manipulate him, to get your own way, to disrupt his career. I have taught Enrico many things since he has been on the island, one of the most important to think with his brain not just his balls."

At his words, she could only turn to Enrico, a silent question in her eyes. *Is that the way you've described me, as wanton, as someone who only wants to manipulate you, to hinder?* He provided no answers, but his shoulders slumped. Dr Gritti had defeated him. No, the truth was worse than that. He'd *allowed* himself to be defeated.

Finding her voice again, she continued to appeal. "My parents will contact Enrico's parents when they fail to hear from me and insist on a forwarding address."

"My dear sister and her excuse for a husband will obey my wishes, no one else's," Dr Gritti was clearly not concerned with any argument she could raise. "Besides, Europe will soon be a mess because of the war. Communications will break down between countries, between people. It will be hard to find loved ones, impossible in some cases."

What was he saying? That she'd never see Albert or her parents again? He couldn't do that, he couldn't! But, as the dream-like scenario she was caught in continued to unfold, she realised he could. "Enrico, did you know your uncle had intercepted my letters?"

Again, it was Dr Gritti who replied. "Of course he knew. I was honest with him."

Still she addressed Enrico. "And… did you plan this all along, you and your mother?"

Enrico rallied. "My mother is innocent!"

So he *was* capable of defending someone, although there was cold comfort in it. "Answer me, did you *plan* it?"

"No." All fight left him. It had been so fleeting. "I planned nothing."

"So it's for the sake of ambition that you'll kill me?"

Dr Gritti roared with laughter, a sound that hurt her ears. "We have no intention of killing you, Charlotte! You too are suffering from hysteria. Contrary to what you think, we are not murderers, we are pioneers." He paused briefly. "Although accidents of course happen when trying to achieve great things, and so many of them. It is unfortunate, I agree. No, we will not murder you. Such a notion! We will do what we do with the other patients. We will *treat* you. Only if you break rank will we take more drastic measures, and a part of you, deep down, will understand that well enough. Comply, however, and there is nothing to fear. You will live, I am sure, to a grand old age on the island."

So, one way or another, they'd get her. She'd die here, on Poveglia, cut off from the rest of civilisation, from her family and her beloved Albert. Enrico had also removed his mask, his normally olive complexion pale. He reached out but only to hold her steady whilst his uncle force-fed whatever drug was in the syringe into her system. As the needle pierced flesh, as consciousness, *true* consciousness began to fade she made one last vow. If Catarina was right about the dead and they were waiting to wreak revenge, she'd lead them. And then she'd leave this island, even if she was dead herself. She'd go home.

PART THREE
Poveglia

Chapter Twenty-One

THERE was a gentle rhythm to the waters beneath Piero's boat that lulled her, the effect soporific, compounded by the thick layers of mist that surrounded them. Passing the raggedy stick men again, as she thought of the wooden pilings that rose out of the water to guide the way, Louise felt caught between this world and the next – unsure what was real and what wasn't. She was in a dream again, although this was a waking dream at least. Last night she'd only realised she'd been dreaming when she'd woken up, the images crowding her mind so vividly and lingering until she'd forced them from her mind. Trembling at the memory, she squeezed Rob's hand. He squeezed back, adding a quick smile before scanning the horizon. The veiled lady had been in the dream.

There'd been mist too. She was somewhere strange; somewhere she didn't recognise but, even so, she knew it to be a stark and barren place, the ground beneath her feet soft but not fertile, far from it. She'd been playing a game, a child's game, even though she wasn't a child in the dream and neither, it seemed, were the people that surrounded her.

"Spin around, spin around!" The shadow figures were saying, their voices high-pitched and bursting with excitement. "Spin around, spin around!"

At the same time hands were reaching out, twisting her, turning her, ethereal fingers that were cold to the touch. She'd been told to close her eyes, was trying to concentrate, to stop her head from spinning. Suddenly she understood the objective of the 'game' – when they finally stopped spinning her, she had to reach out and – still with eyes closed – catch one of them. Then, whomever she caught, it was their turn to stand in the circle, to take her place. She remembered enjoying the game, finding it fun, and then the atmosphere had changed, becoming as cold as the hands that touched her. The voices continued to chant, but their pitch changed too, becoming higher, faster, beginning to grate, to hurt her ears. *Stop it! Stop it!* Despite her irritation, she was determined to make it to the end of the game and then, abruptly, all voices had died away, hands had stopped clawing. Did this mean she could stop, lunge forward and catch the next victim? Relief had surged through her; she'd even smiled. Taking a few steps, she started grabbing, arms waving randomly in front of her, grasping nothing but thin air, big armfuls of it. *Slippery as eels, but I'll catch them. I'll catch someone.* But still the others in the game proved elusive. How much longer should she keep this up? She was getting tired, so tired, which struck her as odd: how could you be tired when you were already asleep? She'd give it just a short while longer; try to be a sport about it.

"Hello, is anyone there? Let me know if you are. That I'm not alone."

She was met with silence – a wall of it. Had her playmates abandoned her? She stopped searching and came to a standstill. God, it was arctic, the very air she breathed solidifying around her. She was going to have to open her eyes and ruin the game. But she had no choice. It needed to come to an end anyway. It had gone on too long. Before she could change her mind, her eyelids sprang open and that was when she'd seen her, the veiled lady standing close, so close, ready to claim her...

"Oh shit!"

Rob turned, a look of surprise on his face. "What's the matter, Lou, do you feel sick?"

"No, no. I... I was remembering that's all, something I saw in a dream last night."

And it had just been in the dream she'd seen her – just the dream. How often had she had to remind herself of that this morning? When she'd opened her eyes for real there'd been no one in the room but the two of them, no sound but that of Rob's gentle snoring.

"Yeah, you were thrashing around a bit. Woke me up a couple of times. You were murmuring too. Was it a nightmare? Must have been. All that drink and..." he paused, looked away but only briefly, "I don't suppose the argument helped either."

She was amazed. He never normally acknowledged their arguments – once cross words were over between them they were never referred to again, and she'd learnt long ago not to press him either, as it got her nowhere, and only led to a fresh argument. Strangely, the fact that he was acknowledging their argument now embarrassed her. She still felt terrible about how she'd laid into him, blaming him for everything, telling him she hated him, hitting him across the face; something she'd never done before. She'd lost control. She couldn't bear to think of the hurt in his eyes, felt so ashamed about it. But she'd gone someway to redeeming things hadn't she? She'd agreed to this at least.

Looking at Rob, he clearly expected some sort of response. "You're right, the argument didn't help. I'm so sorry, I don't want us to argue again."

He shrugged. "We're going to argue, Lou, it's inevitable, couples always do, but yeah, let's make more of an effort to chill out in future, both of us."

She could only agree.

Piero and Kristina were sitting in front, Piero steering the boat. He turned his head round to speak to them. "The mist will clear soon, the sun will burn a hole through it."

His wife nodded sagely as though he were speaking the words of a prophet. Louise didn't have as much faith but she nodded too. They were only trying to be kind. Even so, she couldn't help but wish they'd never gone to that restaurant again last night; had never met the people in front of her; that the question of visiting Poveglia hadn't arisen. But Rob seemed excited, that was the main thing. He'd been thrilled when she'd told him this morning that she'd texted Piero and that he'd replied back, saying the trip was on. He'd even leant across and kissed her – a 'make-up' kiss, tentative as opposed to passionate, but something to show they were on the mend, that another storm had been weathered.

Continuing to glide, leaving one island behind to encounter another, she looked at her watch. It was noon. If the sun were going to burn through the mist surely it would have done so by now? She found herself praying for sunshine, even though she hadn't seen any so far this weekend. The island wouldn't seem so frightening in the brightness of day. She rolled her eyes. *It's not frightening anyway!* But the thought had no impact. The veiled lady might be a figment of her imagination but she'd succeeded in unnerving her. *Venice* had unnerved her, and now Poveglia. She never thought she'd think it, not considering how much she'd wanted to come to this part of the world, but she was looking forward to returning home in the morning, to normality. Perhaps they'd book a beach holiday next time instead of a city break, head to Ibiza, an island saturated in life not death.

"There you are, can you see it," asked Piero, "the bell tower?"

Despite the mist, they could. It was not an unattractive structure – on the contrary, it was even more impressive than when she'd seen it in photos. Tall yet elegant, and with a legend attached to it, a legend she'd read about and which Piero elaborated on.

"They say that one of the island's doctors jumped to his death from that tower," he told them, "the ghosts of so many dead rising up and compelling him to do it. The legend is that he was complicit in employing... erm...how do you say it, *immoral* methods when treating his patients. He used to experiment on them, torture them even; show them no mercy. The people that died, his patients, wanted revenge." He laughed suddenly, as if highly amused. "Ah, the rumours, there are so many here who want revenge apparently, both victims of the plague *and* the asylum. After his suicide, the bell tower was bricked up, and it remains that way to this day. That's one building we won't be able to visit."

Rob was grinning too, loving the spooky story. Kristina,

meanwhile, was gazing at the tower, a strange look on her face. Was she awestruck, Louise wondered, despite having seen the bell tower before? If so, she wouldn't blame her, she was awe-struck too at her first actual sight of the asylum, a row of three buildings, so close to the water's edge.

"Who put the scaffolding up?" she asked Piero, it was covered in it.

"The government. The building is old, crumbling. It needs to be supported."

Louise turned back to the asylum. How would she describe it? Ugly? No, not really. She'd seen far worse in her life. Institutional? Perhaps, but then all large buildings used for such purposes had an institutionalised feel about them, it was the nature of the beast.

As Piero moored the boat, she felt nervous again. The atmosphere was sombre, so subdued. As though the island was lying in wait... but for what? For people to visit, for an injection of life, something to lift it, to erase the sorrow that was so ingrained? Perhaps transforming the buildings into a luxury hotel wouldn't be such a bad idea, gradually the stigma surrounding the island would start to fade and its history forgotten as a new era took over. But then, as she and Rob had already discussed, who'd want to stay here? Would it only attract more ghouls, but this time of the living variety?

One by one they left the boat. One of the 'Proibito' signs was a few feet away. They ignored it. Instead, with a dramatic sweep of his hand, Piero introduced them to the island.

"So, my friends, now you stand on Poveglia, the place where they sent so many plague victims to die throughout the centuries. I am not joking when I say be careful where you walk, there are many graves on the island, mass graves, all unmarked, and why you will find the ground soft beneath your feet. Walk only on the paved areas if you can."

Rob looked entranced. "So, first it's a place of quarantine and then an asylum. Piero, how many years was the asylum in use?"

"From 1922 to 1968, Robert. There is a sign somewhere, we can see if we can find it although I remember it as very overgrown – *reparto psichiatria* – the department of psychiatry. The doctor in question whose work was regarded as immoral was Dr Gritti."

"Was he the one who threw himself from the bell tower?" Louise asked.

"No," Kristina answered, "that was his assistant, Dr Sanuto."

"And did they really kill people?"

"Yes," Kristina frowned as she said it, "I believe it is true that they did. I believe that medical practices during that time were not as regulated as they are now, and that doctors wielded too much power. And look around you," she insisted. "This is an island, so there is no one to hear you if you scream. The evidence seems to support that Gritti and Sanuto performed lobotomies on their patients, trying to cure their madness; that they used hammers, chisels and hand drills, primitive instruments, sometimes sedating them, sometimes not." She closed her eyes briefly. "It sickens me to even think that this happened. But they were the ones who went mad because of it. Dr Sanuto threw himself off the bell tower in the early 1940s, but Dr Gritti committed suicide too, some years later, slitting his own throat whilst in theatre, in the act of performing on yet another poor patient. Such a grisly act and one he committed I think because his guilt finally drove him to it."

Louise was shocked, even Rob looked horrified, how awful if it was true.

"What about the doctors and nurses that came after them?" Louise asked, still curious despite herself. "Were any of them controversial?"

Kristina shook her head. "All I know is that afterwards doctors and nurses came and went. No one stayed long. Except the patients of course."

Of course the patients stayed, they had no choice in the matter.

Louise took a deep breath. Again she felt a sense of deep foreboding, wanted to leave, to escape. The stories the Benvenutis were relating were unnerving her as much as the veiled lady. But she was in the minority. No one had any intention of leaving. She had a few hours to endure yet, but thankfully only daylight hours. And then tonight, ah tonight, she'd make sure she and Rob enjoyed themselves, had a good meal and some fine wine – they'd have earned it. Their final night in Venice would be one to remember. Still wishing the mist would clear and not enclose them quite so greedily, but buoyed by thoughts of later at least, she was keen to get the expedition underway.

"Let's start exploring," she said, the first one amongst them to suggest it.

Chapter Twenty-Two

FROM having examined photos on the net, Louise knew that there were fields behind the asylum, the plague pits that Piero mentioned perhaps, the soft ground. As she walked, she had a vision of that ground opening beneath her, of falling as so many diseased hands reached upwards to drag her deeper into the darkness. When the asylum opened, did the patients know about the island's history? And if they did, did it torment already tormented minds? It would certainly torment her – men, women and children torn from their families, incarcerated, for the good of society, but against their will. A death sentence incurred because you were ill, because there was no cure, because you'd infect others. What must it have been like, being steered across the waters of the lagoon, the doctors terrified too no doubt, the beaks of their masks stuffed with herbs in the hope they wouldn't fall ill too? She asked Kristina if the masks were effective.

"*Medico Della Peste* is what the masks were called," Kristina answered. "They are still used today, but of course in a more frivolous manner, especially during the Venice carnival. It is eerie to see men standing on lonely corners wearing them, especially at night, their eyes on you as you pass, but everything else about them hidden. I have lived in Venice all my life but never get used to that sight. Whether they were effective or not, there is no way of knowing. So many people were struck down, doctors included. Disease was rife."

"But banishing the sick, was that really ethical?"

Kristina shrugged. "If they didn't, many more people would have been at risk." She mulled over Louise's question further. "It was... an impossible situation I think."

It was, and they could discuss the rights and the wrongs of it forever, but in the end it happened, it was part of history. No one could change it.

The middle building of the three had its front entrance boarded up with proibito signs plastered all over it. It jutted out slightly from the other two buildings and there was a side entrance, that particular door rotting so badly it might as well have not have been there. Piero led them to it but it was Kristina who stepped forward and pushed it open, using the rucksack she was carrying as a shield between the door and her body as she did so.

"This room," Kristina explained once they were inside, "is where most people enter the asylum. Maybe we can have something to eat in here before we continue."

Piero had mentioned in his text that they'd provide lunch. She hadn't given it too much thought, but now the prospect horrified her. She had an impression she'd ingest more than just the food they were offering. Rob noticed the expression on her face and raised an eyebrow. Meanwhile, Kristina cleared a space on a desk that still occupied the room and placed her rucksack on it. A sturdy piece of furniture, it was not unattractive, made of some sort of dark wood with two columns of deep drawers running either side of it, some open, some closed. She peered into the drawers that were open, whatever was left in there – it looked like scraps of paper mainly – had not fared well over the years, now little more than mulch. Curious, she opened another drawer, but it was empty – if there'd been any remotely salvageable items they'd have probably been taken by those intent on retrieving a souvenir from the island. There was a tall cabinet too, perhaps used for filing purposes, the wood on it not as intact as the wood on the desk, but chronically splintered as if it had been kicked several times. All of its drawers were open or on the floor, their contents rotting too. It was an office, clearly, but whose? One of the two doctors the Benvenutis had mentioned, or other doctors that came after them? The room had such a derelict feel as if it hadn't been used in centuries, let alone decades. And the air was thick somehow, cloying. With dismay she watched as Kristina opened the rucksack and retrieved four small plastic boxes, one for each of them.

Piero noticed her reticence too because he laughed, a big booming sound that bounced off the walls and flew right back at them. "Eat, eat," he encouraged. "My wife is the best cook in Italy." He took the lid off his box and proudly displayed its contents. "This is *arancini*, a very popular dish in Venice. Have you tried it before? They are rice balls, like risotto, and in the middle of them is my wife's ragu, which she slow-cooks for hours in Chianti. They are delicious, truly delicious!" Picking one up, he bit into it, closing his eyes as if to savour the flavour. "*Perfetto!*" he murmured.

Rob returned his enthusiasm. "It's very kind of you, you know, to go to so much effort. Louise, are you going to try one?"

"Erm… of course."

Taking her box from Kristina, she unwrapped one of the rice balls. She could barely swallow, but she appeared to be the only one having difficulty. Piero was eating, Kristina too, Rob was on his second already, and all eyes were on her, expectant: she'd have to eat at least two of the four balls that had been given to her, it would seem rude otherwise. Gingerly picking up an *arancini* between her thumb and forefinger she bit into it, the rice slightly sticky between her teeth. Despite her misgivings, it was, as Piero insisted, very tasty. She ate the rest of it and then selected another, feeling slightly hungry after all. Smiling her thanks at Kristina, she was about to compliment her too when an almighty bang from above startled her so much she dropped the box.

"What the hell…" she exclaimed, rice spraying from her mouth.

All eyes had flown upwards but no one answered. Silence, stark silence, followed the bang, lasting a good few moments and then Piero started laughing again, although it was not as assured as before. "A chunk of masonry must have fallen," he said. "As I say, we must be careful, the building is not sound."

Louise was as horrified at that as if it had been a ghost responsible. "A chunk of masonry? You mean the roof could cave in on our heads?" Good God, what were they doing here? She turned to Rob. "I think we should go."

"Louise—" he begun.

"It's dangerous here!"

Piero intercepted. "It's fine, we'll be careful." With regret he looked at his food. "But perhaps we should eat and be on our way. It's best to keep moving."

Picking up her box from the floor, she stuffed the two remaining rice balls back into it and closed the lid. "Sorry." She handed the box back to Kristina. Obviously, she couldn't eat them now, couldn't be expected to.

"I've drinks in my rucksack," Kristina said, exchanging the box for a bottle of water.

Thirsty after the food, Louise opened her bottle and then a thought struck her. "I'm sorry to have to ask this, but where do we go if we need the loo?"

Kristina frowned. "The loo?"

"The toilet."

"Ah," Kristina looked at Piero and then smiled ruefully. "There is no working toilet of course, you will have to use the bushes."

"Great." She was muttering again, unable to hide how uncomfortable she was. She took a sip from the bottle and then replaced the cap. "Better not drink too much then."

Rob leant into her. "We're not going to be here long. Just relax, enjoy it."

Enjoy it? Was he serious? How could anyone enjoy this? "Let's get it over and done with," she hissed. "I want to leave by three at the latest."

"Three? That's a bit ear—"

"Rob!" Although her voice was low the sentiment was clear.

"Okay, okay." He looked at his watch. "That gives us a couple of hours I suppose."

Two hours – one hundred and twenty minutes – it wasn't a lot of time, but it stretched ahead like a yawning chasm.

Retrieving a couple of torches and handing them to her husband, Kristina decided to leave the rucksack behind; they'd fetch it on their way out, a sensible suggestion that everyone agreed with. She also left her water behind, and Louise followed suit, not wanting to be weighed down by any more than she needed to be. As Piero led them out of the room that was once an office, Louise asked him what he knew about the layout.

"I have not seen floor plans, I don't even know if they still exist, they probably do, locked away somewhere, but quickly you will get a feel for it. In this building, the ground floor is where the recreation rooms were; the wards are on the upper levels. When we explore it will become obvious what some rooms were used for, there are still giant mangles in the laundry room for example, and in the dining room there are long trestle tables, even a few plates and cups from what I remember." Before continuing any further, Piero handed Rob one of the torches his wife had given him. "But only use it if we need it," he instructed.

The corridor was long, narrow and gloomy, with plaster crumbling and pipes dangling precariously. Louise tried to imagine it as it once was, with young doctors and nurses hurrying along, tending to their patients, but she had difficulty – the atmosphere was just too dead. Piero led them into various rooms, vast open spaces, most of which were empty. She wondered if she'd recognise any of them from the photos she'd seen and certainly there was a hint of familiarity but no more than that. Vines grew in through broken windows, a welcome if strange sight – they lent a much-needed splash of colour.

"The laundry room is interesting," Piero was saying as they entered it and she had to agree. It was still home to giant drums you could crawl into and a mass of copper piping, intact but heavily tarnished. There'd been graffiti on the walls of the rooms where they'd been, but here someone had drawn two life-size bloated figures, outlined in blue, one with a gun in his hand and the other with his hands to his face, his jaw excessively long, his mouth screaming – an Edvard Munch inspired illustration if ever there was one. She found it disturbing, violent and hopeless at the same time, summarising the way that life had been here perhaps. It disturbed her even more to think that teens were the most likely to have drawn it, their minds feeding on the mood that was prevalent, not just capturing it but in their own way *understanding* it. At the thought of teens on the island, she frowned. How did they know they were the only people here, the only living people that is?

"Piero," she asked, turning towards him, "how often do people come to Poveglia?"

He seemed to sense her nervousness.

"Don't worry, where we are docked is where other people must dock too. There is no other landing jetty on the island. To be honest, hardly anyone bothers to come here nowadays. Not even the youngsters. When I was young, groups of us came over but today they get their excitement from computer games. They don't need this."

No one needed this, not really. *She* didn't need it. She could read about it, certainly, but that didn't mean she wanted to experience it. She was only surprised Rob did. With her fears regarding other occupants eased, they carried on exploring, Louise regularly glancing upwards, still afraid that the roof was going to fall down on them. They came to the kitchen next, a huge metal worktable dominating the centre of it, as well as ovens turned on their sides and a butcher's block, blackened with decay. Over the worktable a huge light rig, its bulbs long since extinguished, began to sway gently, their entry into the room no doubt stirring it. The walls were half-tiled; a filthy grey instead of the white they once were and above them a green-like fungus seemed intent on spreading everywhere.

Louise couldn't understand it. "It's been like this since 1968 hasn't it, forty-seven years. Why don't they just knock the entire building down, get rid of it and what's inside it? Why has it been left to stand, supported by scaffolding even? It doesn't make sense."

Piero agreed. "It is strange that it is standing still, as for what the developers are doing I don't know. Sometimes, in Italy, things move slowly."

Slowly? They hadn't moved at all regarding Poveglia.

She looked at Rob. He was peering inside an old cooker, grimacing at how encrusted it was with rust. Kristina was picking up tiles that had fallen from the walls onto the floor and placing them on the worktable, as if she was trying to tidy up – an impossible task.

Traditionally kitchens were jovial places, somewhere to linger, but she didn't want to linger here, it was simply another room to tick off the list. As Piero had said, it was best to keep moving, to keep counting the minutes and the seconds until she could breathe again – fresh air that is, once they were off the island. She'd fill her lungs with it.

They were back in the corridor, some graffiti on the walls at this end, words this time, in Italian; she hadn't a clue what they meant and didn't bother to ask for a translation.

"This way to go upstairs," Piero said, walking forward a few paces and then stopping. He turned to face Rob and Louise, his dark features not as smooth as before, instead concern had creased them. "Upstairs is where the patients were kept, where the wards were. These rooms, many of them still contain beds, even sheets and blankets, personal effects too although most have been taken, but it is important to remember... the beds are empty now, no one remains. It is easy to let your imagination take over."

What a strange warning! Of course it was easy to scare yourself in a place like this but they weren't children, they didn't need to be warned. *Children...* There couldn't have been children at the asylum could there? She had to ask.

Piero looked surprised she'd brought up the subject. "Whatever sources I've read have never made mention of children." He looked at Kristina for confirmation and she seemed to agree. "Of course the plague victims included children, many of them. Have you heard the legend of Little Maria who stands on the shore and stares across the water to Venice?"

Louise nodded.

"Nonsense of course," Piero continued, "just a story made up, but regarding children at the asylum, no I don't think so." He sighed slightly and inclined his head. "But the patients, they were like children anyway don't you think, in need of constant care and attention?"

The comparison surprised her, but yes, yes, he was right, they *were* like children, unable to live life on their own and so they'd been entrusted to the island's carers and, as happened so often with those in authority, some abused that position, in the vilest of ways.

They climbed the stone stairs, all of them keeping well away from what remained of the wrought iron bannister – not wanting to run their hands along it, to touch more than was necessary. They reached a half landing over which presided a broken window before turning and climbing another flight. Graffiti accompanied them some of the way up but it became less so, something Piero pointed out. As if whoever the artists were, their nerve had deserted them. And little wonder. If it was cloying on the ground floor, up here it was worse, far worse. She could *feel* the torment the patients must have suffered – emotions still redolent despite the passage of time, as if no time had passed at all.

"I'm really not sure we should be here…"

Her words faded into nothing as Rob pushed past her to catch up with Piero, mentioning something to him about the interesting 'configuration' of the building. She was about to repeat herself, say she'd wait for them downstairs, that she didn't want to see where patients spent the majority of their miserable lives but Kristina, as perceptive as her husband had been earlier, put her hand on Louise's arm and whispered they'd be okay. Louise still contemplated retreating but then wondered what would be the lesser of two evils, staying with the group or leaving them to wait alone. Neither option appealed. She decided to stay, turning into another corridor, before heading into one of the dormitories.

"One of many," Piero informed them, "and you will notice they are all the same. Uniform. These are the female wards, the men's are at the far end."

As Piero had said there'd be, there were several steel-framed beds, some bare, some with mattresses, thin with barely any stuffing, and even a pillow or scrap of blanket on top. They looked so old, so decrepit, she was sure they'd disintegrate if touched. It was so easy to imagine… so easy… these rooms full of patients, full of madness. *You'd have to be mad to work here.* She'd never do it, not in a million years. She just couldn't. She was too selfish. *Perhaps that's why…*

No, she wouldn't entertain such dark thoughts. Her failure to conceive wasn't punishment for being selfish. Besides, you couldn't compare looking after your own child to looking after people like this; they weren't children they were adults, most of them beyond reach.

The lower half of the room was painted a pale green. Not a pleasant colour, it was pallid, sickly; the upper half the same grimy shade of cream that was elsewhere in the building. The windows were doing their utmost to let the light in but, being as the mist hadn't dissipated, there wasn't a lot of sun to be had. Still, there was no need for torchlight, not yet. Piero beckoned them further into the room, and they all obliged. There were bedside cabinets too, also made of steel – two of them. Rob went over to inspect one.

"Oh my God, look," he said, "there's a pair of spectacles in here!" He placed the torch on top of the cabinet as he reached in to retrieve them, turning them over in his hands. "These actually *belonged* to someone, I wonder if it was one of the patients. It must be, it has to be." Holding them up, he peered through them, squinting slightly, before setting them back down, the care he took almost reverent – something Louise appreciated.

Feeling a need to be close to him suddenly, she started forwards. As she did there was another loud bang. This one not so far removed, it came from just behind her. Screaming, she flew the rest of the way into Rob's arms and wrapped herself around him.

"What is it? What's that noise?" She couldn't bear to look.

"It's one of the beds, Lou, nothing more, one of the legs finally giving way."

He was smiling but for a moment he'd looked anxious

too.

She disentangled herself. Of course there'd be a logical explanation. Everything was in such an advanced state of decay there'd be bangs and crashes on a regular basis. Even so, she was only slightly less nervous as she looked at her watch. They had just over another hour to go. She'd keep close to Rob; wouldn't let him out of her sight. Seventy minutes and then they could sail away. Leave the dead to play tricks amongst themselves.

Chapter Twenty-Three

LOUISE held onto Rob as they continued to explore but, and she was surprised to think it, it was getting boring. As Piero had said, each room resembled the last, some had more vegetation encroaching on them; some had more or less furniture, beds stacked against the walls instead of scattered in a random manner. The one thing she continued to find intriguing was the lack of graffiti. As it had petered out on the stairway, it was in short supply upstairs too. If given a choice, no one wanted to linger.

They'd come to another corridor – there seemed to be an inexhaustible supply of them. Like the wards, they were all the same, no imagination, no care taken with the interior at all. It had been built to purely functional standards. This one led deeper into the building, and was much darker than those they'd walked down before. They would definitely need the torch for this. Piero thought so too. He shone his in front, urging Rob to do the same.

"So what's here," Rob asked, "just more wards?" His use of the word 'just' indicated he was getting blasé too.

"*Si, si, piu reparti,*" Piero turned his head to the side as he replied. Both he and Kristina had been so good about always speaking to them in English but now he seemed to have forgotten, too immersed in his surroundings perhaps. As for Kristina, like Louise, she had edged closer to her husband, one hand clutching at the back of his arm.

What they'd seen so far hadn't been so bad, not really. It had been bearable, and this wouldn't be so bad either. Even so, the deeper they ventured, turning right again and then left, the place as labyrinthine as Venice itself, her unease grew. These wards *weren't* the same, they were different, the doors, unlike those they'd initially come across, closed.

"Can we... can we stop?" She really didn't want to go any further. "I need to catch my breath." She'd said it as if she'd been running rather than walking sedately.

"Of course," Piero said.

"Why are these doors closed? Are they locked?" A part of her didn't know why she was asking. She was better off not knowing. But, Piero, taking his role as 'guide' very seriously appeared keen to provide an answer. As he hurried back towards them she caught sight of his expression, which was more animated than usual, as though he'd come alive.

She clung onto Rob even tighter when Piero brushed past her, the touch of him causing her to recoil slightly. Even Rob tensed. She could feel the muscles in his arm stiffen. There was something more alert in Kristina too.

"We are now entering the high security wing," Piero said, with as much flourish as when he'd first introduced the island to them. "These doors *were* locked, once upon a time, and the most dangerous patients in the asylum kept behind them. But they are not locked now." He selected a door and gave it a hefty shove, shining his torch into it.

"It's a padded cell!" Louise exclaimed.

"It is!" Piero said, as though pleased with her observation. He paused for a moment and then continued speaking. "When I was young I had a bet with my friends, for one of us to sleep the night in a padded cell, to prove how brave we were."

Rob was aghast too. "Did one of you carry out that bet?"

"Ha!" Again Piero's laugh was loud, too loud, it seemed inappropriate somehow. "One of us did, but not me. It was another boy. We didn't leave him on the island, we camped downstairs in the dining room and fell asleep peacefully enough but we were woken in the night by screaming. Of course we rushed upstairs to see what was happening, but it wasn't him. He was sleeping peacefully too. We woke him, accused him of messing around, but he swore it wasn't him."

Louise could feel her jaw drop. "You heard screaming but it wasn't your friend?"

"That's right! It must have been ghostly screaming, *fantasma*, whoo, whoo!" Lifting his hands at the same time as making the sound she was reminded of how he'd done that same thing in the restaurant. She'd found it annoying then, even more so now.

"I want to leave," she said, in no mood to laugh along.

"Leave?" That wiped the smirk from his face. "We have plenty of time."

Louise remained firm. "I said to Rob I wanted to leave at three and by the time we've made our way back, it'll be almost that. We've seen enough, haven't we, Rob? Thank you so much for bringing us, we appreciate it. It's been, as you say, *interesting*."

"But this is what is interesting, this part of the asylum."

Not to her it wasn't. "Rob?" she said, having to prompt him for a reply.

"Erm… yeah, look, I agree with Louise, we've enjoyed looking around, but we don't need to see any more. Do you mind?"

It was a direct question and one Piero couldn't avoid answering. Even so, he stalled for time, looking at his wife, who was staring back at him, stalling too.

Louise had had enough. "Come on," she said, trying not to let panic get a grip – what the hell had they done coming out here with two strangers, people who seemed rational at first but were appearing less so by the minute? "It's difficult to breathe in here."

As she started to walk, pulling Rob along with her, she heard Piero ask them to wait. Instead of obeying, she increased her pace, giving Rob no option but to do the same. She might have found Venice eerie but it was considerably more inviting than this.

"Wait," Piero called again. As she and Rob turned right, he continued to call out. "You are going the wrong way, it's left remember?"

Louise stopped and looked at Rob. Was it left? She could have sworn they needed to make a right turn at this point. Just as Venice flummoxed her, she had to admit the asylum did too. Everything looked the same – it was so damned easy to get disorientated.

"Rob, what do you think?"

Rob shrugged his shoulders. "I don't know, Lou, I… I don't know."

She turned round. Piero and Kristina had caught up with them.

"You shouldn't wander off," he admonished, "you should wait for us."

"We weren't wandering off," Louise denied. "We were making our way back to the boat."

"You will not find it that way," Kristina replied.

"But this is the way, I'm sure—"

"It's not," insisted Piero. "Please, let's not fall out, that would be... stupid. Follow me."

Although she didn't like what he'd just said, the threatening undercurrent, Louise saw they had no choice but to obey him this time. He'd been here before, so had Kristina, albeit a long time ago, they knew the way better than them.

Taking the corridor opposite, Piero started walking down it. Kristina shadowed him as Louise shadowed Rob – two couples keeping close to their partners but not to each other, a frisson of mistrust creating a metaphorical distance as well as a literal one. They walked onwards, past more closed doors, on and on, turning left again, Louise hoping to link to the main corridor, from which it should be easy enough to navigate outwards. At some points the only light was from Piero and Rob's torches, light that was all too easily consumed. They'd been walking for quite a while already, much longer than they'd walked before. What time was it? Nearly three. They wouldn't leave the island at the time she wanted to, the time she'd stipulated. Frustration began to build. She felt cheated.

"Look, that door's open," whispered Rob.

He was right, but if she was where she thought she was – where they *should* be – there'd been no doors open before. Why was one open now?

Piero and Kristina stopped and they did too. Piero looked excited again and was nodding towards the open door. Louise could hardly bring herself to follow the line of his sight and it seemed Rob was also hesitant. In the end, curiosity won out. *Morbid* curiosity. It wasn't another padded cell, as she expected, it was a room with freestanding baths in it, two rows of three, and there were bars at the window, several of them.

"What's this?" she breathed.

"It's one of the treatment rooms," Piero explained. "Come in, come in and see."

They followed him, shone the light on the rusted tubs as well as on one of the walls, which had several panels on it, containing what looked like dials and temperature gauges.

"I don't understand—"

"Surely you know something about the ways in which they used to treat patients," Piero sounded almost arrogant as he said it.

"Apart from lobotomies you mean," Rob, on the other hand, was employing sarcasm.

"Apart from those," Piero agreed, either not noticing or pretending to. "Hydrotherapy was a popular method to treat mentally ill patients." He ran his fingers along the rim of one of the tubs as he spoke. "Some treatments were harmless enough, like warm baths or an invigorating shower, but some were much more extreme. Like mummies, patients were wrapped in towels and soaked in ice-cold water. Others were restrained in the bath for days at a time. There's another room close by, one with water jets. From the position of the manacles on the wall, it is easy to see that patients were bound in a crucifix position whilst being hosed."

Louise held her hands up. "Enough! I've heard enough."

Rob didn't hesitate this time. "Yep, me too. We want out of here."

"Robert—"

"For God's sake, Piero, my name is Rob, just Rob, not Robert. In fact, if you must know, it's Rob*in*, and we didn't pass this room on our way here."

"There are many ways out—" Piero begun but Rob interrupted again.

"No, I'm sorry, the way we went originally, we were right weren't we? You lied to us."

"We didn't lie! Of course we didn't."

Kristina backed her husband up. "This maze of corridors can be deceiving."

"I understand that," Rob continued to argue, "but we weren't wrong. Why'd you make us think we were?"

"We really need to get back," Louise was worried about the rising aggression between the two men. The last thing she wanted was a punch-up, not when they were relying on Piero for a ride home. Keeping her voice low and steady, she pointed out it was the last night of their holiday and that, ideally, they'd like to spend it on their own. They were supposed to be in Venice, not here, on the island of Poveglia, listening to tales of horror. It seemed almost surreal they'd ended up here. "Please, take us back."

Her imploring worked. Kristina leaned over and said something to Piero in Italian, something that prompted him to start explaining. "I just… I wanted to show you the operating theatre, that's all, which is down here too. I don't mean the main theatre, it's a much smaller one, and it has lain untouched for years, even when people still worked here. There is a lot of equipment in the room, a wheelchair, trolleys, syringes and bandages; so much is left on the shelves. Even the plunderers won't touch it. It's the original theatre, you see, the one that Gritti and Sanuto used."

"The one Gritti committed suicide in?" Louise checked.

"That's right."

"And you've been in there?"

Piero looked proud of himself. "I have."

She shook her head. "That's just…" Words failed her.

"But surely this is what you want?" Again, Piero spread his hands wide. "To see such things. And not many people go there, not many dare, you will be in the minority."

Kristina started speaking too. "My husband is right, people are brave when they come here, but up to a point. In the theatre there is darkness, much more than elsewhere in the building. It is… the heart of darkness I think." Looking directly at Louise, she added, "It is said the doctors and nurses that came after Gritti feared to go in there in case his madness was catching." She paused. "So much on the island is infectious."

Finally Rob was as appalled as Louise. "And that's where you're taking us, to the 'heart of darkness'? You think we want that? No way. We don't. Stop playing games and get us out of here."

"But, you cannot leave without seeing it," Kristina insisted. "Truly, it is fascinating."

"Fascinating?" Louise queried. "So you've been in there as well, have you?"

Piero answered. "Yes, we came last year."

She frowned. "But both of you said you hadn't been here in years."

Piero and Kristina couldn't hold her gaze. On seeing that Louise backed away, from them, from the room with the baths in it, from whatever else was close by. "*You're* fascinated with this island, the pair of you, but we're not, not anymore. We'll find our own way out, and wait for you outside." She had another reason for wanting to get ahead of them; she wanted to check her mobile phone reception. Why she hadn't done that before she didn't know. But if they didn't stop playing games, as Rob had said, she'd get a message to their hotel, and get some help, although she sincerely hoped it wouldn't come to that. Not wanting to engage any further with the couple in front of her, she grabbed Rob and turned on her heel. Their 'adventure' had gone too far. Outside the room, she turned to the right and caught sight of something in the distance. At first she told herself that she was mistaken, but very quickly she realised she wasn't, despite her brain continuing to insist. It was a figure, a woman, dressed in white, and staring. Although a scream bubbled up in her throat, it never emerged, instead the darkness closed in, hovering first at the edges of her mind before racing forwards. Her last thought before consciousness deserted her was: *She's here; she's on the island. She's followed me.*

Chapter Twenty-Four

"LOUISE, sweetheart, you're all right. Come on, come back to me."

It was Rob's voice, sounding as if he were talking to her through some sort of muffler, but gradually he became clearer, his voice joined by two others: a man and a woman.

She struggled to sit up, the other voices belonged to Piero and Kristina, of course they did, and she was on an island in the Venetian Lagoon. She was on Poveglia. And then another memory surfaced, the veiled lady; she was on the island too. Who was she? What was she doing here, as though lying in wait? She longed for merciful oblivion again, a refuge, but it refused to come. She was growing more conscious by the second.

"Wh... what happened?"

"You fainted," Rob informed her, he looked around him, as if searching for a reason why. "You're right, the air in here, it's so oppressive."

It was but it had nothing to do with what had just happened. Before she could say anything more, Rob helped her to her feet, a protective arm still around her when he addressed Piero, who, she had to admit, looked concerned too.

"No more bloody nonsense, mate, I'm warning you, just get us out of here and on that boat. When we get back to Venice we'll say no more about it, we'll go our separate ways. We just need to get out." To Louise, he said, "Can you walk?"

She managed to raise a smile at this. "What are you going to do if I can't? Carry me?"

"If necessary."

She was impressed; he meant business. Thankfully Piero and Kristina realised that too. Without another word, Piero started retracing their footsteps. He looked, if not exactly sorrowful, embarrassed and so did Kristina. Something she'd take satisfaction in if she could, but all that concerned her was getting into the open. She was desperate to leave.

At long last the maze thinned out, she thought she recognised where she was: in the corridor that the main wards fed off – they could navigate their way from here alone if they had to, although to do that wasn't a good idea, as they could only get so far without Piero and Kristina. Her mind returned to the veiled lady. Could she really be following her? Was such a thing possible? Had the others seen her too? They couldn't have done. Someone would have mentioned it if they had. She was the only one who'd seen the ghost. *Ghost?* Oh, God, this place was playing havoc with her! But then Venice had done that too, the world's most beautiful city, the most romantic, and the world's most haunted, a prospect that had amused and intrigued her prior to travelling, but not now.

Passing one of the wards they'd inspected, the one with the spectacles in a shelf on the side table, she couldn't bring herself to even glance in. She kept her eyes trained solely ahead. At the top of the staircase she breathed a sigh of relief and with Rob's help descended it quickly. Through the window she was dismayed to register that the light outside – and therefore inside – was failing, rapidly. The last thing she wanted was to be here when it got dark – she'd been promised that wouldn't happen. Not just frustration, she felt a flash of rage. Her life seemed to be full of broken promises, full of disappointment. She remembered a quote she'd read in a book: *My life is like a broken stair, winding round a ruined tower, and leading nowhere.* She came across the quote long before undertaking cycle after cycle of IVF, it could even have been in her teens, and it had resonated with her, the melancholy of it. This place was melancholy. If darkness existed within a person, it would thrive here. She couldn't bear it a minute longer.

"Are we there? Are we nearly at the boat?"

"Lou, it's okay, you know where we are now, it's just down the stairs and along a bit. We need to grab Kristina's rucksack—"

"Rucksack? Who cares about her bloody rucksack? It's getting dark, Rob!"

"I know, I know. But it's still early, it's not even four o' clock, we'll be fine. We'll be back at the hotel soon. We can forget all about this."

Forget? She'd never forget. Even so, she'd be glad to reach the hotel. It seemed like an oasis – a sanctuary. She'd rush in, ignore that damned painting in the lobby, go straight to her room and collapse on the bed. She was exhausted. And in the morning they'd get up and they'd go. A longing for England washed over her, home sweet home, and she was amazed at the intensity of it. It was a small world and Venice but a short plane ride from London, but it felt so different suddenly: the culture, the people, the food, everything.

Continuing to lean on Rob, they re-entered the office, twin beams doing their best to penetrate the gloom.

Kristina walked over to where she'd left her rucksack, then turned around, as though scanning the room.

"What is it? What's the matter?" asked Louise.

"My rucksack," Kristina answered. "I left it here, by the leg of this desk, I'm sure I did."

"Yes you did," Louise agreed. "I saw you."

"But it's not here now," Kristina replied.

"Well, where is it then?" Rob's patience was still on the wane.

"I... I don't know. It's odd."

"Leave it," Rob decided. "It's not important, there's only food in it, maybe you didn't close one of the boxes properly and a fox or something snuck in and dragged it away."

Piero was also looking confused. "Has the desk been moved? It was in the centre of the room before. It isn't now."

He was right. It was definitely more to the side of the room and at a different angle too. Louise pointed to the filing cabinet. "Rob, shine your light over there."

Several drawers had been left open before; some drawers had even been taken out and left on the floor. Now, only two drawers remained on the floor, there were more before, she was sure of it, three at least. Of those two, one of them was now closer to the desk, as if it had been trying to reach out. Frowning, she asked to borrow the torch and walked over to it, kneeling down and shining the light on its contents – just mulch, as it was before, notes, documents, whatever had been in there, ruined. She was about to stand, join the others again, when the torchlight caught the edge of something – a scrap of paper on which the writing was more legible. It was addressed to someone, a letter perhaps, she could make out a capital 'A', an 'l' and a 'b' – *Alb* – but nothing more. She was entranced by it, wondering whom it was to and about the hand that had written it, when Rob, swearing under his breath, brought her back to the moment. As she rose his worried gaze met hers. Things had changed in here for certain, but who'd changed them? Other people on the island could be good news or bad. Either way she didn't want to hang around to find out.

"We need to get to the boat," she insisted.

When Piero and Kristina didn't move, she repeated her words. Rob, clearly incensed by their lack of reaction, raised his voice considerably. "Get us off this bloody island now!"

Piero held his hands up. "I would, I intend to but… we cannot leave without the key."

"The key?" Rob repeated, "What do you mean?"

Kristina stepped forward and laid a placating hand on Rob's arm. "He means the key to the boat. It was in the rucksack."

"In the rucksack? The one you left here?"

She nodded.

Rob's rage peaked. Focussing entirely on Kristina, he gave full voice to his anger. "Why the fuck did you leave the key in the rucksack? Why didn't you take it with you?"

Kristina hastily withdrew her hand. "I thought it would be safer in the bag, just in case I tripped and fell or something, maybe it would roll out of my pocket."

Rob was incredulous. "That's it, that's the reason?" He looked as though he was about to tear his hair out. "Christ Almighty!"

Mindful of how time was slipping away, Louise tried desperately to search for a solution. "Piero," she said, "you must have a spare key?"

He gulped. "I have but it's at home."

"At home?" She was the one who exploded now. "But why did you give the damned key – the *only* key – to your wife? You were the one driving!"

"My wife, she is better at looking after things than me," he attempted to explain.

"Really? Well, not on this occasion!" Oh, what was the use of standing here screaming at the pair of them? She forced herself to calm. "Piero, you said before that if anyone else was on the island they'd have to dock their boat by yours, there's no other landing jetty."

"That's correct." He sounded on the verge of tears, as fearful as them.

"Well, let's go and check then. See if someone else *is* here."

She darted towards the doorway; the others close behind. She expected the fresh air as it hit her to revive her somehow but it was as leaden as the atmosphere inside. Propelling herself towards where the boat was moored, she shone the torch, wishing it would cut through the mist more efficiently. Was there another boat beside theirs? There had to be. But as she drew closer, she realised their boat was alone, hardly even swaying on such still waters.

"Fuck!" she swore. "Fuck! Fuck! Fuck!" She swung around, still trying to find an answer. "Perhaps someone did come but they've left. They came in, played silly buggers, moved furniture around a bit and stole or hid our rucksack, trying to scare us." To Piero she said, "That's possible isn't it?"

"I... I don't know, I suppose. It is strange though, very strange. Why would they do such a thing? For what purpose?"

"Because the people who come here are weird that's why, you'd damned well have to be!"

Piero ignored her insult, jumped onto the boat, and started to rummage around. "But if people have been here with the intention of stealing, why did they not steal what was on the boat? Look, there are things that might be considered valuable. I have a camera on-board, binoculars, my wife's Gucci sunglasses and a medical kit, certainly things that are of more use than food boxes! Why did they not steal the boat itself? The key was in the rucksack, surely they would have looked inside and noticed that."

"If it was just one person, they could hardly have steered both boats!"

Rob's point was valid, assuming that someone had visited the island whilst they'd been upstairs – a *lone* person. But, there was still the possibility that an animal had dragged it off, in which case, it couldn't be far. *But the furniture… what about the furniture?*

Her head fit to burst, Louise turned to Piero again. "You're not mucking us about are you? Playing another one of your games, hiding the key?"

"No! I assure you, we are not. What happened upstairs, I… wanted to show you that's all, so you'd have seen all that was worth seeing here."

"Against our will," Rob pointed out.

"Yes, but… I'm sorry," he muttered. "I meant no harm."

Louise tried to convince herself his apology was meant. "Perhaps it *is* in the building somewhere," she conceded, "or in the grounds."

"But what about the furniture…" Rob was thinking along

the same lines as her.

As tempted as she was to accuse Piero and Kristina of doing that as well, they couldn't have, at no point whilst they were downstairs were they apart. Only upstairs that had happened, and even then, they'd still been close by. She made up her mind.

"Our priority is the rucksack. If it's here, we have to find it."

"Then we split into pairs," Rob suggested. "Start searching."

"No!" It was Kristina who'd objected. "We stick together. It is safer. Much safer."

As much as Louise wanted to get away from them, Kristina was right. Anything could happen in that building. You could fall through a roof or have the roof fall on you. They needed to keep together, but still search widely and efficiently. *What a mess*, she couldn't help thinking, *what a bloody mess!*

Despite being only late afternoon, night seemed to have fallen in its entirety. They needed to come up with a plan and quick.

"Okay, okay, look, we spend an hour searching," Louise suggested. "If no luck, Piero you can phone the police and get them to come and rescue us."

"Phone?" Piero looked at her as if she was mad. "There is no signal on the island."

"What? There must be."

Retrieving her mobile from her pocket, she checked the bars on it as she'd intended to do earlier. He was right, there was no signal, nothing. "Then... what are we going to do?"

"We find the bag, that's what we're going to do." Rob

responded, taking long strides back. Catching up with him, Louise could feel tingles along her spine, little stabs of electricity jabbing at her mercilessly. The building ahead had seemed, if not benign during the day, not overly threatening. In the fading light, however, it loomed like something out of a Hammer Horror movie, hosting a multitude of unspeakable sights and sounds within. And the windows, there were rows and rows of them, like gaping black holes...

She turned her head, refusing to look at the windows. Perhaps they'd only have to search downstairs. If it had been an animal, they wouldn't have been able to haul it upwards. The rucksack would be downstairs or in the grounds. Speaking up, she suggested they explore the grounds first, anything to delay going back in.

"We shouldn't stray too far," Kristina still sounded agitated. "We mustn't go to the fields."

"Why not?" Rob's voice was scathing. "Because they're the supposed plague fields?"

"There's no 'supposed' about it," Kristina said, rallying.

Piero intervened rather than Louise. "What Kristina means, and what I have already told you, is that in the fields the ground is soft underfoot. The people that died here, they weren't transported to the mainland, they couldn't be, even in death there was a risk of infection, they were burnt here, cremated. The mass graves, we are not making that up."

Louise could feel her whole body tense. "Then why do you do it?" she said, her voice much higher than she intended it to be. "Why do you come here, because you do don't you? You're regular visitors, I think. Surely there are better places to have a picnic!"

"We are not ghouls!" Kristina insisted.

"Then what are you?" Louise demanded.

She faltered. "We have… that is, Piero, has family connections to the island."

"Family connections? Regarding the asylum you mean?"

"No!" Piero seemed horrified Louise would think that. "She means family much further back than that, family affected by the plague."

"How do you know? You have records?"

"Of course! The Benvenuti family know their lineage. Family is everything to us!"

Family is everything… His words pierced her. Her and Rob's family would end with them and no amount of travel could make up for that. In fact, right now she didn't care if she never travelled again, it was not the remedy they'd hoped for. England was home, *their* home and the subject of adoption, she'd raise it again, make Rob see it was a valid choice, that they could love a baby born of others as much as one born of them. She certainly could, she knew it. She also knew she couldn't continue without a child to love, never had the desire in her been so strong as now – never had it seemed so *crucial*.

Rob shook her out of the reverie she'd fallen into. "Louise, who cares why they choose to come here, it's of no importance to us. We need to start searching, come on."

"Okay, okay," she replied, having to bite down on a retort. Clearly his impatience had extended to include her. But the fact that they were stranded here, without a boat key, without any mobile phone signal, was not her fault. And he'd better not start acting like it was. She might have been the one who'd found out about Poveglia, but he was the one who wanted to come here, taking 'off-the-beaten-track' to a whole new level.

All four trudged miserably round to the far side of the building. The men had charge of the torches again, and, working as a team, they were aiming the light in different directions, the women busy scanning for any sign of Kristina's rucksack, the incessant mist hindering their task. At the back of the asylum, there was a bank of grass, with stone steps leading downwards into more rough grass, the plague fields, the graves, and not just those that belonged to the diseased either, Louise would bet. How many people who had died at the asylum weren't transported back for burial? Piero had said that in Italy family was everything, but did that extend to include mad members of the family? He had baulked when Louise suggested his ancestry might be marred in such a way.

Side by side in their respective couples, Rob and Louise in front, they negotiated the steps; many were chipped or had chunks missing from them, yet more victims of neglect. At the bottom her feet sank initially but then rested on ground that was firm enough.

"We don't need to go too far in," Kristina said. Louise could tell she was shaking.

"We do if we're going to find that key," Rob replied.

"It's more likely to be in the building," Piero cut in. "If it was an animal, they like shelter, they wouldn't want to be out in the open where they feel exposed."

Still Rob was determined. "We need to do a thorough search."

They moved forward at a tentative pace, their torches making wide sweeps of the ground ahead. It looked empty, although beneath the soil it was perhaps far from that. Louise felt Piero's suggestion that they look inside first made more sense and was about to say so when she heard a scream from behind. For a minute she fancied it had come from *inside* the asylum, but then she realised it was much closer than that. It was Kristina.

She spun around as did Rob. "What is it? What's wrong?"

"Over there!" Kristina could barely get the words out but she managed to point and all three looked to where they were being directed, back over the plague fields again.

"Holy fuck!" It was Rob who'd sworn; Louise could only stare. The mist that had stubbornly surrounded the island all day was moving towards them, a wall of it, as wide as it was tall. She'd never seen mist moving before, not like that, so *purposefully*. But there was something even more alarming, the mist wasn't just a single band of white, there were shapes in it, becoming clearer the closer it got. So many shapes, hundreds of them, their arms outstretched as if seeking help, and solace too, comfort of any sort. Louise was momentarily mesmerised, fear beginning to give way to pity, she wanted to understand them suddenly, those that were appealing to her, their sorrows, what they had suffered, and then the atmosphere changed. Someone yelled for them to run and panic filled the air, as infectious as any disease. Backing away, she joined the others as they fled, wondering all the while if the figure she'd seen in the centre of the mist, the one to whom all the other shapes cleaved to, was the veiled lady, her hands reaching out too.

Chapter Twenty-Five

THEY rushed to put as much distance as possible between themselves and the wall of mist, and arrived at the front of the asylum again. Louise was surprised to find herself still not as frightened as the rest of the group; rather resignation seemed to be the dominant emotion. The figure at the centre of the mist *had* been the veiled lady, she was sure of it. What did she want? Why had she forged this connection between them?

Piero was bending over, his hands just above his knees, trying to catch his breath. Kristina had one hand in her mouth, teeth tearing at her nails. Rob looked bewildered.

"What was that?" he asked, trying to make sense of it. "The way it was moving…"

It was Kristina who finally answered him. "I've heard about the white mist before, how it comes racing towards you. Again, it is the stuff of legend, or so I thought. I have never believed it because I have never seen it." She turned her head back the way they'd come as if checking that the mist wasn't still in pursuit. "I have never seen anything here before."

"Nothing at all?" Louise quizzed.

Kristina shook her head. "This may sound strange, but I have always found it peaceful on the island, quiet, a refuge almost. But then I have never been here after dark. I haven't spent the night." Her voice rose in alarm at the prospect. "I don't *want* to spend the night!"

Piero straightened up, murmured something to his wife in

Italian and she nodded, even attempted to smile at him, albeit bleakly.

"Piero, have you seen that mist before?" Louise continued.

"No, but I have heard of it too. Tales are passed on you know, from person to person."

"What about the figures in the mist, have people mentioned them?"

Piero looked at Louise, Kristina and Rob did too.

"Figures?" Rob queried.

"Yes, figures," she repeated. "Didn't you see…?" No they hadn't, she realised. Once again, that had been reserved especially for her.

Rob quickly forgot all talk of figures. He was shaking his head as if he couldn't quite believe the situation he was in. "What are we going to do?" he asked.

Strangely, Louise could believe it. It was as though she'd been waiting for this, ever since she set foot in Venice – the inevitable – but why, she didn't fully understand yet.

"We need to go into the asylum," Piero answered, "continue our search."

"I don't want to go back in," Kristina was pleading with him.

Before anyone could reply, Louise pointed to another building, a much smaller construction a few feet from the front of the asylum and largely covered by trees. "What's that? I spotted it when we first arrived, I meant to ask."

Piero squinted as he looked to where she was pointing. "It's some sort of living accommodation, a doctor's residence I think. It's the only one of its kind on the island as far as I know – certainly around the back of the asylum there are only the fields."

"But other staff must have lived on the island?" Louise said.

"Probably, but it would have been in the main building, in a separate wing. Maybe if the doctor had a wife, a family, they were allocated the cottage, a home of their own."

"Have you ever explored inside?" she asked.

"No, I... I haven't." Piero looked surprised, as if this was a revelation to him as well. "It's always been the asylum that's interested us I suppose."

"Because that's where all the thrills are?" Rob's voice was curt.

"I... yes," Piero replied. Clearly he'd decided there was no more use in lying.

"Let's go and have a look," Louise decided.

Despite Piero warning that they wouldn't be able to go inside the building due to its advanced state of decay, Louise headed over. An animal could have dragged Kristina's rucksack in there, it was an ideal lair, hidden and therefore undisturbed.

Close up she could see it was indeed a cottage, its terracotta tiled roof caved in along with its chimney. The ground was very soft around the structure and consisted mainly of mud. Time and time again her feet sank into it and she had to work hard to yank them out, banishing the visions she'd had earlier of bodies lying beneath, waiting to claim her. At last they reached the front door, still intact although copious vines covered it, preventing any chance of entry that way at least. In the windows on either side, only lethal looking shards of glass remained. On one wall there was graffiti, but it seemed half-hearted.

"We cannot get in," Piero reiterated, shining his light over the structure.

He was right and, if they couldn't, how could an animal? Surely anything living and breathing would run the risk of impaling themselves trying to jump through a window. Even so, Louise suggested they shine the light in at various points, it was important to eliminate the cottage from their investigations.

Both the men obliging, they peered into rooms long since abandoned and devoid of anything except vegetation, much of which looked withered as if the air inside was too rotten to sustain any form of life. As she suspected it would, the search proved fruitless. They had one more window to look through, on the far side of the house and not easy to reach as trees blocked their path, one of which had probably fallen during a storm long ago, and part of the reason why the roof had caved in. Refusing to be put off, she cleared the way as much as possible with her hands. Rob and Piero copied her, both of them swearing on occasions as branches that felt as sharp as any glass shard dug into them or they stumbled over a root. Kristina hung back, again biting at her nails. They weren't so manicured now.

"Shine the light in there," Louise instructed, wondering if it would make any difference. It was so dark inside she half fancied no light could ever be strong enough to penetrate it. But the torches worked well enough, both of them doing a sufficient job of lighting up the interior. When they did, she wished her initial fancy had held true – what was in the room didn't bear illumination. There were bones, so many bones, piled on top of each other to form a haphazard pyramid, some ivory white, others brown and crumbling – a mixture of old and new – the plague victims and the patients? On top of the pyramid was a skull, staring at them, at her in particular. *With sightless eyes*, she thought. *It's staring at me with sightless eyes.* It was grinning too as if it was finding this whole situation amusing. She only just stopped herself from screaming at the macabre sight, a small part of her, a part that remained stubbornly rational, worried about upsetting Kristina further. Behind her she heard sharp intakes of breath but nothing more – the men were being considerate too.

"What is it?" Kristina called, realising that something was wrong despite their efforts to conceal it from her. "What have you found?"

"N… nothing," Piero returned. "We are still searching."

The quake in his voice told Louise he hadn't seen this sight before, that it was as much a surprise to him as it was to them.

Her eyes travelled from the skull to the wall beside it – again not really wanting to see but knowing she had no choice. That she was *meant* to see.

There were words written on the wall, dozens and dozens of them, some running into each other, some more spaced out. Wiping roughly at her nose with the back of her hand, she read words scribed not in Italian but in English – *'get out'* imprinted in large letters and in small letters, from top to bottom, filling the entire width. And then something different: two more words, precise and neat as opposed to scrawled, on a downwards angle and in capitals: *GO HOME.* As alarming as she found that, what alarmed her more was the something lying at the base of the wall, on the floor, as if 'Go Home' was an arrow, directing her gaze. It was a scrap of material, frayed at the edges – and it was white.

Chapter Twenty-Six

AS all three stood and stared, there was a noise overhead, a loud clap of thunder that made them all jump. Rain started to fall – big fat drops that would quickly soak them to the bone if they didn't react and get out of it.

"Quick, to the asylum!" Piero shouted.

Galvanised into action, she, Rob and Piero started to scramble over the fallen tree and the vine-like vegetation back towards Kristina. She looked shocked at the sudden change of weather too, her eyes wide as she stared upwards. It seemed to take an age to reach her but, when they did, all four turned as if they were one and ran through the grounds, over the sodden, sinking earth, towards the main building that was waiting so patiently. Although it was the last thing Louise wanted to do, to go back in there, be confined, they had no choice – they needed shelter or they'd risk hypothermia remaining in cold, wet clothes all night. *All night?* She'd resigned herself to that fact too.

In the office, she grabbed the torch from Rob and scrutinised the room again, half expecting the furniture to be upturned this time, some ghostly figure responsible, but it hadn't moved a second time. Whether that was a comfort or not, Louise couldn't decide.

"Bloody hell, your weather!" Rob spoke as though the Italians were solely responsible for such contrary elements. "Just when you thought it couldn't get any worse."

Piero stood shivering. "We must start searching."

"Then we split up as I've already suggested," Rob replied. "It's more efficient."

"No, please." Kristina was still insistent. "It is so much safer to stick together."

"It's just a building," Rob argued but Kristina was having none of it.

"It's a dangerous building!"

Rob exhaled loudly, raking one hand through his hair as he did so. All of them were standing apart, in various poses of frustration, Kristina still picking at her nails, Piero pinching the bridge of his nose. As for Louise, so many emotions were fighting for a stronghold: confusion, despair, acceptance and sympathy – the figures in the mist, how they clung to the veiled lady, it moved her. And, after the initial shock, the writing on the wall in the cottage had had the same effect; it seemed like such a desperate act.

Earlier in the day there'd been a crash from upstairs but now there came a scraping sound, like someone dragging one of the metal beds across the floor.

They all heard it but Kristina was the first to react. She almost leapt across the distance to her husband. "There's someone here. There is!"

"There's no one," Piero assured her. "If there was, their boat would still be outside."

"Jesus wept, this is ridiculous!" exclaimed Rob. "I'll go and see."

Louise blocked his path. "Don't." Inclining her head, she whispered, "Kristina."

The other woman was crying again, one hand wiping at her eyes, the other still holding onto Piero. "My rucksack, where's my rucksack? Who took it, who'd do such a thing?"

Piero started speaking to her in Italian, his voice very low and very fast. Louise looked at Rob, who was looking back at her, his nostrils flaring. Whatever the sound had been, who-ever had made it, it had been brief. Silence descended. But it wouldn't last long, she was sure of it. There'd be other nois-es, other sights to endure. According to her watch, it was a little before six – there was still so much night to go.

Piero continued to talk to Kristina, comforting her Louise presumed, but Rob clearly thought otherwise. He stepped forward, not a gesture of solidarity, there was a definite threat behind it. "Talk in English," he demanded. "So we can all understand what you're saying."

Piero looked stunned by Rob's request. "My wife is up-set."

"Talk in English," Rob repeated. "I don't want any se-crets."

"Secrets?" Piero laughed but it was not the boom of earli-er. "I don't understand what you mean, of course there are no secrets."

Something in the way he said it made Louise frown, his voice had risen slightly, but that could just be nerves. Rob was a tall man, he was broad, and Piero, although not slight, was smaller. And Rob was angry, *obviously* angry. He'd had enough of being on the island, but hadn't they all? It didn't do to lose your cool, not in this kind of place. Whatever was here would feed on such emotions and grow stronger. All the books she'd read on the subject in the past, be they fact or fiction, all the films she'd seen, suggested that. Anger, panic and hatred *woke* things from slumber, things that should re-main asleep.

"Rob," she said, "let's get on with our search. The ruck-sack's not outside as far as we can see. But it must be here somewhere. It can't just disappear, that's not possible."

Even as she said the words, she wasn't sure she believed them. At this moment anything seemed possible. They'd entered into some sort of twilight zone in which the 'Italian Dream' had fast become a nightmare, and they the star players. The world was still out there, the normal world, the world she knew, but it was so far away. She clenched her teeth, screwed her eyes shut. *Stay calm.* She'd try but the others weren't faring so well.

Rob was much closer to Piero and Kristina now, standing in front of them. "Louise is right, it's impossible that a bag could just disappear. Are you sure you haven't hidden it, that it's not part of your game?"

"Game?" The word ignited Piero. He forced Kristina's hand from him and squared up to Rob. For a second Louise wanted to giggle, *insanely* giggle. He reminded her of a terri-er, small and brave, but stupidly so, not realising his limita-tions – that in a battle between them the Rottweiler would always win. "You think I wanted this to happen, for the rucksack to disappear, that I planned it? It is an accident, just an accident."

"A *convenient* accident."

"What is convenient about it, Rob? I don't want to be here any more than you do! Not after dark." He flustered. "I admit it is a mistake we've made, a bad mistake and one that I… that *we* will learn from but there's no point in arguing. Time is getting on."

"Then tell me where it is!"

"I've told you, how many times must I tell you, I don't

211

know!"

Kristina stepped forward, wrestled the torch from her husband and started shining it haphazardly around, the light jagged as it bounced off the walls. "It's here," she was muttering, "it has to be here."

"It's not," Rob sneered at her, "unless you've returned it behind our backs."

"Behind your backs?" Piero exploded. "When, Rob, when?"

"Ughhh!" The sound that escaped Rob was guttural. "We need to fucking find it."

Louise interjected, "Rob, come on."

All eyes looked towards the doorway, to what lay beyond. It was so dark, so *unknown*. What if… whatever had been in the mist was now in the asylum, external walls no barrier to such an entity. What if it had drifted through cracks and windows and was now clothed in the gloom of the interior, something black instead of white and therefore harder to spot. Beings that moved, that writhed, that were reaching out, the veiled lady herself, whom she'd already seen upstairs, who seemed to be stalking her, following her from the alleys of Venice to the corridors of Poveglia.

Go Home. If they wanted that to happen, they had no choice, they had to go deeper in, observing Kristina's rule about safety in numbers, even if two of that number weren't to be trusted. The dining room was their first port of call. On the alert for any other sounds, they left the office and trooped towards it, the four of them huddled together, forming a barrier against what might suddenly appear as the mist had appeared. Turning right again, they entered a large room, a few tables and chairs in it as well as plenty of rubble covering the floor and vegetation that had lost all its colour in the low light. Piero and Rob were back in charge of the torches, shining them into every corner. There was a scurrying but before Kristina had a chance to react, Piero was on it.

"*Topi*," he said, "it's just mice."

Mice? He was playing it down. It'd be rats, altogether more sinister creatures.

There was nothing in the dining room, or in the day lounge except more empty chairs. The sight of them causing Louise to shudder, it was easy to imagine patients still occupying them, some sitting perfectly still, others rocking back and forth whilst gazing fixedly ahead – spending hours that way, days, weeks and years. She was relieved to leave and enter the laundry room but her relief was short lived.

As the men shone their torches into the mangles, Louise stumbled into something: it made a clattering sound as it fell to the floor. She looked down, half knowing, half fearing what it might be. She swung round, glared at the others, at Piero and Kristina in particular.

"What are they doing there?"

The other three came hurrying over.

"What is it?" There was a note of hope in Rob's voice. "Have you found the rucksack?"

"It's bones, more damned bones."

Rob looked crestfallen. "They weren't here before."

"No," agreed Louise, "I'm aware of that."

"*More* bones?" asked Kristina. "What do you mean?"

Louise had to remind herself that Kristina hadn't seen what was in the last room in the cottage, that she'd kept her distance. Deliberately? She turned to her, turned *on* her if she were honest. "Did you do this, put these here, you and

213

Piero?"

"No! Why do you keep accusing us?"

"They weren't here before!" Louise repeated Rob's words.

"But as Piero said we've been with you all the time. We are not guilty."

"The cottage could have been rigged up beforehand."

Piero interjected. "Between late last night and early this morning? Oh, come on!"

Rob answered before Louise could, in vehement agreement with her. "You're lying, you're setting us up, probably so you can have a good laugh at our expense with your friends, tell them how you picked on some stupid English tourists and frightened the life out of them. But I'm not having it. I want off this island, give me the key to that boat and I'll drive it away myself. I'll bet it's not in the rucksack at all, it's in your pocket."

"It is not—"

"But how do we know that? You've lied to us about everything else so far!"

"Because I am telling you, that's why!" Piero threw his hands in the air. "What we saw outside, the mist moving towards us, you think I can create that? Impossible!"

"That's just it, I don't know what's possible and what isn't, not anymore," Rob retorted. From one of anger, his expression turned bleak. "This place... it distorts everything. It distorts the mind. It's like... it's diseased or something, still, after all this time." He shook his head, as if trying to remember he had a point to make. "I want to see what's in your pockets."

"There's nothing in them."

"I want to see for myself and then your wife, we'll search

her."

"You will not touch my wife!"

"Then make it simple for all of us and hand over the key!"

Not even waiting for a response, Rob thrust the torch at Louise, reached out and grabbed Piero by the arm. Both she and Kristina moved forward too.

"Leave him!" Kristina shouted. "You mad man!"

"You're calling me mad?" Rob spat back at her. "*Me?* You've got the wrong guy there!"

Although Rob had started the fight, it was Piero who threw the first punch but it wasn't a convincing blow. Louise doubted Rob would even register it. When he retaliated, Louise winced – terrified he'd miss his target and hit Kristina instead.

"Rob, stop, you have to stop!" But the men carried on struggling, too lost in individual fury to take any notice.

Kristina was talking too but in a rapid stream of Italian, Louise was sure there were some prime curses in there from the way she was spitting the words out.

"Rob!" Louise yelled again, stunned at how quickly the situation had deteriorated. But they were under pressure and people under pressure could do terrible things – someone could get hurt, really hurt and then what would they do? Rob had said the situation couldn't get much worse, but it could. Easily. She had to dart aside as his elbow came out to deliver another punch. "Listen to me, please!"

Kristina had to swiftly step aside too, still talking to herself in between sobs and then she bent down, picked up the torch that her husband had dropped and shone it in the two men's faces. "Okay, okay, enough! We haven't been honest with you, I admit—"

Rob's head snapped sideways to look at Kristina. So did Piero's. As for Louise, she looked on wide-eyed, wondering what the hell was coming next.

It was Piero who started speaking, but Kristina hushed him.

"We have to tell the truth," she said. "You shouldn't keep secrets in a place like this."

Chapter Twenty-Seven

BOTH men extricated themselves, making an almost comical show of brushing themselves down as they did and straightening their jackets. Louise shone the torch directly on Kristina, she and Rob wanted answers and wanted them now. As she did, she stepped away from the bones, eager to put some distance between herself and them.

Kristina cleared her throat and took a deep breath. Piero simply looked at the floor, too embarrassed, Louise supposed, to look at either of them. She hoped that whatever his wife was about to reveal really did have something to do with the key, that they'd got tired of whatever it was they were playing at and realised it'd gone too far.

"I am a student," Kristina said at last, still breathing heavily, as if she'd been the one fighting rather than the men.

A student? "I thought you worked in commerce," said Louise.

"I did. I used to, up until recently. Now I am in full-time study."

Rob was also trying to make sense of her admission. "What is it you study exactly?"

"Psychology," she answered, lowering her torch so that the darkness hid her face. "Currently, I am working on a thesis. But... when we got talking to you in the restaurant that was genuine. We are friendly people, *normal* people. We like to go out and meet other people, to make friends. That is not so unusual is it?"

Louise shook her head. "No, no, of course not."

"I'm not sure how the conversation turned to Poveglia, you mentioned it first perhaps—"

"I wasn't the first to mention it." This was the second time this weekend she'd been accused of that. "*You* were the ones who brought the subject up."

Kristina looked at Piero, as if she needed him to confirm that fact. He nodded.

"Well," Kristina continued, "when it was mentioned, you seemed so interested. You'd done a lot of research on the island already."

Again Louise denied this. "I'd read up a bit about it, that's all."

"I was the one who was interested in visiting," Rob admitted.

Louise was grateful he'd got that straight.

"The thing is, when we knew of your interest, we made a connection."

"*Tesoro*," Piero said, "it was me who made the connection." From the look on Kristina's face, she was clearly appreciative of his honesty too.

"I don't understand," Rob replied, "what *is* the connection?"

"The thesis I am working on centres around the science of fear," Kristina tried to explain. "Specifically it asks the question: what is fear? Often, when we are frightened of something or somewhere, it can prompt an expectation in the brain, so easily we imagine things that are not really there because we *expect* to see them. Autosuggestion plays a big part. What others have said they've experienced, whether it is true or not, can shape our own experiences." Knowing she had their full attention, Kristina continued, albeit nervously. "So many myths and legends have been built up around Poveglia, not just over decades but over centuries and, as such, it is widely regarded as the world's most haunted island. People come here because they *want* to see ghosts and some people think they do because their imagination obliges, it creates a spectacle for them if you like. In that way, human beings are very much like magicians. In my thesis, I want to suggest that ghosts are not real, that they are merely a manifestation of the mind, an illusion."

Louise joined Rob in confusion. "So… we're a part of your thesis?"

"In a way, yes, you would be a case study."

"A case…" Rob started but fell quiet, obviously needing more time to digest what he'd just been told. "So hang on, your husband's mind started to work overtime, wondering how he could cash in on the situation. He decided it'd be a good idea to drag us over here, frighten the wits out of us to see how we'd react, whether we'd start seeing ghosts, *conjuring* them. And you went along with it, as you thought it'd be a good idea too."

"We did *not* drag you," Piero growled at Rob, "you willingly came."

"Yes, but not to be a part of your wife's thesis!"

Louise intercepted. "Is that why you took us upstairs, to the high security wing? Why you led us past padded cells and rooms with bars on them, to test our imaginations?"

"Yes," confessed Kristina, "it is widely rumoured that the theatre, the one where Dr Gritti used to operate, is the most haunted room in the asylum. There are those that say they have gone there, but they admit they don't stay long. Even the doctors after Gritti and Sanuto wouldn't go in there as we have told you, for men of science, they let imagination get in the way of professionalism so easily. But we have been in there before, Piero and I, and we have seen nothing. It would have just been… interesting to see your reaction."

Although she knew he'd never do it, Rob looked as if he could hit her too.

Kristina took a step back. "I'm sorry, as my husband said, we meant no harm."

Louise could hardly believe her ears. "So… that story you told us about your friend having slept the night in a padded cell upstairs, how you heard a scream, and rushed up to find it wasn't him, was that to rile us, to get us going?" Piero nodded but it was defiantly so. He clearly didn't like being exposed. "And you said that it's different upstairs, that it's easy to imagine things, thus putting the power of autosuggestion into practise." On a roll, she continued. "Did you arrange for the bang upstairs too, the one that happened when we first arrived here and then later on the scraping sound? Have you got an accomplice with you, already on the island?" That idea took root. "That's it, you've got an accomplice with you haven't you? We've only your word there's no other landing jetty, there could be. After all, if you're going to scare us, you might as well scare us good and proper." Her voice was nothing less than scathing. "You'd get better marks for your essay that way!"

"There is no one else on the island." In contrast to Louise, Kristina sounded weary. "What we did was stupid. We haven't done such a thing before. We are not bad people, I promise. We are not dangerous. It was just… you were too good an opportunity to miss. As for that bang it could well have been some masonry falling, but the scraping sound, I don't know. Look, you cannot deny we have been with you the whole time; we haven't had time to do the things you accuse us of." She faltered slightly. "Please, believe me."

"Believe you?" Rob spat. "There's no way on God's earth I believe you."

"On God's *forsaken* earth."

Rob turned to Louise. "Sorry?"

"Forsaken earth, that's what this is, Rob. There's no God-liness here." Tears sprang to her eyes as she said it.

"Lou," Rob's voice was surprisingly soft, he reached out a hand, meant to comfort her she thought. "I'll tell you what isn't here: ghosts. Kristina's right about that at least."

"But the mist—"

"Was a natural phenomenon, it was nothing more than that. We were all a bit spooked by the disappearance of the rucksack, our minds could have *exaggerated* what we saw."

So he was in agreement with Piero and Kristina, that it was imagination at work, *collective* imagination. But she had stood apart from the collective and seen something different in the mist – the veiled lady again. The first time she'd seen her, in Venice, she'd told Rob about it, but he'd dismissed it so readily, and walked away, not giving it another thought. She hadn't told him about subsequent times. Would he believe such a neat theory if she had?

Rob was addressing Piero. "You've got the key, I know you have. If you don't give it to me right now, don't blame me for my actions."

Kristina rushed to stand in front of her husband. "It was in the rucksack!"

"That's not true. Give it to me."

Piero stayed put behind his wife. "I haven't got it. Accusing me won't change that."

"Yeah, right. We're not as naïve as you first thought."

As Rob made to step forward, seemingly determined that Kristina should not be a barrier to his intentions of hitting Piero again, and to shaking the key from him if he had to, there came a sound like the crack of a whip behind them. *Close* behind them. A huge whoosh of air actually accompanied the noise – Louise felt it brush against her cheek.

Kristina whirled around. "Who's there?" she screamed. "Who's there?"

But there was no one there. At least no one living.

Kristina started sobbing. "I don't understand. I don't."

Piero thrust his hands at Rob. "See, how can I have orchestrated that?"

Instead of stepping closer to Rob for comfort, Louise stepped back. "Have you... have you ever experienced anything like this before on the island?"

Kristina shook her head. "No, I've told you, but we have never been here after dark."

"So you've never camped overnight, Piero?"

"Only the insane would stay overnight."

Louise almost laughed. Did he realise what he'd said? Only the *insane* would stay overnight, and, if you weren't insane, the island would do its best to drive you to it. Certainly her grip on reality was becoming tenuous. So much so that the sound of footsteps running overhead barely registered. Rob, Piero and Kristina, however, acted immediately, moving outwards, heading for the staircase.

"Louise," Rob barked. "It could be their accomplice!"

Instead of following him, she retrieved her mobile phone. As the screen burst into life, she checked reception in the vain hope there'd be some signal, but it was non-existent. Next, she went to her photo gallery, the reason she'd taken it out in the first place.

Rob finally noticed she hadn't joined them. "Louise!" he called again.

"Coming," she said, walking forwards but slowly, taking her time.

The sights and sounds of Venice as she scrolled through were almost a torment, full of landmark buildings, canals, bridges, houses, her and Rob, the two of them smiling, posing, pulling faces. There was even one of the four of them sitting together at dinner last night. The waiter had taken it, their glasses raised in salute. Was it really only last night?

"Louise, come on, someone's upstairs!"

No, not someone, she knew that now. *Something*. The figures that they'd seen outside were no longer in the mist – they had, as she feared, found their way in. So many of them, the victims, but there were other energies too, more malevolent in nature – the perpetrators? All of them with one thing in common: they were excited because there was new energy to feast on, fresh blood. And the veiled lady was here too, leading the way.

There it was! The house over the archway, the one in the painting in the hotel lobby, that she'd found whilst exploring and taken several photos of – expecting, always expecting, but that expectation hadn't come true – until now. Of course there was the possibility that her imagination was playing tricks on her – that she was indeed a prime candidate for study, as Kristina had hoped, but somehow she didn't think so. The veiled lady hadn't been in any of the shots before, but she was in them now, staring, beckoning. *Follow me. Find me. I am here.*

Someone had hold of her arm. "Louise, why the hell are you looking at your phone, it's useless! Something's going on upstairs, we've got to investigate. It might not be an accomplice, it could be animals." He paused, as if struggling to convince himself of that. "I expect it is bloody animals. If they've got our bag we can get it back."

She felt like yelling at him, shouting – *there are no animals up there, there are barely any on the island – nothing can live here, make a home here, be happy here, don't you realise that? Nothing!* But she didn't, she let herself be dragged into the corridor where the other two were anxiously waiting, their eyes darting from her to the stairwell. Again Louise was reminded of those words she'd read a long time ago – *My life is like a broken stair, winding round a ruined tower and leading nowhere.*

The stone steps ahead, they were different, however. They didn't lead 'nowhere' – they led to hell, to so many people's hell.

Follow me. Find me. I am here.

Staring at the steps, she gauged the distance between them and her and then, her mind made up, she pushed a startled Rob off her and started running. Holding onto the bannister this time, using it as a towrope almost, she hauled herself upwards.

Chapter Twenty-Eight

"LOUISE!"

Although she could hear Rob's voice, once again it had that muffled quality to it. They were in an empty building, it should be more resonant than that but he was in a different reality now, and she had entered another. Using the light that was on her phone, she continued to run, surprised at how sure-footed she was, how confident, as if she knew the way ahead, as if she'd trodden it a thousand times. Perhaps she didn't need the light. She could feel her way. And if she faltered, the woman – the veiled lady – would guide her.

I'll follow you. I'll find you. I promise.

If she did, she might also find resolution.

Are you evil?

Would so many cleave to her if she was?

Protect me. Keep me safe.

Would she do that? Could she trust her to do that?

She'd find out soon.

Piero and Kristina had joined Rob in shouting her name, all of them demanding she stop putting herself and them in jeopardy. Their voices were at once angry and bewildered.

"What do you think you are doing?" It was Piero. "Come back."

There was another scream – a man's voice, not a woman's.

The sound stopped her urgent tracks. She had just turned the corner on the half landing, out of sight but close enough to listen, to hear what was unfolding.

"Is it your ankle?" Piero was asking.

"Yeah, I… I tripped. Where the hell did that big chunk of masonry come from? I don't remember seeing it before."

"There is rubble, much debris. It must have been there," Piero replied.

"It wasn't, I'm sure it wasn't. We were only here a short while earlier, I think I'd have remembered, I'd have known to avoid it." And then he cried out again. "Bloody hell it hurts! Help me. I can't get up on my own. We have to get Louise."

"Why did she run off?" Kristina asked.

"How the hell do I know? Get me up. Ah, shit!"

"You cannot stand!"

"No, Piero, I know that!"

"Have you broken it?"

"It's a sprain I think, but a bad one. I can't put any weight on it."

"We need to get you to the day room," Piero decided. "It's the closest room to where we are, and there are chairs in there. You can sit and wait. I'll go after Louise."

"No, I have to come with you."

"How will you do that, if you cannot walk?"

"She's my wife!"

"Rob, be reasonable."

"I… damn!"

"Kristina, will you stay with him?"

"Me? You are going up alone?"

"I won't be alone, Louise is there."

"But—"

"What else do you suggest, Kristina? That we leave her to

roam about? Who knows what will happen. She could fall, hurt herself."

"Piero—"

"*Tesoro*, I know this place, I will find her. Don't worry."

"You'd better find her," Rob interjected. "You'd bloody better. This is all your fault!"

"It is not. You wanted to come here!"

"Please!" It was Kristina. "Don't argue like little boys! Behave like men."

There was a pause and then Rob started speaking again.

"She was looking at her phone in the laundry room, she seemed... I don't know, transfixed by it. I went to get her, brought her to stand with us and then she just... ran. Why?"

"We are wasting time thinking about the reasons why, I need to go after her. Lean on me, I'll get you to the day room first, or Kristina, can you manage on your own?"

"I... I don't think I can, Piero, he's heavy, we need to be either side of him."

"Okay, okay, but hurry, she is getting away."

Getting away? He'd said that as though she were a prisoner.

Breathing deeply, she exhaled long and low through her mouth. Standing beside the broken window, she was reminded it was still raining. The weather hadn't eased, if anything it had got worse – the rain lashed the walls of the asylum, like hundreds of tiny fists furiously hammering. If she looked outside she'd probably see the mist too, surrounding them, cutting them off. But it'd be empty this time – a natural phenomenon, as Rob had said, not *super*natural – its contents expelled and waiting. Now that the others had retreated to the day room, that she knew Rob was being taken care of, she could hear again sounds from upstairs, soft sounds, whispering, but somehow more real than those that had come from downstairs. She imagined shapes and shadows – so many of them – huddled in clusters and speculating about the newcomer. There were footsteps too. Not running this time, but a careful pacing, each step measured; a certain number one way and the same amount back, no more, no less, with the repetition giving whoever was responsible for it a degree of comfort perhaps. She started to move again, climbing the next flight of stairs.

So it was Piero who was to come after her was it? Just him. Piero, who'd been here before, who knew the layout, but never at night, because no one stayed overnight. No one dared. But she'd got a head start at least; the veiled lady had seen to that – in stopping Rob, she'd stopped them all. Except Louise of course, she'd been allowed passage. And there she was, the veiled lady, in the distance, waiting, always waiting. *Follow me.*

"I'm coming," Louise replied, entering the asylum proper.

PART FOUR
Home

Chapter Twenty-Nine

IT'S easy to hide in Poveglia. Like the alleys of Venice, the corridors of the asylum twist and turn, some leading nowhere, but others much more manipulative than that and drawing you in... always in. Perhaps you'll reach its centre, perhaps there isn't one; you might find your way out, or remain lost. So many, thought Louise, remained lost.

Reaching the landing, she passed the rooms Piero had taken them to earlier – the female wards. There was slight movement from within and she turned towards it to see the shapes she'd previously imagined, a whole host of them, filling the void. Outside another ward she faltered. Again there were shapes within, no more than mere outlines, barely distinct from the darkness, but one of them, a woman, with hair that hung in strands and wearing a loose shift, was more in focus. She was the one pacing back and forth, her head bent low, counting each and every step – reciting the numbers as though they were a litany.

Follow me.

There was no time to stand and stare. Piero would catch

her if she did. She turned into another corridor, not the one she'd been in earlier with Piero and Kristina; this one was located at the far end of the main building rather than in the middle. Although different, it too had jagged cracks in the plaster that threatened to gape open like the widest of mouths, eager for sustenance. Up ahead was constant darkness, the torch on her phone unable to penetrate it. All it contained was the veiled lady. She was beacon enough.

"Where are you taking me?" Louise called out.

There was no reply. She hadn't expected one.

She came to a flight of stairs leading downwards. Is that where she had to go? Before descending, she turned around – sure she could hear footsteps, not immediately behind but some way off and getting closer. *Piero?*

Her hand reaching out, she grabbed hold of the cold iron railing and forced one foot in front of the other. The stairs led back to the ground floor, but an area far beyond the recreation rooms. She shook her head. From the outside, the building looked as if it would be straightforward to navigate, but inside it was all too easy to imagine it as a web instead of a vast set of rooms, many of which were secreted away, hidden from the world as much as the patients that used to occupy them. When Piero had led them towards the high security wing, she half suspected they were in the building to the left. Now, she wondered if she was in the other building, the one to the right, close to the bell tower.

Another noise made her jump: a clap of thunder.

It's just the weather, that's all, just the weather.

But her heart was racing, the dark as well as the walls claustrophobic. Instead of being mesmerised by the veiled lady, she had a moment of clarity – the thunder responsible perhaps for returning her to a state of full consciousness. What was she doing? What the hell was she doing, chasing an apparition? Venturing down dark hallways that could be dangerous for a whole variety of reasons... practical reasons. It was madness. Utter madness. She'd been infected; the insanity of others long gone wrapping itself around her like a comfort blanket. Her mind sharpened further. That was it! That was definitely it. She'd found the madness comforting because in it fear had subsided. But now it returned, fear for herself and fear for the others. She should go back, she had to go back. Rob had been hurt, she had no idea how badly. He and Kristina were in one of the day rooms in the main building, one of the rooms they'd been in before perhaps, the one with the empty chairs. What if they weren't empty anymore? What if the shadows upstairs had crept downstairs, and some, like the pacing woman, had become more solid?

Follow me.

Those words! They kept going round and round in her head – as much a litany as the pacing woman's counting. Not just an instruction but also a command. What would happen if she disobeyed? If she turned her back? If she simply refused? Rob – his face was before her, every contour and every line – the man she said she hated, who she blamed for everything, for her failures as well as his. Did she really hate him? Of course not! She missed him. Missed *them*. How happy they once were, before discontent had set in, and bitterness, and anger – anger that had resulted in them coming to this island. If she hadn't lost her temper, if she hadn't hit him, if she hadn't felt the need to make reparation...

Reparation?

Her breath hitched. That wasn't a word she'd normally

use, but it had materialised as vividly as Rob's face had – reparation, amends. They'd argued and she'd had to make amends. Was it significant? Did the veiled lady have to make amends too?

"What do you want from me?"

She was surprised at how much effort it took to voice those words. But she had to find out who this woman was, *what* she was, and why she'd targeted Louise.

"I'm not taking another step until you tell me."

Could a ghost communicate with a living being? Was it possible? Because that's what she was, this figure that was haunting her – someone long dead, a spirit. Could it talk?

The veiled lady was still so far ahead. She hadn't moved. Hadn't risen to the challenge.

"Fuck you," Louise spat, anger dominating again. Not just because of the ghost's insistent mysteriousness, but for so many reasons. For not seeing the bigger picture where she and Rob were concerned; for not being grateful for having each other; for every day that they lived in freedom, glorious, taken-for-granted freedom. With Piero and Kristina too, for bringing her here in the first place, for losing the key, for making her see things. Not the apparitions, but that her anger at the injustice life had dealt her was perhaps… unjustified. Because Poveglia – the building she was standing in and the island itself – defined injustice. Those who'd been confined here, their liberty taken from them due to illness, be it physical or mental, and then mistreated, abused, murdered even, to rot in graves without names, forgotten by those who considered themselves sane, who'd once professed to love them, was the greatest injustice of all. In comparison, hers paled into insignificance. Although she'd come to recognise this, she wasn't ready to accept it, not yet, not when it had torn her apart, when it had driven her towards madness too.

Another clap of thunder sounded overhead, much louder than the last. She turned her back on the veiled lady and, facing the way she'd just come, held her phone up and shone the torch, ready to retrace her footsteps, to find her way to the main building again, bypassing the wards if she could. If she couldn't, she'd refuse to look inside.

Lifting her hand higher, it was a step back she took, then another and another, her eyes widening in horror. The shadows, the shapes, those that had been upstairs, were now in front of her. They were crowding the narrow space, blocking her path. She blinked rapidly, stared again, tried to convince herself it wasn't real, but it was all too real, their silence more menacing than any scream or whisper could ever be. There was simply no way back. This was proof of it. They wouldn't let her – the veiled lady and her charges – not now they had her. She thought of continuing anyway, of barging her way through them. There was no substance to them, so what could they do? If she refused to be frightened, if she kept her eyes shut, there'd be a chance... surely there'd be a chance...

She put her plan into action and recoiled at the clamour as her foot knocked something over. She looked to see what it was: bones, a pile of them. *Freshly* dug bones with dank earth still clinging to them. She was trapped, as surely as any of those who'd been incarcerated here had been trapped – as those in front of her. They'd been trapped too and still were. She nodded her understanding. She wouldn't try and reach Rob, not just yet, or even Piero. Was he still chasing after her? Did she have a hope of being found? All she could do was pray that what little rationale she had left wouldn't desert her; that at some point she'd be able to do what she wanted so badly to do: go home. Just go home.

Certain that the crowd before her were edging even closer, that they'd reach out and touch her if she remained defiantly still – their hands stopping her heart from taking another beat – she faced the veiled lady again and continued onwards.

Chapter Thirty

SHE walked as if in a haze, her mind perhaps not losing its grip but certainly trying to shut down, to protect her as much as possible. From somewhere far behind she could hear her name being called – *Louise, Louise*. Piero hadn't given up, despite having to continue his search for her alone. Perhaps his sense of responsibility was well developed – a point in his favour if she could bring herself to think charitably of him. So what? Let him call her. Let him strain his throat yelling. Right now she knew it was in vain.

Another noise caught her attention: a door banging repeatedly, as if someone was standing beside it, opening it and closing it. Maybe they were, or it could be the wind, snaking its way inside and finding a playmate. Did the mind ever stop searching for logic? Either way, it was too far off to worry about. All the rooms she was passing – some doors closed, others with no doors at all – contained an energy. Although she refused to look, she had no doubt about it – the asylum was wide-awake. The weather seemed only to mourn that fact – continuing to beat at the walls in protest. Bypassing a window, a flash of lightening signalled more thunder to come. The brief illumination caught her eye. Half-expecting there to be figures outside, she saw only towering trees, bunched together, either in a gesture of defence against what was still on this island, or as protection, guarding what lay beneath. Secrets. That's what lay beneath. The island was full of them; secret lives and secret tragedies, layer upon layer upon layer. And lies too. Dr Gritti was the Father of Lies – a pseudonym for the devil, but appropriate, because that's what he was, the devil incarnate. Abusing his profession, his position of trust, experimenting on patients for the purpose of vainglory, then burying their spent bodies in unmarked graves, from which the bones were now being extracted – the dead rising in more ways than one.

"I hope you're the one to rot in hell, Dr Gritti." Although her voice was a low whisper, she was surprised at the venom it contained. Did the burning hatred she felt towards him belong to her or to the veiled lady? Did it matter? He deserved to be hated, to burn.

And he will, he will.

More words, being written in her mind.

Keep walking. That thought was hers at least. *Get this over with.*

As she turned another corner, coldness seized her; different to the cold she was used to. This was able to penetrate, to worm its way deep inside, treading the pathways that led to the very centre of her. It was a dangerous cold, growing claws and squeezing the life from her, but before that, it would feed voraciously.

Follow me!

The words were urgent, more than before – but an urgency borne of what? Was the veiled lady afraid of something? Could this new presence – this *coldness* – harm her too?

Louise looked behind her, expecting to see a multitude of spirits following still. There was nothing but darkness – the doors she'd passed, and the windows, none of them were visible anymore. She stared, willing her eyes to adjust, finally noticing something, some kind of movement. Was it Piero? No, it couldn't be. This thing was writhing, even darker than the blackness and it was cold, so damned cold.

Not wanting to fall into its clutches, she turned back round and her heart almost stopped. The veiled lady was no longer in the distance. She was standing in front of her. There was barely a foot between them. But for once, she was looking beyond Louise, those veiled eyes boring deep, as deep as the cold ever could. Louise swallowed, felt helpless. She was caught between them – the two warring factions – like a pawn in a battle she didn't understand. Tears sprang to her eyes. *I just want to go home.*

FOLLOW ME!

Silent words but she could hear them well enough. They were screamed at her, causing her entire body to jerk. She screwed her eyes shut against the sensation but couldn't stay that way for long. Someone was tugging at her hands, pulling her along, forcing her to move. She had to look, to see what was happening – if it was the veiled lady responsible. But there was no one there – at least no one she could see and the veiled lady was in the distance again. All that was close was the thing behind her, coming closer. As it did, an overpowering stench caused her to retch – the scent of a charnel house, she imagined, the reek of death. Snatching her hands back from whatever it was that held them, she raised one to cover her nose and ran, not needing to be pulled anymore, propelling herself well enough down the corridor, the endless corridor. How long could it go on for? In a nightmare, she supposed, forever. And that's what this was. A nightmare. In it there were no rules, no limits, and no boundaries. She was in the domain of the dead, at their mercy.

Whatever was behind her – the cold, dark thing – had picked up speed too. She didn't want it to touch her. If it did it would drive her all the way into madness.

"Help me!" Her voice was as cracked as the windowpane she'd glanced out of earlier. Who she was appealing to she didn't know. The veiled lady? Piero? God? *But this place is Godforsaken, that's what you said.* She had, but still she found herself hoping.

There was another door banging. Was it the same one she'd heard before? If so, she hadn't come as far as she thought, although it seemed like she'd journeyed for miles and miles, had been apart from the others for hours, or more than that... a lifetime.

The asylum does that. It distorts everything.

Was that her or the veiled lady?

It's a world within a world.

Yes it was. A world *between* worlds, even.

It's a nightmare.

One she couldn't wake from.

It's hell.

And always had been.

The door was close now, so close. Should she go in? Is that what the banging indicated? And if not, what was the alternative? Soon she'd be trapped, her back against the wall with nowhere further to run. What was behind her could then feast as much it liked, she'd be powerless to prevent it – its quarry cornered. Keeping the phone's torch shining ahead she hurled herself into the room. Louder than any thunder, the door banged shut. If she was wrong about this being a sanctuary, there was nothing more she could do about it. The decision had been made. She spun round, half expecting the door to cave in, with what was outside to smash its way through, to claim her. But it remained rigid… for now.

Standing still, she shone the torch around the walls, trying to make sense of where she was: a room, a window on the side wall, with bars across it, some of them intact, some broken. This was a prison that doubled as a home. She was drawn towards the window, and, as she walked, there was a rustling beneath her feet. She shone the torch down, she was walking on pages she realised, pages torn from books, countless books, as if they'd been ripped from their spines in a fury and thrown around. The room was covered in them, half an inch thick in places, forming some kind of curious carpet. She checked the walls again, yet there was nothing on them, no graffiti, no writing. Instead they were relentlessly bare, and above, a cord hung noose-like from the ceiling, all that remained of a light fitting.

This room… she'd seen it before. Not in dreams but on her iPhone. This was the room from a website article about Poveglia, which had been photographed alongside many others, as the person behind the camera chronicled his visit to the island. And the window with blue shutters either side of it, clattering slightly in the wind – the one she'd been drawn to – she recognised that too. It was the window that had framed the veiled lady, just as the window in the house over the archway had framed her. That had been her house. And this had been her room. There was no doubt in Louise's mind. She'd been a resident of both, ending her days on the island, because once confined, you never left. Still unsure whether this was sanctuary or not, she was tempted to run back towards the door, to yank it open, and had to force herself to remain still. What was the point in running?

She knelt and picked up one of the pages. She was

surprised to find not Italian text but English – these books were in English! Although the pages were in varying states of decomposition and much of what was written on them faded, she managed to make out a few sentences. It was a formal, old-fashioned style of writing, the author perhaps dating back to a time even before the asylum was built. She dropped that page, chose another and continued trying to decipher what was written, to see if it was all in English:

... beckoned her ... close ... took up a jewel ... tried its effect...

The rest of the paragraph was illegible so her eyes travelled to where words once again became clear.

"Why... a common labouring-boy!"
"... You can break his heart."
"What do you play, boy?" asked Estella ... with ... disdain.

Estella? This book was *Great Expectations*, by Charles Dickens! And the words belonged to Miss Havisham and Estella, the former a woman who'd shut herself off from society because of a broken heart and who was now urging her adopted daughter to break Pip's heart, the 'common labouring-boy', thus seeking vengeance by proxy. A woman who repented for her actions in the end but too late, sitting so close to the fire, too close, and setting herself alight; her regrets a burden she couldn't endure.

There was a noise from behind her, another rustling, but different to the first. She had to acknowledge it, but not yet. Instead she frantically scanned more pages, searching until she found something more substantial: a cover. Greedily she looked at the title, it was *A Tale of Two Cities* – a tome she'd studied at school. If this room belonged to the veiled lady had she been English not Italian? And had her love for Dickens turned to fury at the end, hence why she'd ruined every page? If she hadn't done it then who had? Someone trying to destroy what she loved? Or trying to destroy her?

Still playing for time, she shone the light on another page.

An Italian Dream
I had been travelling for ... days ... the greatest confusion through my mind ... a solitary road ... it would dissolve... melted into something else.

So many words she couldn't read and what she could didn't make sense, only the sentiment did, the words as broken as the mind that had obliterated them. But she knew the book from which this had been torn too. It was *Pictures from Italy*, and this chapter described Venice. But had he ever ventured through the Lagoon to Poveglia? Had he known there was a flip side of the coin? And this woman, what was her story? How had she ended up here, in this room – this cell? Her name was etched on the inside of the cover she was still holding – *Charlotte Evans*. Not faint at all, but boldly scribed, because Charlotte was precisely that, she understood, a bold woman, strong, unashamed of who she was, with a will cast in iron. A woman who, unlike Miss Havisham, refused to repent – to make *amends*. Perhaps the reason for that was she had nothing to be sorry for.

Letting the cover fall to the ground, she stood and took a deep breath as she squared her shoulders. She knew exactly who was behind her and also that the dress she'd seen her in so many times wasn't a dress at all, not something made from the finest lace but a shroud, thrown over her in death, before she'd been buried – her grave unmarked too.

She'd find out now – what had happened.

As she turned, Charlotte was in front of her again, her hands wide, then coming together behind Louise's back and, like the corridors, drawing her in, their minds melding.

Chapter Thirty-One

FOR so long I was lost – my mind turned inwards, sought out place after place to hide from the starkness of reality – or what had become my reality. I lost count of the weeks, the months and the years. Time is nothing here; it's meaningless and perhaps it always was. In some ways this hinterland I reside in is more honest than the wider world. You are what you are. You're raw. Only a few amongst us wear masks.

Occasionally I see a face float before me – one that I recognise – a young and handsome man wearing an army cap. I see a woman too, her expression pained as if something is worrying her; yet another man, his hand rubbing at his chest, his lips curled in a grimace. Regarding the young man, I almost guessed his name once, something beginning with an A... I tried to sound it out, A... Al... Alb... but that was as far as I got. I see other faces too, faces at the window, crowding around my bed, their hands reaching outwards, ever outwards. Their expressions are so sad – as if they're lost somehow, and in need of comfort. I try to comfort them, I'm willing to, but I simply can't raise my hands in return. I'm too weak and too sad as well. What help could I possibly be?

And then there are the frightening faces, those that wear the masks, their true nature hidden. There are two of them, peering down at me, one man always behind the other as though he's ashamed. What's he got to be ashamed of, I wonder? But the other man, there's no shame in him. He examines me, prods me, makes sure I continue to lie, just lie, doing nothing, seeing nothing but floating faces, or the cracks in the ceiling, or the light bulb as it swings above me, backwards and forwards, incessantly. That's all he wants me to see. But he cannot control me completely. He thinks he can but he's wrong. I still exist. I'm still here, somewhere deep inside, cocooned. And one day the haze will lift. Maybe that's what he's frightened of. Because there is fear in his eyes – he tries to disguise it, but it lurks beneath the arrogance and the bluster. He knows what he's doing is wrong. Should that be a comfort to me – that at least he knows? No, because he carries on regardless. I'll tell you what else I see in him, sitting alongside fear like they are the best of friends; I see madness, utter madness. Of all of us on Poveglia, he is the maddest by far.

"Charlotte, my darling Charlotte, let me hold you, be with you. There, *amore, amore,* do you see? It is not so bad. We can still be together. It is not so different."

She'd been sleeping when Enrico had woken her – so many hours she slept, but then he'd come and shake her awake, whisper into her ear that he loved her, that she was still his wife, that he didn't want anyone else, that he had a 'right' to her. She wondered sometimes if she should be grateful for this? At least she was being touched still, held and stroked. So many within these walls were touched only when it was absolutely necessary, when they needed to be cleaned or fed, and even then with hands that retracted as soon as possible, as if they were vermin, the lowest of the low, barely tolerated. Perhaps they were supposed to be grateful for that too? Being tolerated.

There were those who wouldn't give them that much, who'd expunge them from society; eradicate them.

She used to work the wards; she remembered that, her

brain coming into focus every now and again. Was that because her body was getting used to the drugs or was she being given less, on Enrico's orders perhaps? He certainly liked her more responsive during his visits, hated her lying there like something cold and dead already. If she did, he'd get angry, even though it wasn't her fault, he'd pinch and he'd slap her, tug at her hair. Yes, her dosage was lower, she was sure of it: Enrico still wanted at least a semblance of his wife, as she'd been in the marital bed. That was another thing she was supposed to be grateful for – her room. 'We will have privacy, Charlotte, the kind of privacy a man and his wife should have. And look how pleasant it is. It has a window, a view. If you are good to me you can stay here, away from everyone, from *them*.' He'd uttered that last word so scathingly, but he was more like 'them' than he realised.

She ached inside as much as her body would ache outside when he was done with her. Where had he gone, her handsome husband, the one with the dark soulful eyes and the shy smile? The man she'd fallen in love with at first sight? Was he always a monster deep down? Or had this place – Poveglia – driven him mad alongside his ambition? He wanted to cure madness – she remembered that too – he and Dr Gritti. But you couldn't cure madness; they were living proof. Since he'd been on the island, he'd changed irrevocably, his ideals becoming too extreme. But then she'd changed as well, her naivety gone.

"Charlotte." Enrico was whispering again, his breath hot against her ear and with a smell of something strong on it. Was it tobacco or alcohol? Possibly both. Risking his wrath, she turned her head away and breathed the air on that side but it was no better. The smell of disinfectant was rife, its use obsessive. It burnt her eyes and stung her throat, as the orderlies did their utmost to cleanse what was rotten here – a fruitless task. It was too ingrained, a part of the building, as much as the walls, the floor, the roof, and the very foundations it was built on. A site cursed even before the first brick had been laid.

At first during his visits, Enrico would sit by her side and talk to her about his day. He'd mention how many patients he'd tended to, how smoothly the asylum was running under his and Dr Gritti's care; everyone kept in check, the atmosphere peaceful. That was the word he used – 'peaceful' – prompting a memory of when she'd thought it peaceful too. But she'd been wrong. Catarina had been the one to open her eyes to what was really happening. An Italian woman who could speak English, she'd told her that the island was home still to so many who'd died here; the plague-ridden who'd been banished and not just them, but asylum patients too, the ones taken from their beds and experimented on, that experimentation leading to one thing – death. She hadn't believed her at first, had challenged Enrico, who'd dispelled her fears. And then she'd found the chronicle in Dr Gritti's office. She'd believed then, but too late and Catarina had been taken as well. Challenging Enrico again as well as his uncle, she'd ended up here, at her husband's mercy, her *mad* husband's mercy.

She had turned away but Enrico pulled her face back with his hand, insistent that she looked at him whilst he was speaking, as a good wife must.

"Because you have not been a good wife have you? Not always."

Even if she could, she wouldn't answer him, she'd refuse

to.

"You have been rude to my mother, wilful. And in the bedroom you were not demure."

Demure? What did he mean by that?

"I have discussed your case with my uncle in great depth, Charlotte. He is right when he says your morals are too loose and that you know no boundaries. Perhaps it is my fault, what has happened. I should have been stricter with you from the beginning."

So she was his patient now, as well as his wife? That was new. And her morals were too loose? Why, because she enjoyed sex, because she often used to initiate it? He didn't seem to mind at the time, he'd embraced the way she was. Right up until they'd arrived in Venice. His mother, Stefania, was a monster too, the way she'd wielded her influence over him.

But he is weak… he is weak…

She couldn't move her head only her eyes – the others, the ones she saw crowding around her bed sometimes were in the room with her, speaking to her. She was surprised. They only ever visited when she was alone. Could Enrico see or hear them too?

Her eyes on him again, she realised he was oblivious. He was still talking, taking the blame for her plight, because he'd failed to make her into a decent housewife, one that was content to be told what to do. A shadow wife was what he truly wanted. And now he'd got one. Or so he thought.

He is weak… he is weak…

Still the voices were insisting. He hadn't stood up for her against his mother, and he hadn't defended her against his uncle either. But he did love her – she knew that – in his own twisted way. He had stopped talking, wanted to show

how much he loved her, had risen from the chair and drawn back the thin blanket that covered her. Mentally she braced herself as his hand reached out, parted her legs and trailed a path upwards.

She wished she could scream but it was all she could do to struggle, wriggling her hips from side to side, trying to shake him off.

"Ah, you are enjoying this." Enrico said, seeing what he wanted to see. "Oh, Charlotte, you are so beautiful. Have I told you how beautiful you are? How I love you? You are perfect now, Charlotte. I tell my uncle all the time how perfect you are, that you will not challenge us anymore or put obstacles in our way. Because we are doing nothing wrong, my uncle and I. We are trying to help. And one day the world will realise that."

She hated the way he tried to justify what he was doing, but she hated it more when he started to undress too, unbuttoning his trousers, kicking them off, climbing onto the bed to lie beside her. And still he'd murmur her name, whisper such platitudes of love. But it had nothing to do with love; it was rape. She'd never willingly succumb to him again. He'd push her legs apart, climb on top and force his way inside her, pounding so hard that the metal railing of the bed crashed against the wall in a diabolical rhythm that would continue in her head for hours afterwards. If she closed her eyes, tried to block him out, he'd beat her afterwards, his hand striking her face and bruising her. Sometimes he'd beat her anyway. Or he'd do something worse, much worse. This was one of those times.

Satisfied, he heaved himself off, quickly pulling up the blanket again as if concerned for her modesty. The irony of which never failed to register.

Dressing himself, he made his way over to a table on which her books had been placed – the only personal effects he'd allowed her to keep aside from her wedding ring. He *insisted* she still wear that. He selected one and walked back, his smile so like the one he wore in their early days together. At the sight of it, she had to close her eyes to stop the tears there from pooling. When she opened them he was sitting in the chair, a cigarette dangling from one side of his mouth. The others had come close again too. They'd disappeared during the abuse and she knew why. They didn't want to see her shamed further. But now they were as furious as she was, as sad too.

"The Old Curiosity Shop, Chapter Eight," Enrico grandly announced between puffs. "Business disposed of, Mr Swiveller was inwardly reminded of it being nigh dinner-time…"

On and on he went, the old English words so wrong on his lips. She wanted to scream at him, tell him to stop, she didn't want to hear it, not the words she'd longed to read herself, the words she'd read to the women on her ward, that had ultimately led her to the truth about what was happening here, and the horror of it. The words she'd brought with her because they reminded her of home, of England, of her parents and her brother. They were *her* books, *her* words but he'd taken them over, just as he'd taken her over. A tear fell anyway as he continued to mispronounce. Thankfully, he didn't notice.

He is weak…

Yes he was, of course he was, weaker than her, even in the state she was in.

And together we are strong…

249

Chapter Thirty-Two

THERE were some days when Enrico didn't visit, and that was the only thing I was grateful for. I wouldn't have to suffer his hands all over me, his breath in my face, his voice as he read words that I held sacrosanct, as he mocked me with them.

On those days the others – I didn't know what else to call them at first – would grow stronger in appearance, more and more of them filling the room, all looking towards me. If I could muster up the energy I would smile. There were men and women, so many of them. They poured in through the window, from the fields, and from the graves.

Once or twice I fancied I saw Catarina, maybe Luigina, and the woman who walked back and forth, Gabriela, although when she visited she was still, her face surprisingly pretty, something I'd never noticed. I berated myself for that, for how blind I'd been.

The others were not just from the asylum. I came to understand that. They included all those who had suffered on the island: the rejected and the diseased. What was here before the walls of the asylum had been erected? How had they lived? Or rather not lived. No one lived on the island. Not truly. But I'd tried to make the lives of those I came into contact with easier, to show them a fraction of kindness, and some, like Catarina, had responded – and paid so dearly for it.

The nurse that tends to me daily makes no effort to be kind. Sent in to wash and feed me, she can barely bring herself to look at me, disgust wrinkling that pretty little nose of hers. Her voice belies her stature. It's harsh as she barks orders I can't understand – the language a barrier again. But the others, there's no *barrier between us, between the dead and the barely alive. What medication the nurse administers, I hide under my tongue. When she opens my mouth she doesn't check there, she can't bear to. The haze is lifting, continually lifting. I was afraid at first, I thought the others might fade when I came to but they're still here, they surround me, and they are right, together we are strong.*

"Charlotte, what is wrong, *amore?* You are sick, always sick. Is it what they are feeding you? I can change that; get you better things to eat. I have said it many times, if you continue to be good to me, I will be good to you."

Charlotte marvelled at the concern in Enrico's voice, which seemed so genuine. He really did play the part of the devoted husband to perfection, fooling her, reeling her in, leading her to this. She remained mute. He didn't need an answer, didn't want an answer, just a doll that he could play with, that he could bend and break. But she could speak. When she was sure there was no one outside her door she practiced, whispering at first, her throat unbearably dry, as if it had rusted with disuse. And then she'd practise at a normal pitch, the words flowing much easier after a while. They were nonsense words in the main, sometimes not even that – just sounds, primal sounds, dredged up from deep within, but still a mark of success. She could walk too. She'd get out of bed and cross over to the window. Only once had she dared to open the shutters, cobalt blue in colour, her eyes darting from left to right, checking that no one was outside and would spot her. She had an instinct she'd be all right. After all, who would be out there? A mass burial site, the living would shy away from it, but not her, not anymore. Slowly her eyes had travelled over stone steps, trees and bushes.

Can anyone see me? Is anyone there? Breathing in deeply, she'd waited. There'd been movement beneath the trees: more of them showing themselves. She sent out further thoughts, repeating the words the others had first spoken to her. *Come. Join us. Together we are strong.*

She wanted them, all of them, even those that in life had been capable of wrongdoing, because whatever crimes they'd committed, they'd paid for them.

Content with their response, she'd closed the shutters and returned to her bed on legs that no longer felt so unsteady. Before climbing back in, she'd turn her head to look at the table where her books were. Should she go over to them, select one, open it – run her fingers down the spines of the others? No. She didn't want to. *His* touch was on them.

Enrico brought her back from memories. He was standing over her, wiping her brow with a muslin cloth. "My poor Charlotte, my sweet Charlotte."

He wouldn't rape her whilst she was being sick, would he? Surely he'd give her some respite. When he bent his head towards her and she smelt tobacco and alcohol again – Enrico was living well at least – she couldn't help but recoil. It was even stronger today.

Immediately his expression changed. Became one of suspicion rather than concern.

"Charlotte, what is it?"

Her disgusted reaction had registered. When she failed to answer his voice grew more insistent. Still she kept quiet. Isn't that what he expected, what he wanted?

"Charlotte," he said, grabbing her by the arm and shaking her. "What is wrong?"

Although she made herself go limp at his touch, she knew

she was beyond fooling him. But perhaps the time had come, perhaps he'd be pleased she could talk again, could communicate. Perhaps his love for her would overwhelm his fear of her instead. And perhaps he ought to know what she wouldn't be able to hide any longer. Even if the sickness wore off there'd be other indications of what was going to happen.

"I'm pregnant!"

As though her words were a physical blow, he staggered. "You can speak!"

A wave of nausea paralysed her almost as much as the drugs used to. When it was over, she sat up. "Yes, Enrico, I can speak. I can walk, I can think and I can conceive."

"But... I do not understand. The drugs..."

"Are easy to manipulate. The nurse is easy to manipulate."

Some of his astonishment faded and instead fury edged its way in. He muttered something to himself in Italian. Charlotte had a feeling it concerned the nurse she'd just mentioned. Just as rapidly, Enrico switched to English.

"If my uncle finds out, he will not like it. There will be... repercussions."

Cold fear seized her. She looked around her at the others. They'd shrunk back when Enrico's mood had changed but they were gaining in confidence. And so must she.

"Enrico, I am pregnant, with your baby."

Still he stepped back, shaking his head all the while. "No, no, it is not possible."

"Not possible? Enrico, you come to my room, you rape me – sometimes night after night. You are a doctor, you know how possible it is!"

"But... I..."

She had to know. "Enrico, are you mad?"

His eyes, already wide in horror, seemed to bulge from his head. For a moment he simply stared at her and then he leapt forward and grabbed her by both arms, holding her mere inches from his face. "Why do you say that, why?"

"Let go, Enrico. You are hurting me!"

He had also raised his voice and she was terrified someone might hear.

"How long have you been pregnant?"

"Weeks, a couple of months, maybe more. I don't know."

"Liar! Surely you must know!"

"I don't!" She'd been horrified to realise what was happening but also... something else – something that was completely unexpected, something she hadn't experienced in a long while... hopeful. "Enrico, get me off this island. I need to go home more than ever."

"Home?" He looked at her as if he didn't understand such a word. "My uncle, *Dio mio*. He will not tolerate this."

She reached up to grab his arms too. "He need never know! Not if you get me off this island. Surely he can't monitor every move that you make." She watched as his eyes flickered from side to side. Was he considering her proposal? Hope flared again. "Enrico, my mother and father will look after me. I won't breathe a word about you and what you've done, where we've been. I'll... I'll make something up. War is imminent. It may even have started. Has it started? I don't even know that. But if it has, people will go missing. And that's what I'll say, that you've joined the army, that you're missing."

Still he was quiet and she found herself silently pleading instead. *Please, please, Enrico, send me home.* The very

254

thought of seeing her mother and father again made her feel faint, and Albert too of course, dear Albert, the brother who had called her The Venetian. She knew he intended to join the army but could he have travelled to Venice first when communication between them had ceased? Had he done his best to find her? There was no way he'd realise she was here. Enrico's mother wouldn't tell him or Enrico's father – another weak man. A weakness she had to play on, to try and manipulate.

"Enrico, what you are doing here, perhaps it is noble, perhaps I was wrong, too hasty in my judgement. I should have supported you and been a better wife."

Enrico was looking at her again, his whole demeanour wary.

"This is your child inside me, Enrico, either a big fine boy or a pretty, obedient daughter. Your child, and mine, we are its parents and together we are a family. You know how important family is. I do too. We both come from good backgrounds. Enrico, the three of us can be happy. And in the future we could have more children if you wish, add to our family. But first you have to get me away from here. I need to be looked after properly, to eat good food, the medication you are giving me could harm the baby. I need to go home, Enrico," despite her best intentions her voice began to break. "Let me go home."

"To England?"

"Yes, to England, and then you can join me later. Follow on. But I have to get out of here, if our baby is to live. I have to."

"You want to go to England, leave me behind?"

She faltered. "No… I've just said you can follow me, when

you've finished here, when you've learnt all that you can. Part on good terms with your uncle."

"I should leave? When we are so close to a cure."

"YOU ARE NO CLOSER!"

She screwed her eyes shut, bit down on her lip. Why had she shouted? The last thing she should have done was shouted. Enrico's face became a snarl.

"All you are saying is lies. You are going nowhere, Charlotte, do you understand? You are staying here, with me, and you will take the medication I give you – all of it."

"But the baby—"

"There can be no baby on the island. Either you let me see to that with medication or my uncle will see to it, via his methods."

"So he will experiment on me too, murder us both?"

"If you are not a good girl."

Before she could protest he grabbed hold of her hair and dragged her out of bed, kicking over the bucket she had previously been sick in, its contents splattering everywhere. At the table he stopped, caught her mouth in his vicelike grip and, with the other hand, began forcing tablets down her throat, causing her to retch.

"Nurse," he was calling. "Nurse."

It took a few moments but the nurse came scurrying in, stunned to see Charlotte on her feet. He issued a command and she promptly left the room, returning all too soon with a liquid-filled syringe. Charlotte struggled but the needle went into her arm, tearing the skin slightly she was sure, and then it was as though liquid gold filled her torso, seeping into her limbs and finally shutting down her brain as she collapsed in her husband's arms.

Chapter Thirty-Three

ALL that talk of home, it upset the others and I'm sorry for it. The last thing they want is for me to go. They need me to stay. To look after them, to take care of them, to love them as a mother would, as a mother should – as perhaps theirs didn't. I'm not sure what I was thinking. Not really. It's just… when I found out about the baby, I thought it might change things. Not between Enrico and me, of course not. But I had to say what I did in case there was a chance he'd believe me. It wasn't my life I was thinking of, but the baby within me. You see… she – yes, I'm certain it's a girl – might be half his, but she is half mine too and I had to say what I did in order to save her. A mother has to try. The last thing I wanted was to hurt the others, not when they'd been hurt so much already.

But I understand their upset, their concern, and it was all in vain anyway. This baby won't live, how can she? Already she falters. I'm not sure if Dr Gritti knows I am pregnant, certainly he has never been to see me, but Enrico has increased his visits. Still he rapes me. He seems not to notice my belly. Maybe because it has hardly grown, neither the baby nor me are well nourished. Just lately he's been crying a lot. Instead of reading to me afterwards he remains by my side. He strokes my hair, my face, and he cries. He is talking as he is crying but a lot of it is in Italian so I can't understand. He barely ever speaks in English anymore. And sometimes he gibbers, like a baby in fact, the drool from his mouth staining my skin. I think he is apologising, or at least that's what I tell myself. That deep down in that ruined mind of his, he regrets his behaviour. Even so, what use is sorrow? He's on a pitiful crusade – one that's destroying him too.

But I digress. It can't be much longer before the baby is due, before my body finally expels her and they take her away, to lay in the plague fields, with no ceremony, no fuss, to be forgotten as all of us are forgotten. I don't want that for her. I can't bear to think of it. The others have to help me, they have to promise and, if they do, I will promise something too.

"OhmyGod!" Her cry tore the night in half, she was sure of it. She'd never experienced pain like this. So suddenly it had come upon her. Not creeping up, but leaping like a tiger, catapulting her upright, dissolving the stupor she'd been in for so long and forcing her unmercifully into the present. "OhmyGod! OhmyGod!"

Where was everyone? Why was nobody coming to her aid?

"Help me!" she yelled. "Somebody help me!"

Her hands gripping the sheet, she fought to breathe evenly but it was impossible. Instead it was coming in short desperate pants as she rode each wave of pain all the way to its peak before it subsided, the relief cruelly lasting mere seconds.

Please help me!

They wouldn't leave her alone to endure this, would they? Not if she screamed loud enough, if she screamed the asylum down. Someone would come to her aid.

The door burst open. She thought it might be Dr Gritti, holding a syringe in his hand, determined to shut her up. But you couldn't halt nature in its tracks. This baby was coming and there wasn't a damned thing anyone could do to stop it. It wasn't Dr Gritti it was Enrico and the nurse who usually attended to her – a relief of sorts, albeit a stark one.

Closing the door behind them, Enrico and the nurse started talking to each other in quick bursts of Italian. She gripped the sheets again, her knuckles turning white. Why weren't they rushing straight over to her, seeing to her? What was wrong with them?

"Help me!" Charlotte continued to plead, trying to force her legs over the side of the bed, to stagger to them if she had to, but her body refused to comply.

Enrico again said something to the nurse and she left the room, coming back not long after with towels, one of which she laid roughly under Charlotte's bottom half.

"You have to push," Enrico was saying.

"Push, push." The nurse echoed but Charlotte didn't need telling.

Her body convulsing, she thought she might die. If she did, she could join the others more fully then. Oh, the others, the poor others. She glanced around, there were so many of them, occupying every corner, huddled in groups, their faces contorted with worry.

It's all right. I'm all right.

Even in such pain they were on her mind, and some looked relieved to see it.

Remember what you promised me. Remember.

Of course they would, they wouldn't forget.

She wailed again. Is this how every birthing mother suffered? "*In sorrow thou shalt bring forth children; and thy desire shall be to thy husband, and he shall rule over thee.*" The quote was clear in her mind, an echo of a text read to her as a child whilst at church on Sunday, and something she vehemently rejected. She did not desire her husband, not anymore, and he would *not* rule over her. The children would be her priority. Always.

"The head is coming, Charlotte, push."

Enrico's face was contorted too.

"Charlotte, listen to me!"

How afraid he was, of losing his perfect wife, his doll.

"Charlotte!"

If she thought she knew agony before with the contractions, then the burning as the baby's head crowned nearly caused her to lose consciousness. It was as though she was being branded with an iron. She screamed again and again, and continued screaming until she realised that another cry had joined hers. The sound stopped her own. Only remotely did she realise there was no more pain, that her body wasn't being wracked with it. The baby was here and she was screaming, which meant one thing and one thing only – she was alive! So often she thought its silence in the womb was an indicator that she'd died and then she'd kick again. She was hanging on, despite everything. Was there a reason for that? Could some good come out of this mess?

"Me… give her to me." Struggling to sit up further she found she couldn't, she could only lie against the pillow. Glancing downwards there was so much red – she'd clearly lost a lot of blood in the effort of delivering her baby into the world. It soaked not just her clothes and bed, but the room around her, strangely enlivening it. "Please," she whimpered, feeling like a newborn too, "give the baby to me."

Enrico didn't seem to see or hear her. Instead, he took the baby from between her legs, wrapped her in one of the towels and crossed the room. He was holding her, and not only that he looked enraptured. Rage replaced hope.

GIVE HER TO ME! She screamed the words but only in

her mind. *SHE IS MINE!*

Standing by the window with the cobalt blue shutters, Enrico opened them. Daylight streamed in, which confused her more. She could have sworn it was the dead of night. How many hours had she been in labour? It had seemed like minutes, just minutes. But she couldn't deny it, the sun was bright outside, so tantalising she wanted to bathe in it, feel the warmth of its rays. Let it erase the fever that threatened to engulf her. She knew what Enrico was doing. He wanted to look at the baby properly; he wanted to study her, because even he, brute that he was, was moved by her perfection. And she *was* perfect, she didn't have to set eyes on her to know it. Her head would be nice and round, her arms and legs well formed despite the drugs that had been pumped into her mother's body.

"Give her to me."

The nurse had wandered over to stand by Enrico and the baby, smiling up at him with such pride in her eyes. Misplaced pride, it was as if they were the ones who had created her. But they hadn't. She was the mother – Charlotte Evans – the one who had carried her, who had borne her, who had loved her. And all she wanted in return was to hold her.

When would they turn to her? When would they acknowledge her?

And then the nurse's expression changed. So did Enrico's. Both of them stared at the bundle in his arms, their eyebrows furrowed, comical almost. She wanted to laugh, let laughter be the thing to consume her, to lose herself in unbridled hysteria, but quickly she realised there was nothing to laugh about. The nurse stepped closer, reached out a hand and started prodding the baby, not gently either. The rage building in her reached murderous proportions. If she could she would have leapt from the bed and wrenched her hand from the baby. How dare she touch her? But she could only lie there and stare.

They were talking in Italian again, another thing that fed her wrath. *Talk so I can understand you!* What was going on? Was something wrong with the baby? Surely not, when she'd journeyed this far, when she'd made it into the world.

At last Enrico was looking her way. There was no rapture on his face. He looked like a different man entirely – old and haggard, not handsome at all, with lines she'd never noticed before running deep. He held her gaze for what seemed like forever and then slowly came closer.

Was he actually going to give her the baby? For a short while, when he and the nurse had stood together, she thought she'd died and that was why they were ignoring her. But her heart pounding in her chest at the prospect of holding her daughter for the very first time made her realise how alive she was – and not only that, but, in a life as wretched as hers, she'd achieved something – something great.

Despite her elation, she couldn't help but question. Why wasn't the baby screaming anymore? Why wasn't she wriggling either, her arms batting haphazardly at the air? Newborn babies squirmed, they mewled and they fussed. They didn't lie so quietly. Was she asleep?

"*La bambina é morta.*"

"Wh… what?"

"*É morta, la bambina é morta.*"

Bambina meant baby, she knew that, and '*morta*', she'd heard a word similar, although initially its meaning refused to make itself clear.

With rough hands, the nurse forced her upwards, causing sharp pains to stab at her abdomen. The look of wonder on the nurse's face had gone too, replaced by familiar disgust.

Emulating the others, she forced her arms to move and held them out – a beseeching gesture. *Give me my baby.* If she thought Enrico might hesitate she was wrong. He thrust the baby at her, seemed almost glad to be rid of her. So different to how he'd been a few minutes before. Paying him no more attention, she looked down at the child nestled in her arms. She was indeed perfect but so small – a sprinkling of hair covering her scalp, not dark but fair like her own. Her eyes would also be blue – if she had them open.

Sweetheart, she cooed the words. Would the baby hear them even though she hadn't spoken aloud? *Sweetheart, it's Mother. Look at me.*

Still the baby lay quiet.

Oh, you're a good baby, such a good baby, so bonny, so beautiful.

The pink in her cheeks slowly fading, she was becoming pale.

I'll keep you safe, my English rose. I'll keep you warm.

Why was she growing so pale?

You are mine, just mine. I'll keep you safe.

Never had she been so happy, or so proud. Look at what she'd produced!

Sleep, darling, if you want to, Mother's here. Don't forget that, your mother's here.

Charlotte barely even registered the door bursting open again as Dr Gritti entered. She had to remind herself later what he did, how he had torn the child from her and asked the nurse to 'dispose' of it, how she had heard screaming – *her* screaming, not the baby's, the baby would never scream again. How both doctors held her down, her body no longer limp but thrashing wildly, bucking and convulsing. How the others had crowded round her, not piteous, forlorn or even afraid, on the contrary, their faces were full of anguish, with nothing but a thirst for vengeance in their eyes. She wanted to tell them that vengeance would be theirs but to leave her right now because she was happy still, or at least a part of her was – the part that would forever be holding her baby, gazing down upon her beauty and revelling in such innocence. She'd had that moment and no one could take it from her.

Chapter Thirty-Four

I don't know when I died. But it was after Enrico and after Dr Gritti too, a long time after. The others tell me my husband threw himself from the bell tower, that the demons drove him to it. Perhaps they did – if you can call his victims demons. And Dr Gritti, he died some time later in the operating theatre, just before he was due to experiment on yet another patient. Instead of slicing down with his scalpel, he cut his own throat, his hand forced upwards as his eyes bulged in disbelief. I smiled when they told me that – the demons, the others, my friends and my family. They have such a unique sense of humour.

Those that came after them – the doctors, the nurses – I can't tell you much about them. I'd ceased caring. All I know is that they were frightened of me, scared to come into my room even. They said it had an unnatural feel to it. They only did what they had to do: administer food, more drugs, and keep me clean. And they always came in pairs. Sometimes they would find me in a good mood, still lost in that brief but perfect moment when I first held my baby. At other times I was far from happy as that moment shattered, as I remembered she had taken her first breath not in my arms, but in his, and that he was the only one privy to what life she'd had. Where was she, my perfect child? How had they disposed of her? That word, it tortured me! She was disposed of, as though she were neither human nor a miracle – something untouched by evil, even though evil had played its part in creating her. That was the miracle – and they couldn't see it. Or perhaps Enrico had, but all too briefly. After she died, he reverted back to what he really was and so quickly. Our daughter couldn't save him. She couldn't even save herself.

I waited so many years for her. I would scan the others. Was one of them holding her close? I knew they'd do her no harm. Even so, it wasn't enough. I wanted to be the one to hold her – the phoenix who had risen from the ashes only to be struck down again. She was here, I was here, and the others were here. They had to help me find her, whilst I was still alive.

And so they did.

I don't know when I died because I'd been dead inside since she left my body, although my heart continued to beat. The doctors, the nurses and the orderlies, they were all so easy to fool. The medication they gave me was having little effect, but as long as I remained a mute, they let me be. They hardly even bothered to lock my door anymore. I wasn't going anywhere, I never did. I wouldn't even cross the room to the window, and rarely was I encouraged to. On the table in the corner, my books were covered in dust and cobwebs. Not once did they think to pick them up and inspect their titles. I was not an object of curiosity, and nor were my books – curiosity would have indicated an interest, and these people simply had no interest in what lay beneath.

But I was moving again, I made myself move. When all was quiet, I would force myself from my bed, and place my feet onto the hard, tiled ground. My limbs felt so old, so useless. With a shock I realised they were old – my skin not as smooth as it had once been. There was looseness to it and on my hands were brown spots, so many of them. But my age was of no concern. Only one thing concerned me.

I would circle my bed, stand by the window and even gaze at my books, but I couldn't bring myself to touch them, not yet, not after he had touched them. And then I would move further out of my room – but only at night, always at night, and follow the others, turning left, turning right, keeping to the shadows, the darkness an ally – protecting me. It is easy to hide in Poveglia. But even if it were not, there was so few staff by this time it was hardly a problem avoiding them. There were fewer patients too – the asylum, like everything else, perishing.

I remember when I first arrived I imagined it to be such a noisy place, with patients screaming in grief, anger or self-pity, babbling loudly as they rocked themselves to and fro, screeching in the dead of night, railing at the madness that had gripped them, the harshness of life. But the opposite was true. It surprised me how quiet it was, even those in charge barely spoke to one another. It is still quiet, the drugs doing their job no doubt but that isn't the sole reason, I know that now. All those who have ever had to call this stark place their home are lost within them-selves as well as from the world at large. Perhaps they are screaming, but it is silently, always silently.

I have screamed silently so many times too. But one thing I will not do is to call this place home. I don't belong here. And nor does my baby. Which is why I continue to follow the others, out into the open, into the fields, to find where she's been laid. Several times I've been caught sight of. The nurses' whisper to each other about the woman in white, but I'm no ghost, not yet. But the ghosts that are here will show me where my baby is. They promise me, over and over again, just as I have promised them.

It takes time, some things do. And when at last I find her, it surprises me. She is not in the fields; she is in the grounds by the cottage, her bones crammed into a tin casket. It seems Enrico wanted her close by after all. They pushed her upwards, the oth-ers, helped to release her, one sharp edge of the box already visi-ble in the soil as I fall to my knees to retrieve it with bare hands.

The precious cargo clutched to my chest, I take her somewhere safe, somewhere no one goes anymore, where no one dares but me. I'm not afraid of anything, you see. Not anymore. I will find a place to lay my baby and I will cover her in white as I was covered. Then I will wait for someone to come. Even after all the living have departed, after what life-force I possess has fled too, I will wait for someone who can take her from here, acknowledge that she lived, that she died, and who will bury her elsewhere, on soil that is sacred. Someone who understands the miracle of life and the grief we feel when miracles turn to dust before us. 'Women are emotional beings,' Enrico said to me once, 'some are perhaps over emotional.' It is true, so very true.

My name is Charlotte Evans. I was born in Somerset, England to loving parents. I had a brother, Albert. He teased me once and called me 'The Venetian.' But I am NOT the Venetian, and neither is my baby. She will leave here. And when she is gone, when she is far away, I won't hold back. A woman wronged is someone to be wary of, but be careful if you wrong a mother too – if you tear her baby from her body, from her arms, if you dispose of it. Sanuto and Gritti are afraid, so very afraid and they are right to be. Without her bones this place will be the hell it really is and in hell there is always retribution.

Can you see now, what I want you to do? Find her and I will release you... find her...

Chapter Thirty-Five

THERE was a loud bang, not immediately outside but from further down the corridor. Even so, it brought Louise back to full consciousness and she fell forward, not gently; it was as though she'd been dropped from a great height, landing heavily on her knees, her hands splayed out in front of her. The images she'd seen, that Charlotte had forced upon her, reminded her of an old black and white film, some scenes clear, others stilted. Her voice too had woven in and out, telling her so much except one thing – the most important thing – the location of the child. She cursed the noise that had broken the spell.

"Charlotte, Charlotte, are you still here?" She kept her voice low; not wanting to draw attention from what else might be lying in wait.

There was no indication she was.

Her heart racing she looked around her, at the pages and pages of books. She felt certain it was Charlotte who'd torn them from their spines. Finally touching them again, not in love and admiration as she'd done so many times, but in hatred, in loathing and in fury.

I am NOT the Venetian.

No, she was an English woman who'd married an Italian doctor, who'd been trapped here, confined, imprisoned on an island so very far from home, who'd suffered the worst fate imaginable, who was bent on revenge. If the asylum had closed in 1968, she would have died before that, fifty years ago or thereabouts, yet still she was energised by intent.

Although Louise wasn't sure her legs would support her, she tried to stand anyway, pushing herself upwards whilst glancing left and right. Had Charlotte really flown or was she in the shadows? There were so many shadows. Why was that?

My phone, where's my phone?

She fell to her knees again, scrabbled around for it. She must have dropped it when Charlotte had wrapped her arms around her and possessed her. Her eyes widened. Is that what had happened, she'd been possessed? In a scenario that didn't make sense it made the greatest sense of all. And if so, if that were the case, she'd been possessed from the moment she'd seen Charlotte in the painting in the hotel lobby. She'd been marked, the veiled lady seeing her as that someone she'd waited for, someone who understood. Certainly Louise understood her threat – Find her and I will release you... find her... If she failed, they'd suffer: she, Rob, Kristina and Piero, alongside Sanuto and Gritti.

At last her hands touched something solid as opposed to pages so delicate you feared they'd turn to powder in your hands. It was her phone, no light coming from it because it had switched itself off. With shaking fingers she struggled to turn it back on, praying that the battery hadn't died. It hadn't – there was still a small percentage left. Using the torch facility, she shone it round in a burst of erratic arcs to keep the shadows at bay.

This was where Charlotte had spent the majority of her time on Poveglia – prior to that the cottage with the bones in it and the suite of rooms over the archway too. She thought also of their hotel room – 201. What she thought had just been the curtains swaying could have been her, watching, waiting. *So patient, Charlotte, you've been so patient.*

She summoned up the courage to speak again – praying she'd be heard. "Charlotte, I'm sorry for what happened to you, and I *will* try and help but please, don't harm me, or my husband and friends. We're not the enemy, we're not to blame."

Where had her bed been? In the centre of the room perhaps, the head of its frame pushed against the wall. Not a small room, it was fairly large, but it was soulless, as all rooms in the asylum were, despite being populated by so many souls. The lost, the lonely, and the wronged, they were all waiting to swoop, to do what their mother wanted; the one who had seen behind the façade, the people that they were or could have been, who'd read to them, been kind and, ultimately, who'd stayed. Their devotion would know no bounds.

"Oh, Charlotte, where did you hide her?"

Tears flooded her eyes at the fate that had befallen both mother and child. Charlotte was right; the baby had been a miracle. For the short time she'd breathed she'd represented hope, she'd stopped Enrico on his journey into darkness, and shone a different kind of light. Who knows what would have happened if she'd continued to breathe. Would Enrico have finally found the courage to stand up for his family if not his wife alone? Would Charlotte have forgiven him his weakness in time – for the sake of their child? Would they have returned to England to start again, leaving behind the madness that had consumed at least one of them? Maybe. But the baby had died and with her, hope and forgiveness too, but not a mother's love. That never died.

"Charlotte, I'll do what you ask of me, despite the danger."

And there *was* danger – there was Sanuto and Gritti – desperate to keep the baby here, their only protection against the full extent of Charlotte's wrath. After all, there was only so much a mother wanted her daughter to witness. The darkness that had followed her, the writhing mass that had picked up speed as she had picked up speed, that had only fallen back when she'd entered this room, it was out there, in the shadows too.

She exhaled, and tried to think. Where was it on the island that no one went, not even the living when they'd been here, not for years and years and years? *Think, Louise, think!*

There was another loud bang and the door burst open, it almost flew off its hinges it had been pushed so hard. Louise screamed and took a step backwards, bracing herself for the entity that was Sanuto and Gritti combined, their energy that of the weak and the deluded, the ambitious and the self-centred. All attributes that even in her own darkness she'd never had to battle. She'd battled the same as Charlotte, grief, loss, bewilderment, and anger – especially anger. But all emotions were potent.

She turned her head away, couldn't bear to look as together they rushed at her, as surely they would. They'd freeze the blood in her veins, turn her to ice; a statue that would crumble, be trodden into the ground as so many had been trodden before. Instead, a voice called her name, forcing her to open her eyes to see if she could trust her ears.

"Louise! Thank God, I have looked everywhere! Why did you run off?"

It was Piero, dishevelled and wild looking. A spirit clothed in flesh not shadows, and with a beating heart at its centre. He'd been responsible for the bangs.

"Piero!"

Darting forward, she threw herself into his arms as a lover might and hugged him close. It took a moment for him to react and when he did it was only briefly, relief surging through him, so palpable she could feel it.

"Why did you run off?" again he demanded to know.

"I… erm…" She started to explain but words kept failing her. How could she possibly explain what had happened, would he believe her or would he think she'd gone insane too? A prospect that fuelled her – she wasn't insane and nor was Charlotte! Nor were so many on this island. But they'd been driven to insanity – by those who were supposed to care for them, tend to their needs, help them.

"Louise…"

She shook her head, still couldn't speak. They didn't help, they experimented, Sanuto and Gritti, in the theatre, the one Gritti had committed suicide in, the one subsequent doctors and nurses kept closed ever after, wanting to forget what had happened in there and to *whom* it had happened. Not even looking in its direction as they passed it – keeping their eyes on the ground or fixed ahead. Hiding yet another dirty secret.

Her hands reaching up, she gripped Piero's arms as he gripped hers.

"The theatre, do you know how to get to it from here?"

"The theatre? You mean the old theatre?"

"Yes, that one."

Fear leapt into his eyes. "I think I know, but—"

"No 'buts', Piero. We have to go there."

"At night? There is no way!"

She had to change tack, try a different approach.

"Piero, do you and your wife want to leave the island?"

"Of course!"

"Tonight?"

He looked beyond her, into the darkness, his fear increasing. "Yes, tonight."

"Then take me, because what we need to get off the island, it's there."

His eyes widened. "The key you mean?"

"Yes," she answered. "The key to all of this."

Chapter Thirty-Six

LOUISE could understand well enough Piero's reluctance as they doubled back. Each time he faltered, however, she nudged him, either with words or with the palm of her hand.

"We have to find the key," she reiterated.

He was shaking, she could see that but so was she. Her mind didn't even dare to imagine the prospect of what was to come.

"Is… Rob all right?" she asked him, praying that he was.

Piero turned his head only briefly. "I don't know. I've been too busy trying to find you." Anger was re-emerging, replacing his initial relief. "And the rucksack, how do you know it's in the theatre? How could it possibly be in there?"

"Piero, you don't have to go in with me, I can do that alone. I just need to get there."

"That doesn't explain a thing."

"I know it doesn't, but you have to trust me, I know what I'm doing."

He did stop now, turning to glare at her. "Why should I trust you? Give me one good reason!"

"Because you're the one who brought us here, who got us into this mess!"

"You wanted to come!"

"I didn't! I never wanted to come here, to set foot on such… such… unholy ground. But here we are and here we'll stay, longer than tonight, longer than tomorrow. I honestly think we'll die here if you don't take me to that theatre. Don't ask me how I know, but I do. I know a lot of things, Piero. I've seen a lot of things, things that have taken place, here on the island, how people have suffered, one person in particular. And no, before you say it, I am *not* mad, don't you even dare think it. I don't blame you, for using us as a case study for your wife's thesis, in your own way experimenting on us too, really I don't, but we're in a situation here, a situation I think I know the way out of. Don't argue with me again, Piero, just lead the way. If you don't we're lost, all of us. We'll be joining the lost."

He looked shocked, as if he couldn't believe the way she'd spoken to him, but just as quickly his expression altered as his gaze adjusted, as something caught his attention.

"*Dio mio, Dio mio, che cosa, che cosa?*"

"Piero, what is it, what are you saying?"

The temperature had dropped dramatically. She was turning to ice again. What was behind her wasn't the others and it wasn't Charlotte either. It was those who wanted to stop Charlotte, and by proxy, her, a force acting from the most basic emotion that existed – fear – and who'd be ruthless because of it.

Piero had stopped uttering and was rendered speechless. But still his gaze was fixed; she was the one who had to break the connection now, to stop him from being possessed.

She shoved him forwards and, at the same time, yelled as loud as she could in his face, "RUN, PIERO! RUN!"

It worked. He stumbled back a few paces and then turned and sprung forwards, running so fast she had trouble keeping up with him.

"To the old theatre, remember," she called out, needing

him to guide her, not to change his mind. "If we can get there, this'll be over."

Running up the staircase that she'd descended earlier she thought he might veer off to where Rob and Kristina waited, but he didn't. They were returning to the first floor, to where he'd tried to take them earlier, going all the way this time.

The cold dark thing at her back had kept pace but at the top of the stairs she felt it receding. Why she didn't know, perhaps it was spent, or, more worryingly, it was saving its energy for something else. There was no time to ponder it or to linger. It was getting later and later, the night in its full-ness almost upon them. And, as was the habit of nocturnal creatures, more and more were waking up. The shadows she'd seen in the wards earlier had multiplied, spilling out of doors and into the hallway and all focussed on them, just them. She checked Piero's reaction, but he didn't seem to see them like she could, he was, if not running now, walking very fast, doing what she'd asked him to do, desperation driving him.

Where are you, Charlotte? Why aren't you here too?

But of course she was here, she was everywhere and she was waiting.

Piero continued at a good pace. The building behind her fell away as if it no longer existed. She half fancied if she stopped and took a step backwards she'd fall, her limbs flail-ing uselessly as she struggled for something to hold onto, but finding nothing.

"Piero, are we close?"

"*Si*," he answered. There was such a tremor in his voice.

As they turned again she recognised where she was. This was where the padded cells were, the room with the baths.

Charlotte hated water; she'd gleaned that during the possession. Had they used such a treatment on her? More fool them if they had.

As before, most doors were closed, their locks rusted shut. All had been silent. Now it wasn't. There was scratching coming from behind one of the doors, a relentless sound, as if someone was trying to claw their way out. Piero heard it too and looked towards it.

"Rats," Louise whispered. He'd used a similar excuse earlier, when his wife had been frightened. There was more scratching, *gouging* she'd say, whoever was doing it entombed, buried alive, begging for release. "Ignore the sounds, keep going."

He didn't, he came to a standstill. She was so close to him she had to stop abruptly too.

"What is it?" she asked. "What's wrong?"

When he failed to answer, she peered ahead, following the light of her torch.

Downstairs graffiti was rife, upstairs less so and certainly not this far into the building, but the walls ahead were covered in writing, the same words that had been on the cottage wall – *Get out* – thick and jagged, carved into thick plaster rather than scrawled. Graffiti that hadn't been there before – that was in no way referring to the baby, that hadn't been created by the same hand. It was a warning. More than that – it was a threat.

Piero found his voice. "We cannot go any further."

"We have to."

"No!"

The scratching stopped and a door started to bang instead. Unlike what had happened downstairs, in Charlotte's room, this was not an invitation for her to go towards it, promising a modicum of safety inside, but another threat, compounding the first.

Get out. Go home.

But they couldn't, that was the point. Not if she didn't do as Charlotte wished.

Pushing past Piero she stood in front of him, determined.

"Tell me where the theatre is. I'll go on my own. You stay here."

He looked appalled. "Stay here?"

"If that's what you want."

"None of this is what I want. None of it!"

She pushed her face close to his. "Keep your voice down, control yourself. If you become hysterical, you'll attract it."

His eyes widened. "What will I attract?"

"Gritti. Sanuto. What's evil in this asylum."

"It's all evil!"

"That's just it, Piero, it's not. But make no mistake, evil *is* here and it knows where we are. It's trying to stop us, play tricks on us. We're angry, we're frightened, and that's what it's feeding on. But we're also determined. *I'm* determined. I want to get off this island and I'll do whatever it damn well takes." She took a deep breath, tried to ignore the slamming still going on. "Now are you coming with me or are you staying here – alone?"

Piero was close to tears. "If I come, we run past the door."

"I couldn't agree more."

Keeping to the farthest wall, Louise bolted, not giving Piero time to change his mind.

"Don't look," she called back. "Whatever you do, when we pass the slamming door, don't give in, don't look. That's what it wants, to terrify you, to prevent you from going any further. Shut your eyes if you have to, just while you're going past it."

As they bridged the gap, the door started slamming even more furiously, impossibly so, as no human could keep up such momentum. And then it slowed... the closer they got it slowed. She was right, whatever was responsible wanted them to see what was inside.

"Look straight ahead."

She followed her own instructions, even closing her eyes briefly. There was definite movement; she could sense it, *jerky* movement, as if whoever it was had wires to the head – multiple wires – shocks being administered, over and over again. She sensed the colour red too, coating walls that had once been white – blood – dripping, endlessly dripping.

From behind her came a strangled cry.

"Piero, we're almost past it." Something which should only have taken a moment, but stretched on and on, distorted as everything in the asylum was, the doorway becoming wider and wider, impossibly wide. What was inside was a parody of tragedy; a vision that once imprinted on the mind would be impossible to forget, haunting you in the dead of night and driving you mad. "Look ahead," she reiterated.

It came down to a battle of wills – who would break first, them or the orchestrator?

She was growing tired. Her legs hurt, and her breath was short, playing harder to get with each stride. *Charlotte, you HAVE to help me!*

Lightheaded too, she'd be swamped if she collapsed.
Charlotte, please!

The room's occupant was edging closer, ever closer and, like the others, it had its arms outstretched – all too vividly she imagined long sharp fingernails, ready to lash out, to slash her open, to use her blood as decoration too.

CHARLOTTE!

Like paper crumpling, the door folded in on itself. It was dark again, so dark, despite both torches shining. Coming to a halt she dared to turn her head, relief overcoming her when she saw that what was behind it was at last contained.

She turned to Piero, who was panting heavily. "Are you okay?"

Finally he was able to speak. "I'm... I'm okay," he replied. Making an effort to straighten up, he inclined his head to the left. "We're here, where you wanted to be. It's a few more steps."

Chapter Thirty-Seven

AS they inched closer, every fibre in Louise's body tensed, every thought that entered her head willed her to turn back, to run. But there was nowhere to go. Not without Charlotte's baby. They had to find her, or be *allowed* to find her. The door to the theatre was ajar but it seemed to be straining to shut, invisible forces at work either side.

"Get in quick," she urged Piero.

Once in, the door slammed behind them, causing Piero to jump.

The stench that hit them was the foulest of welcomes. She'd read somewhere once that the smell of fear was shit – the person who'd said it had been a reporter, stationed in one of the world's most troubled regions. How accurate that description was. It really was as basic as that. So many people had been terrified entering here, their collective odour remaining.

Piero had noticed it too; he couldn't fail to. His face was screwed up and he was swallowing rapidly. If she expected something to rush at them once inside she was wrong, but the smell… it was enough to repel anybody – anybody less desperate that is.

The theatre consisted of two rooms, the one they were standing in – an anteroom – and a second further in, separated by a curtain that was hanging in rags. Raising her torch, she saw rows of shelves, some of them empty, their contents looted perhaps, others still with surgical appliances on them – bandages, bottles, syringes all in varying states of decay and covered in a layer of filth. She drew closer, recoiling at the bandages particularly and their intended use, to stem a tide of blood that should never have flowed.

"Help me look," she said to Piero.

He came over to join her. "For the rucksack?"

Should she tell him the truth? Would he freak out? Perhaps not, after all, it wouldn't be the first time he'd seen them tonight. "No, not the rucksack. We're looking for bones."

"Bones? Whose bones?"

"The bones of a baby that was born here."

"A baby? But... I don't understand. Where's the rucksack?"

"It might be here too. I don't know. What I do know is we have to find the bones first, that's what's important. I know I'm probably not making sense but I don't have time to explain, not here, not now. I'll explain later. Please, Piero, just do as I say. Help me look for the bones and then we'll be able to leave. I promise you. We'll get out of here."

Despite her earlier optimism, Piero started to back away from her as if she were indeed mad. Before he could get very far, she grabbed his arm. "Give me ten minutes and then we'll leave and go and find the others. All I'm asking for is ten minutes of your time."

The look in his eyes reminded her of an animal that had found itself caught in a trap, but they were all trapped and she was trying to find a way out of it. He had to help her!

Turning from him, she continued to search and urged him to do the same. She noticed movement, something scuttle, trying to escape the brightness of her torch. She recoiled before realising what it was: a large spider, something that appreciated the lack of human footfall, which thought of this place as a haven. Strange, how the most haunted room in the asylum was also the safest – a hiding place for so much; the good, the evil and – like the spider – the misunderstood. She ignored it and shone her torch into other parts of the room, Piero looking nervously around as she did. The walls were tiled, but many of them had fallen off over the years and lay on the ground either intact or shattered. There was a wheelchair at one end and on seeing it she gasped, expecting a figure to materialise within it, to wheel itself manically towards her. She shook the vision from her head. There was nothing, no chair-bound figure and certainly no bones. Charlotte's daughter might be in the other room, the one obscured by the curtain.

"We have to go in there," Louise said, nodding towards it.

Piero stayed where he was.

"I'll go first," she continued, "but follow me, I need the light from your torch too."

Inching closer she had to force herself to pull the curtain aside, not wanting to touch anything so drenched in death. She hadn't expected it, not here, but in the room beyond there was graffiti, just the one word but in letters half as tall as her: *Hell*. Who'd written that, she wondered, the living or the dead? She wouldn't be surprised if the latter. The walls also had what looked like smears on them, some travelling from top to bottom. And on yet more shelves were the tools of the trade.

She hadn't noticed Piero come to join her, she only realised when he stepped back, stumbled and lost his footing, his torch crashing to the floor.

"Blood! There is so much blood!"

His cry was halfway between a yell and a sob – he crashed to the floor, his back sliding against one of the walls, his chest heaving.

Louise rushed over to him.

"Piero, it's not blood, it's spray paint. I swear to you, just spray paint." It had to be.

But Piero wasn't listening; he kept shaking his head and insisting over and over again, his language alternating between English and Italian – blood, *sangue*, blood, *sangue*.

She was confused. "You've been in here before, Piero, you know what's in here!"

"No," he insisted, gesturing erratically around him, "not this part."

So what had he done, got as far as the anteroom and then bolted? Probably. She'd bet it was the same for most people.

"Look, I won't be long, but the bones, I have to find them."

Swapping her phone torch for his – the beam was brighter – she swung round. In the centre of the room was an operating table, placed under a massive circle of lights that could be adjusted and pulled forward. The bed was horrendous enough but what she found worse were the straps hanging from it, what they implied beyond contemplation.

"Charlotte," she cried out, deciding she had to speak, regardless of what Piero thought. "You wanted me to come here, don't abandon me now. Where are the bones?"

She wanted to scream into the silence, fill the void.

"Charlotte! Where's your daughter?"

It was Piero who started screaming, startling her at first

until she realised whom it was.

"Over there! Who's that? Who's that?"

She shone the light to where he was pointing, but could see nothing.

"By the bed, there's someone bending over it. Who is it? Dr Gritti?"

She was standing by the operating table but, because of his words, she stepped briskly away. Was it possible the doctor could materialise? She could still see nothing.

"It is! It's Dr Gritti. He's... he's operating."

"Piero, there's no one—"

"The patient underneath him, she is struggling so hard to escape. She is begging him to stop, pleading with him, over and over again. But Dr Gritti, he has no mercy."

It was like listening to the rants of a mad man, like looking at one too. Piero had shrunk back against the wall, his hands tearing at his hair. She wanted to help but she couldn't, she still had work to do. She turned back and stopped dead. The dark energy that had been behind her before, that had tracked her, almost touched her, was in front of her, and close, so close, its shape becoming more and more discernible. He was a tall man, imposing, in scrubs and a mask, his dark eyes glaring at her. Not sightless eyes, they were eyes without a soul, with no trace of humanity in them at all. Eyes so different to Charlotte's but just as fixated. As she stared back, the figure raised his hand; in it he held a blade, not rusted at all but catching the light and glinting dangerously.

Behind her Piero screamed again.

"The blood. Oh, the blood."

But whose blood did he mean? The patient's? The

doctor's? Hers?

Waiting for him to strike she noticed another figure behind him, an extension of him almost, refusing to come forward – Dr Sanuto, still attached, still hiding, still weak.

She tried to step backwards but her legs were leaden and refused to move. She tried to raise her arms but they wouldn't comply either. They remained tight under her chin.

Would her voice work at least? It seemed not.

Charlotte, you know what it's like to be abandoned. Don't do the same to me!

The corners of the room were writhing as Piero said the patient had writhed, as Dr Gritti and Dr Sanuto had writhed in the darkness behind her.

"What… what's happening?" Piero could obviously see the others too.

Moving forward en masse, the writhing shapes also became more discernible – she could see faces and a mixture of expressions; the most common one was loathing. Looking again at Dr Gritti she could see fear in his face too, and in that of the doctor at his coattails – fear and something else – hope? If they could stop Louise, Charlotte would contain herself. And right now, as stricken as she was, she'd be an easy target.

There was a slight rustling, a noise to the side of her. As if caught in freeze-frame all were still on hearing it – all except one. From out of nowhere came Charlotte, drifting forwards, not rushing – she had no need to rush – and as solid as any living person. The veil of her shroud was thrown back to reveal her face – old and withered, line upon line etched deep, her thin, pale lips twisted. At the sight of her, Louise was able to galvanise herself into action and jumped aside, out of Charlotte's path, tripping as she did over some debris, falling forward and smashing her head against the tiled wall, knocking some contents from the shelves above to the ground, one item in particular – a syringe; a dirty, used syringe.

The impact momentarily stunned her. She could hear her name but couldn't work out who was calling. She forced her eyes open; had to see what was happening, she couldn't remain in ignorance. What was the point, the mind would continue to taunt her anyway. Charlotte was like some kind of dreadful angel, and, as her arms closed around Dr Gritti, the others closed around her, lending their strength, their energy, their anger – so many of them keening, making a sound unlike any she'd ever heard before. And all the while Sanuto cowered. Perhaps Charlotte would destroy him too, but not until her daughter had been removed. This wouldn't be over until then.

Struggling to her feet, Louise grabbed the torch that had fallen a little way from her and shone it round. Where the hell was the baby? They had to find her. In frustration, she started banging the wall with the handle of her torch – perhaps there was a secret cavity behind the tiles, one that Charlotte herself had gouged out in the last years of her life.

"Piero, where would she be?" she yelled above the ghastly chorus.

Although he had cowered like Dr Sanuto had cowered, thankfully he proved braver. Despite what was unfolding, what he could see and what he couldn't, he forced himself to his feet, and, keeping as far from the centre as possible, crept closer. Like her, he started banging the walls. The tiles fell easily, but underneath it was solid, no dark hiding place at all.

"Where is she? Where is she?" Her cry was one of pure

frustration.

Piero grabbed her arm. "Stop! Stop what you are doing! Look above."

Did he mean look on the shelves, as they'd done in the anteroom? What was the point?

"She won't be there."

"Why not?"

"Because it's too obvious."

"But, Louise, rarely people see what is in front of them."

She looked at him in surprise. He was right! And if anyone knew that, it was Charlotte.

With renewed determination, she started grabbing at what was there, pushing it aside, looking for a box amidst the carnage, a tin box, a casket, the one that the others had pushed upwards, expelled from its woeful place of burial with skeletal hands. She touched something hard and unyielding, something cold. It fell to the floor, made a clattering sound. Immediately she bent down, so did Piero. He reached it first and yanked the lid off.

"What is it, Piero? What have you got?"

He tore his gaze away to look at her. "Bones," he said. "I've got bones."

Chapter Thirty-Eight

TOGETHER they peered into the box. The baby – what remained of her – was wrapped in a length of white material, either a dress or a shroud. The latter probably as there'd have been no clothes for her on the island, no provision made at all. They didn't want to disturb her too much – it seemed sacrilege to do so – but something caught Piero's eye.

He pointed. "There's something placed on top."

She caught sight of it too, reached in and retrieved it. It was a small gold wedding band – small enough to fit on her finger: Charlotte's then, not Enrico's. She must have slipped it in there, wanting to give her child something. To keep it safe, Louise put it on. Meanwhile, Piero placed the lid back on the box, afterwards making a sign of the cross. Again he surprised her. It wasn't a hurried action; his manner was reverent. Nonetheless, she was aware of mounting pressure in the atmosphere, waiting to explode.

"We've got to get away," she whispered, nodding towards the curtain.

"What about the rucksack?"

"We can't stay, it's impossible." She shone the torch from left to right. "Besides, the rucksack's not here, we'd have seen it if it was."

"But where is it?"

"I… Piero, I don't know."

"Then there is no escape!"

"Maybe not the island, but we can escape the theatre. We have to!"

Although he was still agitated, he couldn't disagree. They were at the epicentre, there'd be a higher degree of safety elsewhere, surely.

"Piero, if we can make it through the night, we can find a way. We have to get outside."

"Yes, yes, of course, of course."

Relieved that he'd agreed, she clutched the tin to her chest as they stood and hurried forwards. Another shape emerged, not the others, not Dr Gritti, but Enrico Sanuto. Forced onto the front line.

Grinding to a halt, she stood and stared as he too materialised fully. He was not a man whom you'd attribute such sin to. His features were at once boyish and endearing. Only as you stared further could you see beneath them. He had no real depth, nothing that held you or elicited compassion. He was superficial; a man whose emotional development had been stunted perhaps, who could only follow those with great passion, even if that passion frightened him. He was certainly frightened now. He was beseeching. Holding out his hands, he wanted what he'd been complicit in disposing of so many years ago – his daughter. Unsure what to do, how to avoid him, Louise looked around, at those crowding behind her, her eyes searching for Charlotte, but she was gone, and Dr Gritti too – as though she'd swallowed him whole. Her eyes rested on Piero. She knew what he was thinking – that they should keep going and circle around him. Impossible! He was coming closer, his attention on what she held.

She clutched it tighter.

"You want your daughter, don't you, but only because you fear your wife and what she'll do to you. I'll tell you what she'll do to you, Enrico Sanuto – she'll destroy you, just as you destroyed her, just as you deserve. There is no protection, no hiding, not anymore. With or without the baby, Charlotte is coming for you. A woman can only wait for so long."

His shy, studious mask slipped, revealing something far less wholesome. His eyes grew bigger, so wide she was sure they'd pop from their sockets. She could utter no more brave words, only continue to stare, her mouth open; a part of her still marvelling at the imagination and the tricks it could play, another part certain that this was reality, the kind that existed just below the surface but which could so easily emerge. Piero too was transfixed. As she'd done in Charlotte's room, Louise closed her eyes, trying to shield herself.

Nothing happened. Unable to resist, she opened them again to see Charlotte blocking Enrico's path. Louise seized her chance. Reaching out to grab Piero, she pushed him against the wall, away from husband and wife, from what was about to be unleashed.

Dressed from head to toe in white, again her veil pushed back, Charlotte wasn't the crone that had dealt with Dr Gritti but a woman in her early twenties and beautiful, as she'd been when she'd first met Enrico perhaps – brimming with joy and anticipation. Enrico had come to a standstill too. He seemed mesmerised, her face stirring in him a memory of a time when he was also young and handsome, when ambition hadn't yet found him such a willing victim. Incredibly, a smile started to play around the edges of his mouth – his dark eyes narrowed and started to smoulder. Louise looked at

Charlotte. There was a smile on her lips too – a *sensual* smile – the chemistry between them making the air crackle. She was amazed. Was it possible she was going to forgive him? That the love that had once existed between them could rear up to carry them forwards? That they could redeem each other and therefore themselves? In a night where anything was possible, she was beginning to think so and then Charlotte's smile began to change, from sweet and sensual, from loving, it widened into the rictus she'd seen before. No, anything was *not* possible. There was no love in this woman for Enrico. He'd killed it stone dead.

Not wanting to see how the final scenes played out between them – even the others had fallen back, giving husband and wife the privacy they were entitled to – Louise started to run, knowing that Piero would follow, both of them eager to put as much distance between them and the theatre as possible. Despite this, the cry as they fled tore right through her and she knew it tore through Piero too. It was a cry of agony, sheer and utter agony, embodying every pain and every sorrow that was ever inflicted within these walls. It seemed to brand her. She'd never forget it. It would be the thing that would haunt her long after she left these shores, *if* she left these shores. A cry that would go on and on, and which was just the beginning – Charlotte would make sure Enrico's suffering lasted as long as hers had. He'd not get away lightly. Not anymore. He was the one with amends to make, he and Gritti both, and they would – they'd pay. So often vengeance is portrayed as black, something dark and full of shadows. But Louise knew better. Vengeance is white. And it is terrifying.

As they continued to run, she feared the building would

play tricks on them again, that corridors would run on and on, that doors would open and shut with inhuman force, that more graffiti would start appearing, that the walls would seek to contain them not expunge them. But with each step her confidence grew. She was beginning to recognise routes, landmarks even, her subconscious having taken it all in, her mind making a map of the interior – a map that was both a blessing and a curse. Would she wander down these routes even when she'd escaped them, in her dreams, in her nightmares, when she was awake too, returning to them time and time again, a part of her trapped, always trapped? A sob escaped her at the thought. Not just a possibility, it was a likelihood.

Keep running; keep running.

But there were some things you couldn't run from.

"Louise, this way."

They were on the landing outside the wards now, the men's wards directly to one side of them and the women's wards ahead. There was movement inside each room still but unless it was just wishful thinking, it had lessened.

There was another cry. She tensed to hear it, but it wasn't coming from behind her, it was coming from in front – a voice she recognised. Two voices. Rob and Kristina.

"Louise, where are you? Come back, come back now!"

"Piero, you must come back."

Piero shouted something in Italian, but whether they'd hear it or not she didn't know.

Reaching the section with the women's wards, she was compelled to stop. She looked inwards, expecting to see the pacing woman reciting her litany of numbers, but instead she saw the outline of a woman sitting by a bedside, plus a woman in the bed too. As she stared the vision increased in depth. It was Charlotte who was sitting, holding a book in her hands and reading from it. The bed's occupant was elderly and she was lying against her pillow, her eyes half-closed but her general demeanour one of contentedness. As Charlotte finished reading, the woman opened her eyes and leaned forward. Charlotte reached out a hand and readily the woman took it, highlighting a bond between them, one that had started with words. There were other beds lining the walls, figures in them too but none as clear as Charlotte and the elderly woman. Louise understood what she was trying to tell her: that this was a bad place – of that there was no doubt – but in it peace and friendships had been possible. Like the birth of her baby, good had found a way to triumph, if only for a moment, one bright and glorious moment. It had shone. *That* was what she should remember whenever she thought of Poveglia. It would offset the horror.

Charlotte, won't you come with us too, find a way?

She sent out the thought, wondered if it'd be heard. It was. Two words formed in her mind, simple words that spoke volumes.

I promised.

Piero was getting agitated. "Louise, why have you stopped? We must go."

As quickly as it appeared, the vision vanished. There was nothing in the room but a sliver of moonlight through an open window, indicating that the rain had stopped, that the mist had lifted. It fell on the elderly woman's bed and caressed it.

"Louise!"

"Yes, yes, let's go."

She bounded down the stairs, trusting in instinct to avoid

any obstacles. Kristina was at the bottom, still shouting frantically before sobbing in relief at the sight of them. As Piero drew closer, his wife threw herself into his arms, reciting his name over and over.

Sidestepping them, Louise rushed into the dayroom, eager to see Rob, he was in the chair they'd helped him to but, on seeing her, he struggled to rise.

"Don't," she called. "It's okay, stay there. I'll help you to move in a minute."

Rob took no notice and stood anyway, wincing as he limped towards her, as she was caught in his arms too.

"Thank God you're all right. We've been so worried about you. Why'd you do it, Lou, why'd you run off? Are you okay? Are you hurt? Did you see anything? I tried to come after you but I couldn't. I even tried to crawl. I didn't get very far. This bloody ankle, I don't know what I've done to it, sprained it or something. What's in your arms?"

Although delivered in a rush, each word he uttered was a comfort – he was alive, she was alive and they were hugging each other. She had to tell him what she held, but not the full story, not until they were off the island.

"Bones? But—"

"Rob, I'll explain fully later, but right now we still need to find the key."

Rob beamed at her. "That's just it, it's here. We've found it. That's why we were shouting out, making such a racket. We were trying to get you to come back. We've got it!"

"You've got it… but how?"

"We were getting so agitated, wondering what had happened to you both, that we devised a plan of our own. Kristina was too frightened to explore alone, but if I crawled to the door and just kept talking to her, anything, nonsense speak, it didn't matter, as long as she could hear my voice she'd continue exploring. Apparently, it's the silence that freaks her out the most, which is something she could put in her thesis perhaps." He paused to laugh and, impatient, she had to remind him to go on. "Anyway, she went back to places like the office and the dining room, only stood in the doorway mind and shone the light in but there was nothing, absolutely nothing. When she returned she was so down-hearted, she shone the light at me to explain how useless it had been and then she gasped."

"Gasped? Why?"

"Because that's when she saw her rucksack! It was behind me, right behind me, tucked under one of the chairs. Either we didn't check this room properly or we were too panicked to notice it was here. I suppose that can happen. Panic can blind you."

Trying to absorb what he was saying, she looked to where he'd said the rucksack had been – it wasn't there now. The blood drained from her. "Oh no, don't tell me it's gone again!"

Rob hugged her to him again, the tin pressing against her chest as he did so. "Kristina's got it on her back. She won't be taking it off in a hurry, I can tell you. As we first thought, it must have been animals that did it. The bag's been ripped into and a couple of the food boxes are gone, the one with the most food in probably, but the key was still there. Thank God."

Kristina and Piero burst into the room. "The key," Piero shouted. "We have the key!"

Louise looked from them to Rob – he still thought it was

animals responsible? If only he knew. But he would, he'd know soon enough, he and Kristina both.

"Can you help me with Rob?" Louise asked Piero, determined to keep moving.

All four of them left the dayroom and made their way to the office – Dr Gritti's office, it had to be – and subsequently the exit. As they entered, the furniture had been moved again. This time the table had been upturned, the filing cabinet too and all its drawers scattered across the floor, the wood even more splintered than before.

"What the hell—" Rob began.

"Who did this?" Kristina was stunned too. Clearly worried that blame would start being apportioned again, she quickly added, "I didn't. It was nothing to do with me..."

Louise reassured her, "We know it wasn't you, Kristina. We know."

"Louise—" Piero urged.

He was right. "Come on, quickly." Her voice was urgent too.

Passing one of the drawers, she was reminded of what she'd seen before: a scrap of paper with the letters 'Alb' on it. Was it Charlotte's letter, one of many she'd written to her brother, which had never been sent, which Dr Gritti had intercepted? Where was it? Louise wanted to remove it from the island, to remove as much that belonged to Charlotte as possible. But it would take time to find it, time they didn't have. Perhaps it didn't matter – she was taking the most important thing of all.

As they left the building and stood on the path outside, there was relief on everyone's faces. The rain had stopped but there was a freshness that lingered.

The boat started instantly, Piero putting it into gear and steering them away. Navigating the waters back to Venice, all kept their eyes on the island.

Kristina eventually spoke.

"What's that?" she said, pointing. "It seems like a light has come on in the building."

Louise scrutinised the building, now so far away.

"That's not a light," she answered. "That's fire."

"Fire?" Rob was alarmed. "We'd better inform the police when we reach the mainland."

"No!" Both she and Piero said it at the same time but he deferred to her as she continued. "We don't mention it to anyone. We leave it. Sometimes anger needs to burn."

Epilogue

LATER, much later, when Rob and Kristina had had time to absorb all that Louise and Piero had told them, they decided on a plan. It was too risky to smuggle bones back through customs to England so they'd bury the baby in Italy. Louise would have loved to transport her to Charlotte's homeland but that might well involve the authorities and the bones being taken from her – after all who would believe their story? They could take the cloth she'd been buried in and the wedding ring – that was enough to create a shrine with, at least. Initially, Rob thought it strange about the ring, that Charlotte had enclosed it in the casket, 'you know, considering what happened between her and Enrico.' Louise reminded him that primarily it was a symbol of love, of hope. Besides, it was all she had to give.

Piero knew where to bury the baby – in the Tuscan countryside he grew up in, near the village of Fuchecio. "It's a peaceful spot on my father's land, beneath a cypress tree."

"And we can have a marker?" Louise had asked.

"Of course, but what name should we put on the marker? You haven't said."

That had stumped Louise. She didn't know the baby's name, or if Charlotte had even bestowed one on her. After some debate, they decided to call her Charlotte too, in memory of her mother. It was also suggested her middle name should be Maria, after Little Maria – the young girl that stood on the shores of Poveglia, pointing back towards Venice. Whether she was real or not didn't matter – it was simply a way of paying homage. Charlotte Maria Evans (the choice of surname another deliberate gesture) was laid to rest in the shade of a cypress tree on land that was fertile, where flowers grew and bees hovered. Her name was carved into a wooden cross, beside which Kristina placed a lantern.

"It's an Italian tradition," she explained to Louise and Rob. "We don't leave those who have passed in the dark. When night falls, the lantern is switched on."

"But who'll do that?" Rob asked. "Who'll switch it on?"

"We will," Piero had replied, placing an arm around his wife. "We've decided to move out of the city, to live in the country instead. My father has plenty of land, and he'll be glad of our company, as we will be of his. We can build our own house too, something we have both wanted to do for a long time. We don't want to put it off any longer."

Louise agreed. You had to live life whilst you could.

Having cancelled their flight to stay with Piero and Kristina for a week to oversee the burial of Charlotte Maria, it was time to return home, the pair of them hoping, as they walked through security that her mother would have approved of what they'd done. They might not be bringing back her bones, but they were bringing back her memory.

"Tessa, Tessa, come on!"

Whilst they waited for Tessa to return, Rob and Louise linked arms. Emulating Piero and Kristina, they too had sold their London home and now lived in the Sussex countryside, yearning not only for peace but also for grass and trees – a land that was soft rather than urban, and easy on the eye.

They'd bought a barn conversion close to the village of Ditchling and had discovered lots of gorgeous country walks close by, either along the ridge of the South Downs, the air still laced with salt from the sea, or in woodland glades, like the one they were in now, the ground a mass of bluebells and wood anemones. This was their favourite spot, within walking distance of their house and quiet, so quiet – the perfect place to plant forget-me-nots close to the baby's shrine, the seeds of which she'd also sent to Kristina so she could plant them beside her grave too.

For a long time Louise had tried to trace Albert Evans, but she'd drawn a blank. He would most likely be dead anyway, she reasoned, but she'd continued in the hope he'd had a son or a daughter she could have talked to. Rob even suggested that in the search she might find a family connection to her own: 'That's why she chose you, because you're a descendant or something.' But Louise didn't think so. The reason she'd been chosen was because of the similarities between them, which had acted as triggers. There were so many – even a few between Rob and Enrico, which Rob had frowned at when she'd told him – but the greatest of all was anger. It was this that had truly united them. It had sprung from the same well.

In the end she'd given up her search. Perhaps any true descendants of Charlotte didn't need to know the fate she'd met. It would only hurt them. *They* knew. That was enough.

Their walk at an end, they gazed down on the shrine. As Louise always did when they stood in this spot, she tried to make sense of her feelings.

"It's like there's peace in me now, as if I can rest too."

"You can," Rob replied. "Our lives are different."

"They are, they're more fulfilled."

Reaching out, Rob put his arm around her. "We've got everything we could ever want."

"I know. We're so lucky."

Both of them were quiet – remembering those who weren't so fortunate.

"I'm not sure if this is the right time to bring this up," Rob was definitely hesitant, "but the developers who've brought the island of Poveglia are going forward with their plans to build a luxury hotel on it. They've already bulldozed what remained of the asylum after it caught fire and work on the new build is due to start soon."

At his words, Louise inclined her head. "Is it on the net, what they're doing?"

"It is, but it was Piero who told me. Apparently he's been asked to get involved."

"And is he?"

"He's thinking about it." Again Rob faltered. "He thinks it's definitely a good idea, that it will breathe new energy into the place, erase the past entirely."

Louise shook her head. "You can't erase the past entirely."

"I know, Lou, but it's best not to dwell."

It's best not to dwell? She turned back the way they'd come, facing the winding path that led towards home. "You're right," she said as Rob fell into step beside her. "And Piero's right too, the island needs to be transformed."

Rob was clearly relieved she thought so, and that she wasn't protesting the land remained sacrosanct. It was, after all, a graveyard. "Maybe it'll be a happy place to visit one day. Maybe we'll even go back, check out this luxury hotel."

She came to a standstill. "Go back?"

"Well… I thought—"

"No, Rob, we're not going back."

Rob shrugged. "Okay, I was just saying…"

"There'd be no point."

"No point. What do you mean?"

"Charlotte's not there."

"Charlotte? How'd you know that?"

"Because I do, I feel it. None of them are. That's why there'd be no point."

"Sorry, I don't understand." He looked thoroughly confused.

Seeing that, she broke into a grin. "Well, it's just another luxury hotel isn't it? And, quite frankly, you can go and stay in one of them anywhere."

Absorbing what she'd said, he laughed too and they continued walking. "Quite right, no point in going over old ground. It's new experiences we want."

She snuggled into the side of him. "Or we could just stay at home."

"That's right, we could."

"With Tess."

"Yeah, with Tess." He turned his head. "Talking of which, where is she?"

Louise looked round too. "I don't know, the little scamp!"

Again they called out, their voices in unison, hers high, his low, breaking the silence. Worry started to nag at Louise when there was no sign of her. She moved away from Rob and continued to call. "Tessa, where are you, sweetie? Come on, we need to go home."

Biting at her lip, she looked at Rob.

"Where can she be? She never goes far."

"Something must have caught her attention."

"But what?"

Rather than wait for an answer, Louise started walking briskly in the direction they'd just come from, back towards the shrine. "Tessa!" Her voice had grown stern. "Come on now."

The only other sound was her breathing grown heavy, even the birdsong had ceased as if they too were listening for Tessa's return and would only sing again afterwards.

"Tessa!" God, where was she? "Come on, stop playing games."

She caught a glimpse of something, a flash of white. Her breath, having quickened, stopped altogether. *Could it be? Was it her?*

With shoulders so tense they shot darts of pain upwards into her neck, she turned slowly towards what she'd seen, all the while hoping and praying.

The slightly cumbersome frame of the Old English sheepdog came bounding out from behind a clump of trees, as happy to see her owners, as they were relieved to see her.

As the dog threw herself at Louise, she hunkered down to meet it, letting it lick her face all over in greeting. "Where'd you go, Tessa? Did you see a squirrel maybe? You had us worried. We thought something had happened to you, that you'd been spirited away."

She laughed as she said it but a part of her *had* thought exactly that, maybe even Charlotte herself, not satisfied with what they'd done after all, not seeing it as enough. And so she'd take Louise's baby, the *only* baby she was ever likely to have.

No! She'd never do that. She'd never inflict that kind of pain.

And if anything happened to Tess, it would be painful. It was amazing how much she and Rob loved her; how she completed them.

Rob started ruffling Tessa's ears, fussing over her. "There you are, you big furball. Honestly you do worry us sometimes. You shouldn't go off like that."

Helping Louise to rise, he patted the dog again before resuming their journey home, the three of them, walking together through the woods. A family.

The End

A note from the author

Keep in touch via my website - www.shanistruthers.com - where you can subscribe to my occasional newsletter and keep up-to-date with book releases, competitions and special offers. I'm also active on Facebook and Twitter, it'd be great to hear from you!

Also by the author

If you've enjoyed This Haunted World Book One: The Venetian and want to read more paranormal fiction from Shani Struthers, check out her bestselling Psychic Surveys series (if you haven't already!): Book One: The Haunting of Highdown Hall, Book Two: Rise to Me, Book Three: 44 Gilmore Street and Book Four: Old Cross Cottage. In the Psychic Surveys series there will be six books in total, plus several supporting novellas, including Eve: A Christmas Ghost Story and Blakemort. If you prefer romance with a hint of the supernatural, there's also standalone novel, the ghostly Jessamine. They're all available from Amazon in e-book format and paperback.

Eve: A Christmas Ghost Story (Psychic Surveys Prequel)

What do you do when a whole town is haunted?

In 1899, in the North Yorkshire market town of Thorpe Morton, a tragedy occurred; 59 people died at the market hall whilst celebrating Christmas Eve, many of them children. One hundred years on and the spirits of the deceased are restless still, 'haunting' the community, refusing to let them forget.

In 1999, psychic investigators Theo Lawson and Ness Patterson are called in to help, sensing immediately on arrival how weighed down the town is. Quickly they discover there's no safe haven. The past taints everything.

Hurtling towards the anniversary as well as a new millennium, their aim is to move the spirits on, to cleanse the atmosphere so everyone – the living and the dead – can start again. But the spirits prove resistant and soon Theo and Ness are caught up in battle, fighting against something that knows their deepest fears and can twist them in the most dangerous of ways.

They'll need all their courage to succeed and the help of a little girl too – a spirit who didn't die at the hall, who shouldn't even be there...

Psychic Surveys Book One:
The Haunting of Highdown Hall

'Good morning, Psychic Surveys. How can I help?'

The latest in a long line of psychically-gifted females, Ruby Davis can see through the veil that separates this world and the next, helping grounded souls to move towards the light - or 'home' as Ruby calls it. Not just a job for Ruby, it's a crusade and one she wants to bring to the High Street. Psychic Surveys is born.

Based in Lewes, East Sussex, Ruby and her team of freelance psychics have been kept busy of late. Specialising in domestic cases, their solid reputation is spreading - it's not just the dead that can rest in peace but the living too. All is threatened when Ruby receives a call from the irate new owner of Highdown Hall. Film star Cynthia Hart is still in residence, despite having died in 1958.

Winter deepens and so does the mystery surrounding Cynthia. She insists the devil is blocking her path to the light long after Psychic Surveys have 'disproved' it. Investigating her apparently unblemished background, Ruby is pulled further and further into Cynthia's world and the darkness that now inhabits it.

For the first time in her career, Ruby's deepest beliefs are challenged. Does evil truly exist? And if so, is it the most relentless force of all?

Psychic Surveys Book Two: Rise to Me

"This isn't a ghost we're dealing with. If only it were that simple…"

Eighteen years ago, when psychic Ruby Davis was a child, her mother – also a psychic – suffered a nervous breakdown. Ruby was never told why. "It won't help you to know," the only answer ever given. Fast forward to the present and Ruby is earning a living from her gift, running a high street consultancy – Psychic Surveys – specialising in domestic spiritual clearance.

Boasting a strong track record, business is booming. Dealing with spirits has become routine but there is more to the paranormal than even Ruby can imagine. Someone – something – stalks her, terrifying but also strangely familiar. Hiding in the shadows, it is fast becoming bolder and the only way to fight it is for the past to be revealed – no matter what the danger.

When you can see the light, you can see the darkness too. And sometimes the darkness can see you.

Psychic Surveys Book Three: 44 Gilmore Street

"We all have to face our demons at some point."

Psychic Surveys – specialists in domestic spiritual clearance – have never been busier. Although exhausted, Ruby is pleased. Her track record as well as her down-to-earth, no-nonsense approach inspires faith in the haunted, who willingly call on her high street consultancy when the supernatural takes hold.

But that's all about to change.

Two cases prove trying: 44 Gilmore Street, home to a particularly violent spirit, and the reincarnation case of Elisha Grey. When Gilmore Street attracts press attention, matters quickly deteriorate. Dubbed the 'New Enfield', the 'Ghost of Gilmore Street' inflames public imagination, but as Ruby and the team fail repeatedly to evict the entity, faith in them wavers.

Dealing with negative press, the strangeness surrounding Elisha, and a spirit that's becoming increasingly territorial, Ruby's at breaking point. So much is pushing her towards the abyss, not least her own past. It seems some demons just won't let go…

Psychic Surveys Book Four: Old Cross Cottage

It's not wise to linger at the crossroads...

In a quiet Dorset Village, Old Cross Cottage has stood for centuries, overlooking the place where four roads meet. Marred by tragedy, it's had a series of residents, none of whom have stayed for long. Pink and pretty, with a thatched roof, it should be an ideal retreat, but as new owners Rachel and Mark Bell discover, it's anything but.

Ruby Davis hasn't quite told her partner the truth. She's promised Cash a holiday in the country but she's also promised the Bells that she'll investigate the unrest that haunts this ancient dwelling. Hoping to combine work and pleasure, she soon realises this is a far more complex case than she had ever imagined.

As events take a sinister turn, lives are in jeopardy. If the terrible secrets of Old Cross Cottage are ever to be unearthed, an entire village must dig up its past.

Jessa*mine*

"The dead of night, Jess, I wish they'd leave me alone."

Jessamin Wade's husband is dead - a death she feels wholly responsible for. As a way of coping with her grief, she keeps him 'alive' in her imagination - talking to him everyday, laughing with him, remembering the good times they had together. She thinks she will 'hear' him better if she goes somewhere quieter, away from the hustle and bustle of her hometown, Brighton. Her destination is Glenelk in the Highlands of Scotland, a region her grandfather hailed from and the subject of a much-loved painting from her childhood.

Arriving in the village late at night, it is a bleak and forbidding place. However, the house she is renting - Skye Croft - is warm and welcoming. Quickly she meets the locals. Her landlord, Fionnlagh Maccaillin, is an ex-army man with obvious and not so obvious injuries. Maggie, who runs the village shop, is also an enigma, startling her with her strange 'insights'. But it is Stan she instantly connects with. Maccaillin's grandfather and a frail, old man, he is grief-stricken from the recent loss of his beloved Beth.

All four are caught in the past. All four are unable to let go. Their lives entwining in mysterious ways, can they help each other to move on or will they always belong to the ghosts that haunt them?

CPSIA information can be obtained
at www.ICGtesting.com
Printed in the USA
FSHW020321240521
81763FS